PENGUIN BOOKS
After Beth

Elizabeth Enfield is a journalist and regular contributor to national newspapers, magazines and radio. Her short stories have been broadcast on Radio 4 and published in various magazines and anthologies. *After Beth* is her fifth novel. Keep up to date with what Elizabeth is up to at www.elizabethenfield.com.

CW00953665

After Beth

ELIZABETH ENFIELD

PENGUIN BOOKS

PENGUIN BOOKS

UK | USA | Canada | Ireland | Australia
India | New Zealand | South Africa

Penguin Books is part of the Penguin Random House group of companies
whose addresses can be found at global.penguinrandomhouse.com.

First published 2021
001

Copyright © Elizabeth Enfield, 2021

The moral right of the author has been asserted

Quote on page 293 from *A Little Life* by Hanya Yanaghara reproduced with
permission of the Licensor through PLSclear

Every effort has been made to trace the copyright holders and obtain permission

Set in 12.5/14.75 pt Garamond MT Std
Typeset by Integra Software Services Pvt. Ltd, Pondicherry
Printed and bound in Great Britain by Clays Ltd, Elcograf S.p.A.

The authorized representative in the EEA is Penguin Random House Ireland,
Morrison Chambers, 32 Nassau Street, Dublin D02 YH68

A CIP catalogue record for this book is available from the British Library

ISBN: 978-0-241-53551-6

www.greenpenguin.co.uk

MIX
Paper from
responsible sources
FSC® C018179

Penguin Random House is committed to a
sustainable future for our business, our readers
and our planet. This book is made from Forest
Stewardship Council® certified paper.

For my family, in all its forms . . .
With love

PART ONE

There are many Beths in the world, shy and quiet,
sitting in corners till needed, and living for
others so cheerfully that no one sees the sacrifices
till the little cricket on the hearth stops chirping,
and the sweet, sunshiny presence vanishes, leaving
silence and shadow behind.

— Louisa May Alcott, *Little Women*

Events Unfolding

'I'm off now. See you later, Mum.' Beth is standing at the back door, a large beach bag over her shoulder, dressed in denim shorts, trainers and the sweater I was looking for earlier.

'Is that my jumper?' I look up at my eighteen-year-old daughter from my position kneeling on the grass by the back wall of the garden. I am preparing the ground for a blanket-sized wildflower meadow.

It's a beautiful late-summer's day, the kind of day when the world and everything in it feels overwhelmingly magnificent: blue skies, vast horizons, and Beth framed by the doorway about to head off to the beach with Chloe, where low tides will reveal huge swathes of sand.

Beth, on the cusp of life, her horizons as limitless as the day.

'You don't mind, do you?' She tugs at the hem of my jumper. 'I've packed most of mine.'

It's a rhetorical question.

I don't mind. It's kind of flattering. When she was too small to borrow my clothes for anything other than dressing up, I remember her asking if, when she was bigger, she could wear them.

'By the time they fit you, you won't want to!' It had seemed so unlikely, at the time. I certainly never wanted to borrow any of my mother's.

'Just make sure you don't leave it at the beach,' I say, thinking that the one advantage of Beth's being away will be that my clothes will remain exactly where I left them.

Beth's about to leave home: a year's Nuffield Research placement at Stamford University before coming back to read physics at Cambridge. A year investigating gravitational lens theory in Connecticut before immersing herself in a world that may be geographically closer but will be a million miles away from mine. Because what do I understand of the light from distant stars and the way matter bends and distorts it?

'I'll see you later, then,' Beth says, again.

'Be careful on the roads,' I say. 'And don't forget your helmet.'

'I won't.' She turns to go, then adds, 'By the way, Chloe might come back for supper.'

'Okay, that'll be lovely.'

I went back to my weeding, anticipating the tiny wild-flower area bursting into bloom next spring, the profusion of betony, toadflax and field scabious that would greet Beth on her return. It was something to look forward to. I busied myself unearthing clods of soil where thicker grasses grew now, pausing briefly when my phone pinged a text alert.

It was from Beth, already at the beach. *Hi Mum ☺ I put a shirt to soak in the sink and forgot to hang it out. Could you please???? Sorry. Forgot and want to take it with me. Love you XXX*

I told her I would and went upstairs to the bathroom, lingering as I ascended, looking at the framed photographs that hung on the walls of the staircase: Patrick holding

Beth, wrapped in a hospital blanket, his look slightly anxious but hers steady, meeting the camera lens as if she'd been expecting just this moment throughout the long hours of her delivery.

'This one's an old soul,' my mother had said, with an air of authority, when she saw her. 'She's been here before.'

It's hard to work out how much of what my mother says she actually believes: old souls, angels, Heaven and Hell are all part of her vernacular.

Beneath that picture is a similar shot but this time it's Beth, aged three, holding baby Alfie, my brother's younger son, the cousin who's almost a little brother to her. He's resting on her lap and she has one hand on his head and the other holding his hand but she's looking questioningly at whoever took the photo, as if afraid she might not be doing this baby-holding thing quite right.

Two stairs up, Beth's sitting in her high chair prodding curiously at the cake in front of her. Her first birthday. Patrick was away. I'd taken the photograph so he wouldn't miss the occasion, or any of the other moments IKEA-clip-framed beside the stairs: the look of delight when she took her first steps and one of slight trepidation on her first day at school.

Towards the top of the stairs, she's feeding geese, unafraid of their honking upfrontery. And, in another photo, she's dressed as a Moomin for World Book Day – a papier-mâché feat that I cursed during its production. Most of the photos were taken before she was eight, when she became self-conscious and began to turn away from the camera or pull such faces the images weren't worth framing.

This was about the same time as Patrick and I began to lose sight of each other. A pang of regret. It never quite goes away.

At the top of the stairs there's one of her at the beach, about six now, emerging from the sea, wet hair and a huge smile. It was taken not long after we moved here from London when the beach was still the 'best thing ever in the whole wide world!'

Where had the time gone, I wonder, as I walk across the landing, remembering how, earlier this week, Beth tried to explain Einstein's theory that time is an illusion, that the past, present and future all exist simultaneously.

But how can that be?

I'd nodded, not really comprehending. What more evidence of time's relentless march forward do you need than the speed at which children grow up and move on?

I go into Beth's room, trying to remember what I came upstairs for in the first place, taking in the contents of her wardrobe, lying in haphazard piles on the floor. I sit on the edge of her bed and no sooner have I done so than Tiger, who'd been curled up on her pillow, gets up, stretches and resettles on my lap.

I hadn't wanted a cat but after her father left I'd given in to Beth's insistence that we get a kitten and call it Tiger. 'It's ironic.'

'It's just going to be the two of us for a bit,' I say, stroking him, feeling grateful to him for being here now.

Beth's $E = mc^2$ wash-bag is in the middle of the floor, stuffed with toiletries. It was a birthday present from Evan, her first proper boyfriend.

I know she'll miss him more than she does me when

she goes away, that trying to sustain the relationship over the next year with the Atlantic Ocean between them will be difficult.

I'll miss him too and her other friends: the comings and goings, the tales from college, the unwashed coffee cups clustered by the sink in the mornings, the bread disappearing overnight. I'm missing it all already: missing Beth and the past eighteen years and wondering at the speed of them.

Beth's hairbrush is lying on the floor beside her suitcase. I pick it up and pluck out the strands of caramel-blonde hairs trapped between its bristles. Her hair is wavy, a softer version of Patrick's defined curls, and golden, like his hair when I first met him, but a shade or two darker.

I remember then that I came up to retrieve Beth's shirt from the basin in the bathroom, but as I leave her room, the doorbell rings and instead I go downstairs to answer it, slipping the strands of hair absently into the pocket of my cardigan.

It's Martin, Chloe's father, unshaven, wearing a polo shirt and pinkish shorts. It must be a working-from-home day.

I'm not expecting him.

'They're not back from the beach yet,' is my slightly unfriendly greeting.

'Can I come in?' he asks.

And from the way he says it, I know that something is wrong.

Later that Monday

Hospital corridors are always endless and white. Martin chaperones me along them with a nervous running commentary.

'Just along here. Here we go.'

The waiting area outside A and E is surprisingly quiet, not the Dante's Inferno one expects from watching hospital TV dramas. There's a mother with a toddler in a pushchair, holding an ice pack to his forehead. An old man sits slumped in a chair, his shirt unbuttoned, as if he arrived in a hurry, but is showing no obvious signs of distress, and a younger man in a smart suit is standing by the window, scrolling down the screen of his phone.

Only the ice pack hints at an accident. Only the way my heart is racing, emergency.

Chloe is standing outside the double doors of A and E, and Nadia too, an incongruous-looking mother and daughter: Nadia, a teacher, in a slim skirt and navy shirt, Chloe beach fresh in T-shirt dress and plimsolls but pale and shivering.

'Cate.' Nadia comes towards me, her arms open and I allow myself the awkwardness of the embrace, which feels more like an obstacle to seeing my daughter.

'Where is she?' I look at Chloe, salty and sun-kissed, the straps of her swimming costume visible above the line of her dress: a reminder of the day that has been but no longer is.

'She's in there.' Nadia nods towards the double doors and I brush past her towards them.

But Nadia is at my side, her hand on my arm. 'They told us to wait here. They said someone would come out in a minute.'

'But I'm her mother.' I shrug off Nadia's hand and the sympathy it conveys.

I grab one of the door handles, expecting it to yield, but it only rattles, locked above the keypad for which I have no code.

'They said they'd be out as soon as . . .'

I stand on tiptoe and peer through the frosted glass. There is movement inside. I knock on it. But it's tough, hardly makes a sound. I try the door again.

'Cate?' Nadia is pleading. 'It won't be long.'

'What happened?'

Martin had told me a version as he drove me to the hospital but I need to hear it from Chloe. She was there. She witnessed everything.

Chloe's expression is one of shock. 'She went for another swim. She wanted to swim to the sandbar.'

When the tide is out the sandbar appears, like an island rising in the midst of the sea. At low water, you can sometimes walk to it. When it's a little higher, people swim there. All the time.

Chloe is giving me facts. I want an explanation. 'There were these boys playing cricket there.' Chloe tugs at the strap of her swimming costume. 'She was standing up and talking to them.' She lets go of the strap and it pings against her chest but she grabs it again as she resumes. 'I wasn't watching. I saw her there, and then I went back to reading my book. It was only when the boys started waving and shouting that I realized something was wrong. I couldn't see Beth anywhere – and then the lifeboat was racing out . . .'

She pauses, swallows. 'I knew it was for Beth.'

There must be some mistake, I tell myself. She must have got it wrong. Beth will walk in at any moment and explain, surely. She's a strong swimmer. She practically grew up at the beach.

'But the lifeboat crew got to her quickly?' I'm retelling the story, before I've even heard it. Beth gets swept away but the lifeboat gets there in time. They pick her up. They bring her in. It's all going to be okay. Someone will walk out through the locked double doors at any minute and tell me they've given Beth the once-over and she's fine.

'Well, it was out there for a while, looking.' Chloe blinks and swallows hard again, then looks at her father.

She opens her mouth to speak. She pulls the strap of her swimsuit, half choking herself with the action.

'She wasn't breathing when they brought her out of the water,' Martin says quietly, helping her, repeating some of what he's already said in the car.

'They did CPR on the beach,' Chloe says, looking away to the double doors, which remain resolutely locked, trying to hide her tears from me.

'But I don't understand,' I say. Any of it. 'She swims there all the time.' None of this makes sense.

Martin is saying something about a rip tide. About it

pulling her out to sea. I can hear the words and see his mouth moving but it seems all wrong, like watching a TV recording that is slightly out of sync.

CPR. Resuscitation. What do these words have to do with two teenage girls spending an afternoon at the beach?

The double doors open. Finally. A woman in uniform comes out.

'Can I see her?' I'm desperate to see her.

'Mrs Challoner?'

'Yes,' I say, although my name is Tierney. Beth has Patrick's name but I will be Mrs Challoner if it gets me to Beth faster.

I follow her through the double doors.

All those television programmes you see, *Doctors*, *Casualty*, *ER*, *Green Wing*, they do nothing to prepare you for the reality of seeing your child lying lifeless but alive. No amount of make-up can create the drained pallor of someone in this position. No amount of rehearsing can perfect the absent look.

Beth is dwarfed by a maze of tubes and monitors, her hair pulled back from her grey and sunken face.

'Beth, sweetheart.' I put out my hand to touch her cheek, which feels dry and rough, where usually it's so smooth.

Nothing. No sign of response.

I stroke her hair, which is salt-encrusted and lacking its normal lustre.

I bend down and kiss her forehead, like I used to when she was little. 'Darling. It's Mum . . . Beth!' My voice becomes louder. It's almost an admonishment, born of desperation. 'Can you hear me?'

I increase the pressure of my hand on her head. I'm

not being gentle enough but I must get some response from her.

'Beth. Please. Come on now.'

Nothing.

I look at her. The beauty spot on her cheek, the sprinkle of freckles that have darkened and spread over the summer, the wispy down around her hairline, all the familiar details of my daughter are still there.

But her eyes are unfamiliar. Beth's eyes are a peculiarly unique shade of bluey-green. There's warmth to them, inquisitiveness and knowingness, as if the world they see is at once pleasing, enticing and familiar. Beautiful eyes. But now, although they are open, they are not registering – not the ceiling, not the doctors, not me. 'Beth?' What am I asking?

I need to hold her, to lift her torso and clasp it close to mine, to feel her warmth, to make her better. I have to do something. But there are so many wires and tubes.

'Sweetheart.' I take her hand and find it cool and clammy.

The outline of her legs, unmoving, is visible beneath the sheet and I put my hand on her knee, the way I used to when she was little. She'd pretend it wasn't her leg at all and try not to react but could never stop herself squirming and laughing.

She doesn't do that now.

'It's okay, lovely girl.' It is my job to reassure her. 'You're going to be okay.'

The medics by her bedside have moved away a little. They are conferring quietly a few feet from her bed.

'The doctor will be with you in a minute,' says the

woman who ushered me in, kindly but without the reassurance I crave. 'I'll bring you a chair to wait.' She produces
an orange plastic one, which she places next to the bed,
the ubiquitous Robin Day stackable classic that is the only
familiar thing in the ward. Even though Beth is there, on
the bed beside me, I feel utterly alone. Scared and alone.

Then and Now

Martin had phoned Patrick when we got to the hospital, a call I couldn't face making myself. We'd been supposed to meet at the airport tomorrow. I had been dreading waving Beth off at the departure gates but looking forward to the lunch we'd planned together beforehand: to playing happy nuclear families briefly, to watching Patrick press a wodge of American currency into Beth's hands at the very last minute and make some joke about 'a fistful of dollars' before she kissed us both and disappeared beyond the gates.

Would he have put his arm round me and squeezed me to him, as I tried not to cry, and told me she was a brilliant girl and I should be proud of her? Perhaps he'd have trotted out the let's-have-a-coffee-in-our-pleasant-coffee joke. He'd seen a sign saying this somewhere in Morocco, years ago, a poor translation from the French, which had become part of the family lingo.

Maybe we'd have talked about how much I was going to miss her, how I knew it was a beginning for her but nevertheless . . .

None of what I thought might happen tomorrow was going to happen now. We aren't going to be waving Beth off anywhere for a while.

My phone beeps. There's a missed call from Patrick. And a message: *Be strong, Cate. With you very soon, PXXX.*

And, despite the circumstances, I still feel the familiar mixture of warmth tinged with regret that never quite goes away, despite the years we've been apart.

'Mrs Challoner?'

I look up when I hear the unfamiliar name again.

'I'm Dr Takis, the consultant in charge of your daughter's care.'

The tone of his voice is reassuring. I am grateful to him for that.

'Is she going to be okay?'

'Mrs Challoner.' This constant repetition of a name that is not really mine adds to the sense of unreality. A Welsh name, meaning 'blanket-maker'. Patrick used to say he was descended from a long line of blanket-makers, although his father worked at a hotel in Scarborough.

'Cate,' I say to Dr Takis.

'Cate.' He pauses. 'Your daughter was submerged in the water for some time, during which she would not have been taking in oxygen.' He looks at me, questioning, as if to make sure I'm taking it in. The oxygen of his words.

'Yes.' I nod. 'They told me she wasn't breathing when she was picked up by the lifeboat. But she was resuscitated?'

'Yes, that's right.' His tone is kindly and might be patronizing, were it not for the fact that I need to understand.

'At the moment her lungs are not working by themselves.' He nods towards the bed. 'The ventilator is breathing for her. She's not able to breathe for herself.'

'But that will change?'

'We don't know yet. It's too early to tell.'

I feel as if I've been punched in the stomach. I expected reassurance.

He looks at her notes. 'For the next day or so, we need to make sure her blood pressure, heart rate and body temperature are all stabilized. And she'll be given a CT scan and organ check.'

'So there could be damage to her organs?' I'm still reeling with shock from his earlier statement.

'Beth's body has undergone a significant trauma,' he says gently. 'What we need to do here in A and E is make sure she is stabilized. We need to keep her comfortable and give her body time to recover from the initial shock. I know it's difficult but I'm afraid I can't make any long-term prognosis yet.'

'So how long will she be here? When will you know more?' I'm casting around for some more tangible piece of information.

'As soon as a bed becomes available, she'll be transferred to the intensive care unit. The doctors there will carry out further tests.'

'Okay.' I nod miserably. I need to be patient.

Beth shouldn't be here. She is too still, too unresponsive. There's a child crying loudly at the end of the unit, a middle-aged man groaning in the bed next door, doctors and nurses bustling with the urgency you'd expect.

Beth doesn't belong here.

She should be at home finishing packing while I make supper for her and Chloe before they go off to the pub with friends. She should be coming home with Evan, spending her last night with him before she goes away. 'We'll get you home soon,' I say to her now, taking her hand again, feeling the lightness of it in mine, stroking her slim, lightly tanned fingers, examining the milk spots on her nails, trying to fix all these tiny details. 'We'll get you home soon, Beth.'

An hour later, Beth is transferred to the intensive care unit, and shortly after, Patrick arrives, as fast as the trains from London allowed but not fast enough.

'She's just along here.' I can hear the nurse and then the familiar softly spoken voice, with its slight trace of accent.

'Caitlin.' He acknowledges me with a brief look and a light hand on my arm but his focus is on Beth.

'Hello, love.' His voice breaks slightly. 'Look at you. I'm a bit worried I might upset the circuitry here.' His Yorkshire accent becomes more pronounced as he speaks, the way it does in times of stress. He bends over the bed, kissing her face, pushing a stray strand of hair away from her forehead, taking her hand.

I watch him as he makes his own assessment of our daughter. His hair is still the same golden blond, flecked with grey now but only a little, and the lean wiriness of his body is not yet offset by middle age. Only his hands give this away, lined and dark as they clasp the paler golden hand of his child.

'Look at you,' he says again to Beth. 'You've given everyone quite a shock.' His voice cracks. The early bravado is gone. 'Jesus, Beth. What happened to you?' He leans in closer, then moves away, as if better to take her in. Then, still holding her hand, he reaches out and takes mine. 'Caty.'

He takes a deep breath and I look at him, see that he's blinking back tears. I swallow, refusing to allow myself any. I have to be strong for her.

'I'm sorry, Caty. It's just she looks such a mess.' He laughs now, the kind of half-laugh people use to overcome fear.

'I know.' My voice falters this time, and he turns to give me a hug.

'She's strong, Caty. She's a strong girl. She'll pull through. We'll get through this.' Each sentence is punctuated by a sharp intake of breath.

'Yes.'

I allow myself to believe him, because to believe anything else is impossible.

But the moment is broken. Einstein's singular time moves on, as it always does.

'Excuse me. I just need to check a few things.' The nurse is hovering at the end of the bed. 'It won't take a moment.'

I move out of her way.

'What happened?' Pat asks, and again his accent is pronounced. 'Tell me what happened.'

I repeat what Chloe and Martin have told me.

'It just doesn't make any sense,' Patrick says when I've finished, echoing my own thoughts. 'She was such a strong swimmer, she could have let it sweep her out and swum back. What made her go under?'

'I don't know, Patrick,' I say quietly. 'I just don't know.'

'How long was she . . .' Patrick pauses '. . . in the water for?'

I know why he paused. He cannot quite bring himself to say 'under the water', 'drowning'.

'She was out there swimming for a while,' I say. 'And probably under for a few minutes.'

It sounds like nothing. In all that space-time, all the infinitesimal moments, what difference could a few minutes make to the way the world turns?

All the difference. A few minutes without oxygen is not nothing. It is everything.

'She's strong,' he says again, putting his arm around my shoulders.

There is no word in the English language that adequately sums up the continuing relationship you have with the other parent of your child, when the two of you are no longer together. But the fact that Patrick is here now, that he is the person I want to be here now, more than anyone else in the world, says it all. Patrick is the only person who can really understand what I'm going through, the only person who can share it by experiencing a near-identical set of emotions.

Early Evening

'Her blood pressure's low.' The nurse swishes aside the nylon curtain that separates her bed from the rest of the ward.

We stand apart and back, allowing her space to replace Beth's notes in the holder at the foot of her bed.

'I'm going to get one of the doctors to take another look.'

We move back to the bed. I take her hand and Patrick holds her face. 'Beth,' he says, moving closer. 'Beth.'

'Don't,' I say. He's shouting. He sounds cross.

'Sorry.' He moves back a little. 'I just want to know if she can hear me. There must be something, some way of finding out if she knows what's going on. If she knows . . .' His voice falters.

'What?'

'That we're here.'

We watch, in vain, for signs of life, some spark of the person she was just a few hours ago.

'Did she wink?' I think I saw some facial movement.

'Did she?'

'I'm not sure.' I've raised Patrick's hopes. 'I'm sorry.'

'It's okay.'

'Mr and Mrs Challoner?'

This doctor has a closed face. His mop of thick dark hair hides half of it, his eyes are ensconced behind thick glasses, and he remains tight-lipped as he looks at

Beth's notes and the various monitors to which she is attached. He was here, in the intensive care unit, when they first brought her up. He helped attach her to a new set of monitors and machines while I watched, helplessly. He was the one barking out numbers, which a nurse recorded in the notes he is now studying, as if he's forgotten already.

He checks one of the monitors. 'I think we need to increase the saline drip,' he says to the nurse, who adjusts the flow from the bag of liquid suspended next to Beth's bed.

Only then does he give us his attention. 'Shall we go to the relatives' room?' It's more of a command.

He heads to the double doors of the intensive care unit.

We follow reluctantly. I suspect the relatives' room is a bad-news room. The décor suggests this. More orange plastic chairs lined along the wall. A grey sofa, albeit one that looks as if it may have been rescued from the pavement outside. A coffee-table that may once have had a wood veneer but is now all particleboard, stained with coffee rings. Peeling grey-painted walls decorated with posters warning relatives that as well as their loved one lying critically ill, they, too, are at enormous risk: of cancer, of type 2 diabetes, of a heart attack or stroke, or being raped while under the influence of alcohol, of measles and flu and MRSA.

There's bad news everywhere. And in the corner a drinks-dispensing machine, which this doctor is looking at intently.

'Do you want tea or coffee? I'd have tea, if I were you. The coffee's undrinkable.'

I think this is a joke, delivered without a hint of humour. I suspect he may have been absent on the day they taught bedside manner.

'No, thanks,' Patrick says.

'Tea, please,' I say, hoping, if I do as the doctor says, it will miraculously bring my daughter round.

We are gestured towards the sofa, which is as uncomfortable as it looks.

Patrick takes off his sweater and I register the familiar scar on his forearm, caused by having to extract a grub worm in Rwanda. Beth has a birthmark in the same place, as if her gene decided to imprint the memory of this incident on her unblemished baby skin.

'So, Mr and Mrs Challoner.' The doctor looks at Beth's notes as he waits for the drinks dispenser to do its stuff. 'I'm Dr Such.'

He comes over, notes in one hand, plastic cup in the other. 'You're probably going to be seeing quite a bit of me over the next few days.' His tone gives nothing away. 'Your daughter's condition is currently very serious.' He looks at her notes through the glasses that are so thick I can't see his eyes. 'She's still needing a ventilator.'

'But given time,' Patrick nods in the direction of the ward, 'she'll be able to breathe again by herself? The ventilator is helping her get there?'

Dr Such looks from Patrick to me. 'At the moment, Beth is showing very little sign of response, but we hope that may change over the next couple of days.'

'So she'll start to come round?' There's a ray of hope.

'Not necessarily.' Dr Such dashes it. 'It's possible, yes, but I can't tell you that for sure.'

I have not touched the tea I'm holding and I jerk the cup in my agitation, sloshing liquid over the side and onto the floor.

Dr Such takes a tissue from his pocket and bends to wipe it up, taking his time, as if it's important.

'Why?' I ask. 'Why is everything a possibility? Why does everyone say it's too early to tell? Why can't you tell us anything more definite now?'

'Cate.' Patrick reaches his hand out and puts it on my forearm.

'What?' I shake him off.

'I'm sorry I can't be more positive,' Dr Such says.

The apology is the first sign from him that he is aware this might be difficult for us.

'But it's too early for a prognosis. Beth will be monitored closely during the night, and in the morning it's possible there may be some change. If not, we'll carry out tests to see where we are.'

'What tests?' I say brusquely.

'In a drowning situation,' Dr Such begins, 'and depending on the length of time the brain has been deprived of oxygen, a patient's response may be delayed. We'll see how she is in the morning and she'll be given an EEG, which should tell us more.'

'EEG?' I'm out of my depth.

'An electroencephalogram. A test to assess brain activity.' Dr Such explains the abbreviation.

Patrick puts his hand on my knee and we remain silent, allowing it all to sink in.

'Do you mind if we have a few minutes to ourselves?' Patrick asks eventually.

A few minutes. I hate those three words. A few minutes. That's all it takes. To make all the difference.

'Of course.' Dr Such gets up. 'I'll be here during the night and we'll be keeping a very close eye on Beth.'

'And we can stay with her?' I ask, my voice small. Pleading.

'I'm afraid we can't allow visitors during the night. The area around the bed needs to be kept clear,' he says. 'There's a room next to this with recliner chairs where you can sleep if you wish to remain at the hospital.'

'We do.' The thought of leaving Beth here on her own is impossible to countenance.

'I'm sorry I don't have anything conclusive to tell you,' Dr Such says, and leaves the bad-news room.

'We need to get back to her.' I half stand.

'Just a moment, Caty.' Patrick stops me.

'But what if there's been a change?'

'Please,' he says, inclining his head towards the sofa. 'I just need to take it all in. Please.'

'Okay.' I sit.

'I can't believe it,' Patrick says. 'I spoke to her on Sunday evening. She was so excited.'

'She was so looking forward to going away,' I tell him, pulling my cardigan around me even though the heat is getting to me. 'And do you know what the stupid thing is?'

'What?'

'I sat on her bed while she was at the beach, crying my eyes out because she was leaving. Can you believe it? I was crying because I was going to miss her.'

'Of course you were.'

'It's all I want now. For her to be well enough to be

24

going somewhere. I'd be happy for her to spend the rest of her life in Timbuktu as long as she's fit and healthy.'

'I know.' Patrick takes my hand and squeezes it.

I'm about to say that we should resume our vigil beside Beth's bed when his phone vibrates in the pocket of his trousers. There's a message and I see it's from Rachel before he bends forward obscuring the screen. 'I'd better call her,' he says. 'I'll just go outside.'

I get up and hurry back to the unit, where Beth lies apparently unchanged. I take her hand and press it. Still nothing. Or is there? Is her skin, which was ashen and grey, a little brighter? Or is it just the evening light?

I look at her, the way I used to when she was first born, fearful that if I took my eyes off her, something might happen. I used to think that if I could just see the almost imperceptible rise and fall of her chest, then no harm would come to her, that if I monitored the tiny smiles that appeared to form and then unform, almost as quickly, that I was doing my job as a mother.

'Do you know I'm here, sweetheart? Blink if you know it's me. I'm here. Let me know you're still here too. Please.'

I can't bear the lack of response. I could cry again, weep like a baby because my baby isn't going anywhere, but what would be the point?

I have to be strong. Because she could come round in the morning.

I smooth the fabric of the hospital gown she's wearing, straighten the sheets as much as I can in a vain attempt to make her more comfortable.

I'm fussing with a hospital corner when Patrick returns.

'Rachel sends her love,' he says, coming to join me. 'She'll try to come down in the next few days.'

I nod, as if acquiescing, although I don't really want her here. Patrick's new partner, a photographer like he is, a woman who understands him and his work in a way I never really did. But Beth has been a big part of her life too.

Patrick stands next to me while I look at Beth, scan her face, searching desperately for a sign of the person she was when the day began, when her hair shone and her eyes sparkled and her smile radiated a happy anticipation of life. I find only its absence.

'You should try to get some sleep,' Patrick says, a few hours later, as we go through the pretence of settling down for the night.

In the room outside the ward, adjoining the relatives' room, are a couple of rows of high-backed chairs, which can be made to recline. It looks a bit like a residents' lounge in an old folks' home, and in the half-light I can already see a couple of people I noticed on the unit, attempting to doze.

Patrick and I head for two beside a window, which is firmly shut. We remain silent as we work out how to adjust them.

There's a shelf under the seat, like the ones life jackets are stashed in on planes. On it, I find a grey fleece blanket, with 'HOSPITAL PROPERTY DO NOT REMOVE' stamped in capital letters along the edge – as if this is a luxury hotel and the blanket is something we might be tempted to take away with us. I pull it up to my chin, telling the world I am 'NOT TO BE REMOVED', and try to get comfortable in the chair. I doubt that either of us will sleep.

It's just before midnight. I've been here since three o'clock. Nearly nine hours. A day that has felt like a lifetime.

In the Morning

Patrick was gone when I stirred from a brief doze, which had been a long time coming. I got up several times during the night, went to the bathroom, even when it was not necessary. Stood outside the locked double doors of Intensive Care, as if simply by standing there I could somehow get through to Beth. And then I must have nodded off without realizing and I'm awake and it's ten past seven. I jump up, eager to get back to our daughter.

The nurse lets me in and I rush to Beth's bed, expecting to find Patrick already there, hoping to see him turn and tell me she's awake.

But it's just Beth, lying still and quiet as if she's simply sleeping, her eyes closed now, the vacant stare of yesterday hidden behind the mauve of her eyelids.

'Sweetheart. It's morning now. You've been asleep a long time. Can you hear me? Do you know that I'm here?' I smooth her hair and kiss her forehead, as if she's a much younger version of herself and had been woken in the night by a cough or nightmare.

She doesn't respond.

'Morning,' a nurse chirps, too cheery, as I look around for Patrick. 'I'm just going to squeeze past you and make sure everything's okay here.'

I stand up but I keep my eyes on Beth.

'Did you get any sleep?' the nurse asks, sliding past me.

'Not really. How is she?' I watch her adjusting tubes, moving dials, monitoring monitors, unsure what any of it means.

'She's been stable overnight,' she tells me. 'The doctors will be round to see her later.'

'Do you know when?' I want someone to tell me something more than that she's stable.

'They start their rounds about eight thirty.' She's busy, not really paying me attention. I should let her do what she has to do but I'm so anxious for something.

'Is there any change?' It's been a whole night. There must be something someone can tell me.

The nurse speaks kindly. 'Everything's as I would expect it to be.'

'Okay.' I feel admonished. Too many questions – but what else can I do?

'I'll be here for a good ten minutes, if you want to get yourself a coffee.' It's almost an instruction.

'Okay.'

I hold Beth's hand for a few more moments, then reluctantly leave the unit, in search of caffeine and Patrick.

He's not in the bad-news room. Or the chair room.

'Cate?' I'm only vaguely aware that someone has just walked past me, a brief flash of navy blue. 'What are you doing here?'

'Sophie?'

My brother Joe's wife in her doctor's uniform. With the shock of the past eighteen hours, I hadn't thought to let my family know what's going on, but it's a relief to see her, a familiar face, someone who knows Beth, who knows the hospital and the things that go on in it. I feel bad now, that we haven't let anyone know.

'What's going on?' she asks.

'It was all so sudden,' I say. I'd seen her a week ago, when she and Joe hosted a farewell barbecue for Beth. Joe, the eldest, with his reliable doctor wife, two sons and a big house, which somehow all combine to make him head of our family.

'What was?' Sophie asks gently.

'It's Beth.' I abandon my thoughts of explaining why we'd not called anyone earlier. 'She's in intensive care.'

'Oh, Cate. What happened?'

I fill her in as we walk back together towards the unit.

'I'm on shift in a few minutes but is it okay if I come in for a bit?'

'Of course. I'd like you to see her.'

Sophie's being there gives me hope. In the circumstances you clutch at whatever you can.

'Sophie?' Patrick's back, at the foot of Beth's bed.

He looks up as soon as we go in and I register the night's stubble on his chin. Patrick's almost always clean-shaven. Wherever he is in the world, no matter if there's no running water, he hates not shaving.

'Where were you?' I ask him.

'I couldn't sleep. I went outside for a bit.' He answers me, but is looking at Sophie as he speaks.

I wonder when he last saw her. Patrick and Joe remained friends when we split up. Patrick sometimes stays there at weekends, in the garden room they built as Joe's home office before a company expansion forced him to find bigger premises. Beth would go there for the weekend rather than London, getting to spend time with her cousins as well as her dad.

'Have they scanned her yet? Done an EEG?' she asks now.

'We were told she'd have one later today.'

'That should offer a clearer picture. Do your mum and dad know?'

'Not yet,' I reply. 'It was all so sudden and I know I should ring them but I thought maybe we should wait a bit and . . .'

'Yes?'

'I don't know if I can.' My voice falters.

'Do you want me to call them?' She looks from me to Patrick. 'Or Joe can speak to them. They'll want to know.'

'It's just that telling them makes it seem so . . . real.'

'I'm so sorry, Cate. This is impossibly hard. But she's in the best place.' Sophie undoes her hair from the elastic that holds it up in a coiled bun and lets it fall to her shoulders briefly, then coils it up again. She curls her lips in and holds them briefly, recomposing her face, trying and failing not to let the shock show. 'She has the best chance here.'

'Do you think so?' I seize on this. 'The doctor keeps telling us not to get our hopes up.'

'I'm sorry, Cate. It's not my area. I can't tell you anything with authority.' She pulls her eyebrows together as she speaks, creating furrow lines along the bridge of her nose. 'But I do know the doctors here will be doing everything they possibly can for her.'

'But it might not be enough.'

'You have to hope that it is. Come here.'

She hugs me. Holds me tight, as if that alone will make everything okay.

'I'm sorry,' she says, after a few moments. 'I have to go now, but I'll call your parents before I begin my shift.'

In the Early Days . . .

I didn't have to tell Patrick when I got pregnant with Beth.

We were sharing a flat in London, and although he worked away, his presence in the home we shared was always tangible.

The shaving foam in the bathroom, the striped towelling dressing-gown on the back of the bedroom door, the locked cupboard in the hall where he kept his photographic equipment, and the framed photo of the herd of zebras crossing the Serengeti were all reminders.

I was in the kitchen making dinner. Steak. A clue in itself, perhaps, because for the past few weeks I'd been craving meat in a way that was unusual. I was young for all this, for my generation anyway – to be living with someone, expecting their child aged twenty-seven.

'Hello,' Patrick called from the hallway as he took off his coat.

I knew better than to come out of the kitchen. This was part of his homecoming ritual. He needed the space to transition from his working day to home life. I concentrated on the steak, moving it around and occasionally stirring the potatoes in another pan.

'Hi.' Eventually he appeared in the doorframe, filling it with his own.

'Hi.' I looked at him, taking in all the features I could

see with my eyes closed, wondering how they would trans-
mute to the child I was carrying.

'Are you okay?' He sensed my scrutiny.

'Yes.' I exhaled, unaware until I did that I'd been holding my breath.

And that was it. 'Caty?' He stepped towards me and I
nodded before he took me into his arms and held me so
tightly I struggled to breathe.

I knew he knew.

Maybe everyone thinks in the early flush of a relationship that they understand each other intuitively.

'I can't believe it,' Patrick said after a while. 'We're
going to have a baby.'

It felt impossibly magical.

This thing, this renewal of life, which kept on happening time after time and place after place in myriad forms,
was happening to us. It was so simple and yet so miraculous.

Discovering you're pregnant, being pregnant, seeing
the first glimpse of your baby via an ultrasound scan is
like a strange collision of past, present and future: the
past of your parents and their ancestors, and the life that
your unborn child will lead begin to unfold slowly in the
strange timeless chamber of your womb. That, for now, is
its present but already the genes of past generations are at
play, shaping and anticipating a future the child's parents
can only guess at.

I envisaged a child so like the one Beth was to become it
was almost uncanny, as if I'd been expecting her, without
knowing it, all along.

When we went for the first scan, at twelve weeks, the

image that appeared on the screen and the photograph they gave us, the one I still carry in my purse, did little to sharpen Patrick's impression of the baby, other than that it was there. It confirmed mine.

I was already dreaming about her future, which was unfolding in the way her tiny fingers were beginning to unfold. It was a happy future but one that scared me too.

'How will we manage?' I asked Patrick repeatedly during my pregnancy, worried about where we would live, how I would work with a baby and with Patrick away so much.

'We'll find a way,' he replied each time. 'We'll work everything out and it will be wonderful. I love you, and whatever happens, however you feel about work once the baby is born, I'll be there to support you both.'

I never dared tell Patrick that I worried I might not be able to love the baby as much as I loved him. I worried I might not have enough love in me to go round.

I needn't have worried.

As soon as Beth was born, I was consumed by the fiercest, most overpowering love I had known.

How is it possible, I wonder as I look at our daughter now, that a child conceived so easily, who is loved so much, can be lying here on life support?

I go back through the events of the previous day.

We'd had breakfast together in the garden: muesli, yoghurt and raspberry muffins from the deli near my office. Beth had fed crumbs of hers to a blue tit that had landed on the table, hopped about hopefully and then flown off in a dizzying display of acrobatics that had made her laugh.

'Do you think birds have sugar rushes?' she'd asked, as the bird fluttered and looped the loop around the garden.

'I suppose it's possible,' I replied, as the bird calmed, came back and looked hopeful again.

'Here, birdie.' Beth had given it another morsel of muffin and giggled as it repeated its frenetic flying routine.

'I think they must,' she'd concluded, after a few more crumbs had been consumed. 'I'll have to look it up.'

I'd taken the day off work because it was Beth's last day at home. We'd gone into town later that morning to buy a few last-minute necessities, toiletries, a calculator, new underwear and a towel. They weren't really necessities but the ritual of doing this with her was – for me anyway.

Beth went up to pack after we got home, and I'd gone out into the garden. I'd shouted up the stairs to ask if she wanted a sandwich when I went in to make one for myself but she'd called back that she'd get something at the beach.

And then she'd reappeared, just before she left.

What had I said to her? Something about wearing my jumper and being careful on the roads.

What might I have said or done that would have changed things?

Here and Now, in the Midst of it All

We have to get out of the way when the technician arrives later in the morning to do the EEG. There isn't enough room beside her bed for us to stay while several small electrode patches are attached to her scalp and the signals from her brain, transferred via wires, amplified and recorded.

'It'll take at least half an hour,' the technician explains. 'Your doctor will talk the results through with you afterwards.'

So Patrick and I wait anxiously in the bad-news room. Patrick is by the window, rolling his sleeves up and unrolling them as he strides backwards and forwards over the linoleum, and I sit on the grey sofa, wishing he would stop, wanting to tell him to be still, wishing time would speed up and Dr Such would arrive with some good news.

'What news?' I practically spring up and pounce on him when eventually he opens the door.

He pauses and raises his hand, almost imperceptibly, as if holding back the force of my anxiety, like Canute trying to hold back the tide.

'Shall we sit down?' He waves towards the sofa. 'I might just get myself a coffee, if you don't mind.'

I do. But I suspect Dr Such has not slept any more than we have, that he's been there for emergencies during the night and has been doing his rounds since early morning. Perhaps this is his first dose of caffeine for the day.

'Anything?' he asks.

I shake my head.

'No,' Patrick says, coming to sit beside me on the sofa, then taking my hand and squeezing it so that I forgive him his earlier pacing.

Good luck, his touch seems to say, as if we have the wherewithal to influence whatever Dr Such is about to tell us.

'So,' he elongates the vowel as he walks over to us, pulling one of the plastic chairs opposite the sofa, interview format. 'I'm afraid it's not good news,' he begins, stopping to clear his throat. 'I've had a look at the results of your daughter's scan with the neurologist and at the moment there's very little sign of activity.'

'But there is some?' I am insistent.

'Not as much as we would hope –'

'But this can still change?' I interrupt. I almost believe if I ask these questions I can make it change, force Beth's brain back into action.

Dr Such takes a sip from the polystyrene coffee cup he's been balancing on his lap, then puts it on the floor. 'There are circumstances, which, at this relatively early stage, could still change.'

'Yes?' This is good news. This is almost good news. Enough for me to seize on it.

'Beth was sedated to allow ventilation when she first arrived at the hospital. It's easier for everyone if the patient is sedated while they're being stabilized.'

'So the drugs are partly responsible for her lack of responses?' Patrick asks, his reactions more formulated than mine.

I look at him and smile. It's a brilliant question. Why had I not thought this? Why had anyone not told us?

'They could be,' Dr Such says, speaking slowly and raising his voice a little, the way people speak to foreigners. 'Hypothermia can also mask the signs of brain activity.'

I look at Patrick, wondering what he is hearing. Dr Such's manner is so matter-of-fact, so un-bedside, it's hard to assess the impact of the facts he delivers.

I try paraphrasing: 'So you're saying we need to wait for the effects of the drugs and hypothermia to wear off before we see any improvement?' I'm going to stay hopeful.

'I'm not going to raise your expectations,' Dr Such parrots.

I feel out of my depth. How appropriate. We live on an island surrounded by sea and our language is full of watery metaphors. We swim against tides. We try to keep our heads above water. We go with the flow or paddle beneath the surface. I'm out of my depth.

Dr Such, whom I'm beginning to think of as 'Dr Fucking Such and Such', starts to speak again. I look up at the wall in front of me. A poster asks if I'm aged between forty and seventy-four. I'm forty-five. It urges me not to 'miss life's precious moments' and find out if I'm eligible for a health check.

The most precious moments of my life have been with Beth. My health is irrelevant. It's hers that's important.

Early Afternoon

The hospital is already beginning to feel horribly familiar: the ward, the relatives' room and the bathroom at the end of the corridor outside, with its cracked tile above the washbasin, stained enamel, and the Picasso print of a seascape with pigeons above the bath, positioned hopefully, as if it might fool anyone into thinking it was a real view. I have not washed or brushed my teeth or changed my clothes.

My focus is on Beth, my Beth, my girl, but in the absence of any response from her, it's impossible not to take in the details of the other patients: the snippets of conversations with doctors and nurses, the anxious exchanges of loved ones.

In the bed next to Beth's an elderly woman, in her seventies I'd guess, has pneumonia and septicaemia, and on the other side, a young woman in her twenties. She has epilepsy and her latest seizure, during which she was rushed to hospital, lasted over twenty minutes. I don't know her prognosis but I suspect it is not good. Twenty minutes is an epileptic eternity. That much I know.

During the night, a young man was admitted after a suspected drug overdose. He's in the bed next to the middle-aged man who had a heart attack at the weekend.

These people and their relatives are my new neighbours.

'How old is your daughter?' asks the woman whose

daughter has epilepsy, as we entreat each other to go first with the drinks dispenser. There is nothing to do except watch and wait and measure out the day with coffee cups.

She has long, perfectly highlighted golden hair and manicured fingers, and is wearing wide-legged trousers and a loose white T-shirt. She manages to look glamorous, somehow, even here.

'Eighteen,' I say. Too young, I think, to be here. 'And yours?' It's like first-day-at-school introductions. Next we'll be asking where they went to nursery, inviting them back for a play date and asking if there's anything they won't eat.

'Twenty-seven,' she says. 'It's her birthday on Sunday.'

That's five days away. I can guess what her mother is thinking.

'It's not the first time she's been admitted, but her seizures have been getting worse.' She removes the coffee from the dispenser tray. 'She calls it her break-dancing routine. And this last one was one hell of a routine.'

'Oh.' I'm shocked, not quite sure what to say.

'She jokes about it. It's how you deal with stuff, isn't it? I'm Anna, by the way.' She extends her beautifully manicured hand with its scattering of rings.

'Cate.' I smile but I have to force it because I'm new to being so close to death, too new to it to inject any humour into the situation. I press the combination of letters that will give me a coffee with milk but without sugar.

'See you back at the coalface,' Anna says, with the air of someone who is more used to being in this situation than I am.

Waiting

'I might go for a cigarette,' Patrick says, mid-afternoon.

The last couple of hours have been punctuated only by Beth's drips being changed, her monitors checked and the nurse suggesting we might want to get something to eat. Neither of us can face a trip to the canteen. But this inertia is oppressive.

I know Beth is being 'stabilized' but it feels as if she's being ignored.

'When will the doctors be back?' I ask the nurse, as Patrick stands up, patting his pockets.

'They'll check on her this evening, unless there's an emergency,' she says and then, hurriedly, 'She's fine. You can take a break.'

I shake my head. She makes it sound like . . . Well, it doesn't matter what she makes it sound like.

'Want to come?' Patrick asks.

I shrug and walk with him out through the unit.

'I bought a packet at the station,' Patrick tells me semi-apologetically, as we move along the corridor postered with warnings of what smoking will do to him. 'I couldn't face this without something.'

Patrick smoked when I first met him. He'd given up after Beth was born but still had the occasional relapse.

'You shouldn't smoke, Daddy. It makes you go disgusting inside.' Beth had been horrified when she first discovered his dirty secret. She was about six at the time and already her school was impressing the risks upon the children. When I was six we used to make clay ashtrays for our parents in art classes, not alert them to the dangers of smoking.

There are no posters on the wall warning you not to swim, no statistics for the number of people who drown each year.

My dad, a merchant seaman, never learnt to swim despite all his years at sea. 'It's the people who go swimming that get into difficulties,' he used to say.

Patrick taught Beth to swim as a baby, using a method that was unorthodox and a little ahead of its time although she was immediately at home in the pool. He held her close to his chest at first, and he would swoosh her gently in the water, supporting her in the crook of his arm, allowing her to enjoy the sensation of weightlessness the liquid afforded. Getting bolder, he would swim on his back, kicking out of the shallows, holding her on his stomach, her head held high as she locked eyes with him, as if she thought that alone would keep her safe.

I sat nervously in the tiered seating by the side of the pool, watching Patrick as he became more confident, swishing her through the water with speed and in circles, creating gentle waves, which showered her as she passed through them. She didn't mind. She laughed and squealed and thumped the surface with her hands. And when Patrick lifted her high above his head, then dunked her, the laughing and squealing crescendoed and she shook her head, the way dogs do, to remove some of the water from her eyes.

And then he let go of her.

But he knew what he was doing and Beth kicked back up to the surface of the water and the safety of his arms, emerging once more with a smile on her face.

She loved it and, despite my initial misgivings, I loved watching them together, father and daughter, playing in the water like aquatic creatures.

'Babies are born with a diving reflex,' he said, as he wrapped her in a towel by the side of the pool. 'They instinctively hold their breath underwater and they'll instinctively swim to the surface too.' Beth was still smiling from under the hood of her towel. 'Harp seals teach their pups to swim when they're two weeks old,' he'd added. 'They need to be able to swim in case the ice breaks.'

I must have smiled at the time, moved by the way father and daughter were in the water together.

But we are not harp seals, I think now. And we let the ice break.

The smoking area is a small quadrangle between the various hospital buildings, about twenty feet by ten, with a flue pumping out warm air from the inside. A plastic bucket filled with sand for butts has been placed near one of the walls.

It's grey and damp from overnight rain, the only colour a cluster of dandelions poking up hopefully between the paving slabs.

There's nowhere to sit, nothing to look at beyond breeze-block walls, a section of guttering and a few discarded Coke cans and coffee cups littering the gravelly ground.

44

Patrick nods to a man who is probably the same age as him but looks a whole lot older. He's in his dressing-gown and slippers. Others are a little more dressed, among them a doctor, his white coat unbuttoned, lighting a fresh cigarette from the end of one he's just smoked, unheeding of the warnings on the walls.

Anna, the mother of the epileptic girl, stands against a wall pulling her cardigan around her, as if it's freezing, even though it isn't.

I check my phone while Patrick smokes.

There's a text from Mum. It's not punctuated and reads like a stream of consciousness: *Dear caty joe called and told us news about beth how worrying how is she and how are you we are going to get the train over and Joe will drive us to the hospital lots of love and praying for her mum.*

When we return they are there already, standing outside the double doors to the intensive care unit. Mum looks smaller and more silver-haired than she does in my mind, and Dad more stooped. He is leaning on his stick, as Mum presses the bell. They don't see us until we're right behind them.

'Mum. Dad.'

'Oh, Caitlin, there you are,' Mum says, as if they'd been looking everywhere, as if everything is normal, but her voice gives her away.

'Mum.' I feel like a child again, when her presence was always reassuring, would always make things right.

She gives me a hug but it's too intense. Things are not right. 'We've just arrived,' she says, and I hear it, all the pent-up anxiety she is trying not to let me see.

Dad mouths something I can't hear.

45

Mum pats Patrick's arm uncertainly, never quite sure how to be with him now. His relationship with my parents has never been entirely straightforward. In the early days he was convinced my mother didn't like him but it was more complicated. She did. But she worried about the amount of time he spent away and how I would cope.

To me, Patrick's job as a wildlife photographer and the places it took him were part of his allure. To my mother it was a worry.

'Patrick.' Dad puts his hand out to shake Patrick's. Formal.

Patrick takes it, then holds the door open for all of us. 'I'll wait in the relatives' room,' he says. 'Give you a bit of space.'

'Oh, but we don't want to . . .' Mum begins.

But I want to be alone with them now.

'They don't allow more than three people around the bed,' Patrick explains. 'It's okay. You go through with Cate. Is Joe coming up?'

'Oh, yes,' Mum says, as if she's forgotten about him. 'He was just looking for somewhere to park the car.'

I lead my parents slowly towards Beth's bed, knowing that, whatever they've prepared themselves for, they're in for a shock.

Beth is my mother's first granddaughter and I think she fell in love with her almost as much and as immediately as I did. She was at the hospital as soon as Patrick had called. She helped a lot in the early days, when Patrick was away, and later, too, when we moved out of London and nearer to her and Dad.

'You're Granny's favourite grandchild,' I heard Alfie telling her once, citing as evidence that Mum had asked Beth to help her in the kitchen.

'That's because I'm a girl and Granny is sexist!' Beth had replied, laughing.

'Ned's her favourite eldest grandchild, I'm her favourite female grandchild and you're definitely Granny and Grandpa's favourite youngest grandchild!'

And my favourite nephew, I had thought, without meaning to. No one admits to having a favourite, but although I loved Ned, there was something about Alfie. He had an endearing vulnerability about him. Perhaps it was just because he was the youngest and perhaps because by the time he was born I already suspected that I'd never be able to have another child.

'Oh, Lord,' Mum is saying now, looking at the mass of machinery and Beth, who seems to get smaller every time I see her. 'Can I touch her?' Mum looks anxious and uncomprehending.

'Of course.'

'Oh, my darling angel.' She takes Beth's hand. 'Dear sweet child, just look at the state of you.'

Dad hesitates for a moment before he goes up to the bed, leaning heavily on his stick as he stands there. 'Susan,' he says, placing his hand on my mother's shoulder.

'I'll ask the nurse to bring you chairs,' I say, leaving them and going to the station.

When he brings them, they sit, both at a loss for words, and then my mother starts praying quietly, under her breath but loud enough for me to hear the cadence of the 'Hail Mary' she is murmuring. My parents are Catholics still, but I am lapsed. I envy them now, having something to sustain them, other than hope.

'So what do the doctors say, love?' Mum asks, when she has finished.

I fill her in, staring at the grey paisley pattern of her skirt as I speak. Not wanting to look at her, instead focusing on the folds of fabric that are more familiar to me than this setting.

This is one of my mother's best skirts. She wears it to church. She's worn it here. And Dad is wearing a tie, as the occasion requires one.

'Caty,' Mum says, taking my hand, adopting her familiar no-nonsense tone.

I explain that the hypothermia and sedation may have affected the results of the tests.

'She's such a bright girl,' Mum replies, as if she hasn't been listening. 'She's always been such a bright girl. And she's a fighter.'

I look at Beth's face, masked by the breathing apparatus, her eyes closed, no sign of the fierce intelligence that lies behind them. 'Yes,' I say vehemently. 'She is.'

Early Evening

The cat behaves as if he's been abandoned for weeks rather than just over a day when Joe drives me home to pick up a few things.

Mum and Dad are still at the hospital with Patrick.

And Beth.

Joe had spent a few moments with her, then offered to take me home. I recognize his need to be doing something, rather than just standing around, feeling helpless. 'Has he been fed?' he asks, as Tiger follows us into the kitchen, miaowing and getting in the way.

I bend down and pick him up, remorseful for threatening to get rid of him when Beth went away. I hold him in my arms and am glad of his warmth.

'Yes. Nadia, Chloe's mother, has the spare key. They've fed him.' And tidied, I notice. The washing-up, which was piled in the sink, is now stacked on the draining rack, and this morning's post is on the kitchen table, with the packets of wildflower seeds I'd been ready to sow in the garden. I wonder if Nadia has been round with the vacuum as well. The house feels a little more cared for, a little less abandoned. And it's the sort of thing Nadia would do, on top of all of the other things I asked her to do: call work, call the university in Connecticut where the professor who was to be supervising Beth's placement would have been expecting her to let him know when she had arrived. Feed the cat. Close the windows. Bring the milk in. She's probably watered the garden too. I hope so, although it feels wrong to be worrying about it now.

'Shall I make you a coffee?' Joe asks, going to the kettle. 'And something to eat?'

'I don't want to be too long,' I say, unsure what to do now that I'm here. Tiger begins to squirm in my arms and I put him down.

'Just sit for a bit,' Joe says. 'Beth's fine. Mum and Dad are with her. And Patrick. Have a bit of a break. You need to look after yourself, too, or you won't be any good for Beth.'

I sit and Joe opens cupboards. He knows his way around my kitchen. It felt odd, at first, having them so close by when he and Sophie decided to move here from London, as if we hadn't grown up properly, and with Laura, Mum and Dad only a short drive away too.

But we've always been close. Joe and I shared a room until he was ten, when he took Laura's smaller room and she came in with me.

'I love this picture,' he says, closing the cupboard where I keep the coffee and pointing to one of Beth's paintings tacked to the door.

'Her Georgia O'Keeffe.' I smile. A close-up tiger-lily, a school assignment from years back, the vibrant oranges and browns faded with years of exposure to kitchen sunlight.

I'd stuck practically everything she'd come home with on the kitchen walls, taking things down to make way for new bits. But there was still a carefully curated selection: an ode to Marmite, from when she 'did' Shakespeare, a story she wrote about a 'Careful Cat' that never risked any of his nine lives, and a personal timeline, created in a history lesson.

Joe was looking at it now, tacked in the space between the bottom of the cupboard and the work surface. To the left was her date of birth. Then a picture of a baby, an inch or so to the right another baby, Joe's Alfie – 'My cousin is born!' Further along a seagull and then a cat. Not such an event-filled life when she drew it. Getting a kitten was significant and so, too, the shock of a seagull flying into the living room through an open window. Beth had screamed the place down and the gull had responded with angry cries and furious wing-flapping. It had taken me a few minutes to chase it out of the back door, much longer to calm Beth.

The line stretches out into an unknown future.

'What's going to happen to her now?' I say to Joe, as he looks at it, absent-mindedly spooning coffee into the cafetière.

'Don't think too far ahead,' he says, coming over and setting it on the table. 'Take the next few days as they come and hope that the signs improve. Here, drink this.' He pours coffee into one of the cups that were a gift from him. Joe runs a company supplying crockery to cafés and restaurants and, by default, to most of his family. 'And then have a shower. You look awful and you're beginning to smell!'

I manage a smile.

'I think you've finished that cup.' He watches me trying to drain it, long after it was empty. 'Do you want another?'

'No, thank you.'

I get up, ready to head upstairs to shower, change and pack a bag that's better suited to a prolonged stay in hospital than the one I grabbed when Martin appeared at the door.

'I'm going to make you some pasta.' Joe has already taken a packet out of the cupboard.

'Okay, thanks.'

I go upstairs, wondering, but without real interest, whom Joe is calling almost as soon as I have left the room. 'Hi, it's me,' I hear him say. 'I'm afraid something's come up.'

My room looks tidier, the bed neatly made, where I don't think it had been. The patchwork quilt, which my godmother made me for my twenty-first birthday, is placed neatly across the foot. The towels in the bathroom are also neatly folded. This is what women do when they want to help, something to make what you're going through better.

I look out of the window and there's a solitary magpie sitting on the fence and I murmur, 'Good morning, Mr Magpie,' as my mother does whenever she sees a solitary magpie. She says this offsets any sorrow.

Beth's bedroom is thankfully exactly as I left it, filled with the anticipatory mess of the trip she'd been about to embark on. I look at the clothes strewn across the floor and wonder if she'll ever again wear anything other than a hospital gown. Should I bring the Venetian glass horse that is on her bedside table, a gift from Chloe after a holiday? Or the film canister in which she keeps her earrings? A photographer's daughter, Beth has kept things in film canisters long after they stopped being ubiquitous containers for school dinner money. Or the books she'd been reading? Carlo Rovelli's *Reality Is Not What It Seems* and Richard Yates's *Revolutionary Road*, the latter because she wanted to read something set in Connecticut. I'd kept quiet about my misgivings on the comparisons she might draw between the Wheelers' troubled marriage and her parents' failed relationship. There weren't many to be made but I worried she might.

I put them both in the bag, telling myself I could read to her. And the green shawl Patrick bought me in the market in Kathmandu when we first met. A dark green woollen wrap embroidered with tiny gold flowers, Beth had loved it as a child, fingering the delicate petals of the flowers with such delight that I'd said she could have it. She used it as a blanket when she was small enough that it covered her child's quilt but latterly she wrapped it around her shoulders when she sat reading in bed. I packed her lion too, a toy Patrick had brought back from a trip, this one to Africa.

'She kept hold of that?' Patrick asks when I take the lion out of my bag.

I try to put it on the end of her hospital bed, when we go back. It seems childish but it might make her feel less alone during the night when Patrick and I have to leave the unit.

But the nurse intervenes: 'I'm sorry but we can't allow that. Soft toys harbour too many bugs. It's an infection risk.'

'Oh. Okay.' I put it back in the bag. 'I suppose the same goes for this?'

I pull out a corner of the shawl. I want to put it over her, over the hospital sheet, make her feel more at home.

'I'm afraid so.' Her tone is brusque and I feel defeated.

Mum and Dad have said goodbye, for today, and Joe is driving them back to the station.

I've been away for a couple of hours and the things I brought with me, hoping they might make Beth more comfortable, are banned.

'Any change?' I ask Patrick, searching hopelessly for some sign, as if my brief absence would have been enough to effect something.

'No, Caty,' Patrick says. 'I've been here all the time. She's still the same.'

'Oh.' I feel deflated. I half believed that if I left her, if I allowed myself not to be there when she came round, she might.

'There was something, though, while you were out,' Patrick says.

'Yes?'

'It's not Beth,' he says quickly. 'It's the man at the end, the one who had a heart attack.'

'Has he gone home?' Had I registered an empty bed as I walked past?

'No,' Patrick says. 'I'm glad you weren't here when it happened. It was . . .'

'What?'

'He didn't make it.' Patrick shakes his head sadly.

I feel my legs begin to give way and I sit on the end of Beth's bed. He was in his fifties, still relatively young. His heart attack was out of the blue.

'That's terrible,' I say.

It's too near. Too real. Too close to Beth.

'Are you okay?' Patrick asks, putting his hand on my

shoulder. He's concerned that I'm upset by the proximity of death and I daren't tell him I'm relieved. I feel guilty but I'm relieved that it's a fifty-year-old man I don't know who didn't make it through the afternoon, as if his death will offer some protection against the possibility of Beth's.

Going Back

I take out of my bag the shawl I brought in but was not allowed to leave with Beth as we try to settle down for another night in the hospital. Using it, instead of the hospital regulation blanket, will make me feel closer to her even though I cannot stay with her.

'Is that the shawl I bought you in Nepal?' Patrick asks.

I nod, thankful that he still remembers. I was twenty-two. A year out of university, with a linguistics degree, several temping jobs under my belt and a better one lined up: an editorial assistant for a small London publisher of history books. With a month until it started, and enough money saved to do something, I had, on a whim, booked a trip to Nepal, tracking red pandas in the eastern Himalayas.

'We also have a photographer from *In the Wild* magazine on the trip,' the group leader told us, as we gathered in the lobby of a small guesthouse in Kathmandu.

Moments later he appeared, the photographer, wearing his camera slung around his neck, like a professional badge, and a rucksack over his shoulder. Patrick Challoner.

There was something about him, a difference that I could not quite put my finger on. He looked taller than he actually was, a lean, angular physique lending him height that in reality he did not possess. And his hair, which curled in loose coils down the nape of his neck, was almost golden. He was tanned too, the colour of his skin emphasizing the peculiar green of his eyes. He looked like a man who was confident of his place in the world. I felt unsure of mine and a little annoyed when he took the empty chair next to me.

'Hi,' he said, cockily, I thought, as he sat down and the guide resumed his talk.

And then I noticed, as he picked up the metal teapot and began to pour himself a cup of mint tea, his movements were awkward and he spilt a little. He was nervous and I immediately warmed to him.

'Patrick.' He'd sat next to me again at dinner, offering his hand this time.

'Cate.' I took it.

'Ah.' He smiled, as if I'd answered a question.

'What?'

But the guide was tapping a glass with a fork, asking what we'd like to drink with our dinner, recommending the local beer. And after the meal, the instructions for the following day: we'd be leaving at nine, taking a minibus to the foothills of Kanchenjunga, the third highest mountain in the world. If we wanted to explore the city before we left we'd have to be up at dawn. Kathmandu woke early but we might need the rest. If we went out this evening we shouldn't go unaccompanied. We would meet for breakfast at eight.

I walked out into the hotel lobby, aware that Patrick was only a few paces behind me.

'Have you been to the square yet?'

'No,' I said. 'I walked around a bit before dinner but I didn't get very far.'

'It's better at this time of night,' he said. 'Want to take a look now?'

'Okay.' I wondered at the slight trace of accent and followed him outside where he paused to fish a packet of cigarettes from his pocket.

'Smoke?'

I shook my head and watched as he took a lighter out of his pocket, flipped it open and lit up.

'Let's go.'

I fell into step beside him as we headed off through the narrow maze of streets that took us to the magnificent Durbar Square and the old Royal Palace. The city was an assault on the senses. Awe-inspiring architecture, vivid colours, aromas of spices mixed with hashish. Everywhere people, animals, vehicles. The whole place teeming with life. I defy anyone to stand in the square and not to feel affected by it all.

But the thing that affected me most was Patrick.

During the ten days that followed, Patrick began slowly to fill a space I had not even known was there.

Trekking from our base in Dobate, we moved through the forested foothills of the eastern Himalayas, in single file or falling into step alongside others. Increasingly I found myself walking beside him, eliciting facts about each other and our knowledge of the world as we took in our surroundings.

He knew what to look for.

'Look.' He pointed out a small chestnut bird with a black-and-white cloak around its shoulders. 'A spotted laughing thrush.' He raised his camera and a series of shutter clicks sent it fluttering into the surrounding rhododendrons. 'We'll see more.' He shrugged 'They're fairly common. Here and in Bhutan. And they have a lovely song.'

'How does it go?'

'A kind of *wu-it, wu-u, wu-u, wi-u, wi-u*.'

I laughed.

'They have better voices than I do,' Patrick said.

I liked his voice. It was soft, with the slightest trace of that indeterminable accent but gentle and soothing to listen to. 'Have you always been into birds?' I asked.

'Not until I reached my teens.' He smiled.

'I meant . . .'

'I know. Yes, from quite an early age. I remember going to feed these ducks that weren't ducks and asking my dad what they were. He didn't know but he had an *Observer's Book of Birds* that he gave me.'

'What were they? The ducks that weren't ducks?'

'Terns. Not that exciting, really, but the book opened up a whole new world.'

On the third day of our trip we were rewarded with a sighting of the hitherto elusive red pandas. We climbed steadily through the alpine forests with our local guide, Tashi, who had grown up there, learning to read the landscape around him before the alphabet. He paused often to examine a patch of disturbed leaves or scrutinize the bark of a tree, and eventually led us to a clearing where the foliage was less dense. Here the sunlight penetrated the canopy of trees and an adult panda lay stretched out across a branch, as if sunning itself. Our presence sent it climbing higher into the trees but we waited.

'Be still,' Tashi urged.

Patrick crouched in the undergrowth, pointing his camera towards thick clusters of bamboo, silently alerting the rest of the group to two more red pandas, dining on the shoots that surrounded them. They were beautiful creatures, a deep russety red, with cream and black ringed tails and jet black eyes. There was something almost spiritual about seeing them up close in their natural habitat.

The encounter lasted only a few moments but it stayed with me.

'You can't put it into words, can you?' Patrick said, higher up the mountain path.

'No,' I said, thinking. 'But there's a line from *The Little Prince*.'

'What is it?'

'"The most beautiful things in the world cannot be seen or touched, they are felt with the heart."'

'Yes,' Patrick said. 'That's exactly right.'

I knew then that the sense of euphoria I felt was not just because of the sighting: it was being with Patrick, the ease of being with him, the sense of understanding we seemed to possess.

I'd started to fall in love, to move towards a time when I would be happier than I'd ever thought possible.

Early Next Morning

In the morning my eyes are red, the bags underneath them more pronounced. My skin is dry but perspiring from the heat of the hospital and my hair is plastered with sweat to the side of my head.

And Rachel arrives. Early. At the start of visiting hours. Before the doctors have done their rounds. Before Beth has been given the further tests we've been promised. Before I'm ready for her to be here.

She looks like someone who has not spent the past night sleeping in a reclining chair in a room that is stiflingly hot, never dark and never quiet. She looks concerned, but fresh and well.

I hear her before I see her. Her American accent cuts across the hum of the ward as she asks the duty nurse what she should do with the huge bunch of flowers that cannot be brought in.

'Didn't you tell her that flowers aren't allowed?' I say, as Patrick gets up.

He seems not to hear me.

Rachel is wearing black trousers and a cream jacket over a white shirt. Her short white-blonde hair, a legacy of her Scandinavian roots, is pulled back into a neat ponytail. She looks groomed, the way New Yorkers do. The way Brits have yet to master. And she looks out of place.

'Can you give them to someone else here?' she's asking

the nurse. 'There must be plenty of people who want flowers.'

I look away as Patrick reaches her and they embrace.

'Rachel's here,' I tell Beth. 'She wants to see you, sweetheart.'

'Hey, Caitlin.' Rachel is approaching the bed, arms open. I stand up and she hugs me awkwardly, although I am the one who makes it so. She smells clean. I catch a trace of sandalwood and a whiff of mint as she kisses my cheek.

'How are you doing? How's Beth?' She glances nervously towards the bed.

'I've been better,' I say. 'And Beth? Well, you can see for yourself.'

I see the shock register and the uncertainty: Rachel, unsure what to do or say when usually she is so confident.

'Hey, sweetie,' Rachel says, looking at Patrick, as if for permission.

'You can come here.' I move away from Beth. 'I need to go to the bathroom.'

I let Rachel access the bedside and she smiles apologetically. 'Don't go on my account.'

'I'm not,' I say.

As I head for the door, I hear Rachel saying to Patrick, 'Jesus, poor Cate.'

Rachel and Patrick go for a coffee when my younger sister Laura arrives later, apologizing. 'I'd have come earlier but there was no cover until this afternoon.' She teaches at a primary school in the neighbouring county.

'It's good to have you here now.'

Laura's presence is somehow more comforting than anyone else's. She doesn't ask too many questions. She just sits with me and Beth until Patrick and Rachel return, and the nurse tells us all to clear the bed while another EEG is carried out.

Laura leaves. She has to get back for a parents' evening but promises to come again tomorrow. Rachel absents herself, while Patrick and I wait on the bad-news sofa for Dr Such to come and speak to us, to translate whatever results the scan has yielded.

He sits down opposite us. Serious. No suggestion of coffee to delay the news. Just stark delivery.

Rachel returns to find us both back at Beth's bedside, stunned and sombre.

'Has something happened?' She detects the change in us where there is none in Beth. Still.

I grip Beth's hand, which I'm holding, tighter. I can't look at her. I can't quite bear the disparity between the mental image I carry of her in my head and the reality of the way she is now.

'They're going to do another test tomorrow morning,' Patrick tells Rachel. 'But . . .'

'Patrick,' I plead. 'Not here.'

I don't want the words spoken in front of her. Because, despite everything we've been told, a part of me still thinks, still hopes, that everything will be fine.

'Patrick?' Rachel looks at him.

'Let's go outside,' he says to her. 'Is that okay, Cate? Will you be okay for a bit?'

I nod. But I will not.

'I'll be straight back.' He puts his hand on my shoulder before leaving.

'Beth,' I plead with her. 'Sweetheart, please.'

I'd been hoping so hard for something, something better than the news we were given.

The Morning After the Night Before

I don't remember sleeping during the night but I suppose there were moments when I must have dozed off, when my mind was free from the reality of it all. Perhaps I had dreams, which I no longer remember, that everything was okay. That time had rewound, that Beth had never gone for a second swim, that the ache that feels as if it will split me in two is duller, that I'm missing Beth because she's in America.

Someone has left a copy of *Psychologies* magazine lying open in the bad-news room, evidence that something has changed since we were here yesterday, since Dr Such told us unequivocally that, whatever happened, Beth would be brain damaged.

I know now that I've been kidding myself, thinking she might just wake up and be back to normal. We're never going to get her back, not the Beth we had.

'Live the Life You Have,' says the headline in the magazine, and beneath it a couple of explanatory sentences:

'It's not always possible to change your life but you can change your attitude to it. The key to happiness lies in accepting the cards you've been given and learning how to make the most of them.'

It's almost as if someone left the magazine open deliberately at these pages. I snap it shut.

It's beginning to feel like *Groundhog Day*, this constant

returning to the bad-news room. The incessant waiting for the results of more tests, for Dr Such to appear and explain them to us.

'I'm afraid I don't have good news,' he begins this morning, pushing his thick glasses up his nose, frowning slightly as they reach the bridge. He clears his throat. 'In a situation like this,' he resumes, 'we keep repeating tests, looking for, hoping for signs of recovery.'

'But you said yesterday that, whatever happens, she'll be badly brain damaged?'

It's a statement I phrase like a question, hoping he might tell us he was mistaken.

'It's more serious than that.' His voice has an edge to it. It's not unkind. It demands our attention.

I look up and catch his eye but he looks quickly down at the floor. I follow his gaze, which seems to be focused on a tear in the corner of the grey linoleum, revealing a patch of darker floor beneath.

'I'm afraid it's no longer just brain damage we're looking at here,' he says. 'The stark truth is there are no signs of brain activity at all. I'm afraid that what you're looking at now is . . .' He looks up and we look at him.

Despite the circumstance, despite his lack of bedside manner, I feel sorry for him, and sick, stifled, unable to breathe until I have heard what he has to say.

He puts his hand over his mouth and moves it slowly down, as if smoothing a non-existent beard. '. . . brain death,' he finishes, barely pausing before he explains further. 'Beth's brain is not functioning at all.'

I hear the words but the full weight of them does not hit me. Not immediately. A kind of numbness passes over me. My brain is tingling, like pins and needles, but right inside my head, distracting me from the impact of what he has said.

Dr Such does not speak. Not immediately. His mouth is closed but he moves it, as if he is preparing the words that are about to come out of it.

'One of my colleagues will carry out another assessment later this morning to confirm my results.'

He pauses, as if to make absolutely sure we're taking all of this in.

I'm struggling too.

'If brain death is confirmed, there is no chance of her making a recovery. I'm so sorry.'

His voice trembles as he speaks and this has more impact than the words themselves.

'But there must be . . .' I begin, my voice taking on a pitch and tone that are wholly unfamiliar to me, underscored by desperation. Some hope, I think but cannot say, something to try to cling to.

Tears are forming but I'm not going to let them come. Not yet. There will be more tests later this morning and a different doctor.

'I'm very sorry,' he says, and I stand up, before he can say any more, and push past him. I have to get back to Beth.

What Hope Remains

It's easy not to believe in miracles until a miracle is the only thing left to believe in. I know my mother has been praying for one. She's seen Beth, heard what the doctors have to say. She trusts them and their medical knowledge, but she does not put all her faith in them. That lies elsewhere. So she has been praying for a miracle, something that will change the situation in a way that nobody understands.

And in the absence of hope from anywhere else, I find myself wishing, if not praying, for one too. Me, the sceptic, the woman who, when paddle-boarding became a thing, suggested that maybe Jesus had been an early enthusiast.

A new doctor comes to examine Beth later: Dr Tregowan, a woman, younger than me, in her thirties. We've been told that she is the consultant who will confirm brain death. Unless a miracle has occurred.

She explains this herself too. That she is looking for brain stem reflexes. She is fresh-faced and pretty, this doctor, curly blonde hair scraped back from her face in a way that would be severe were her features not so soft. And she speaks with a slight accent, which I think may be Cornish.

She starts to draw the curtains around the bed, expecting us to leave. We know the procedure.

'Please can I stay?' I beg.

'The tests are distressing to watch.'

'I know, but I'm her mother. I want to be there for her.'

'I'd like to stay too,' Patrick says quietly, and I exhale.

We stand as she moves to Beth's head, takes a torch from the pocket of her coat, shining it in Beth's eyes before she holds one open, takes a tissue and strokes it across the cornea.

I wince and look away.

She applies pressure to Beth's forehead and pinches her nose. No response. 'I'm going to test her airways now.'

It's painful to witness but I cannot look away as she removes the tube from Beth's windpipe and waits, I don't know how long for – a few seconds but it feels like longer before the doctor moves her head, almost imperceptibly. It's a no. There is nothing, she is telling us wordlessly before she reinserts the tube back into Beth's airways. There is no gagging, no coughing, which are the signs you would expect from someone whose brain is still alive.

There has been no miracle.

She writes something on Beth's notes before turning to us.

I feel Patrick's hand taking mine. Grasping it. I hear my own sudden noisy intake of breath because for several seconds I forget to breathe. We remain motionless, stunned, waiting.

'I'm so sorry,' Dr Tregowan says, and the tiny nano-sliver of hope that had been there disappears. The prospect of a miracle I'd dared myself to think might happen is obliterated.

'What did you write?' I ask accusingly. 'What did you just write on Beth's notes?'

'I wrote the time,' she says. 'And I confirmed that there are no signs of brain activity.'

Patrick's hand is still in mine. He squeezes it so hard it hurts. I don't care. I understand. He needs to curl his hand around something and crush it. He needs that release. Let him break every bone in my hand, I think. Let him.

I hate Dr Tregowan. What gives her the right to do this to us?

'No!' I shout, shaking my hand free of Patrick's, stepping closer to Beth, trying to pull the tubes from her mouth myself as Dr Tregowan tries to restrain me. 'Breathe,' I say to Beth, pulling away, trying to get to her. 'Just breathe. Stop this now. Don't give up. You can't just give up like this.'

I am thumping my hands on her chest, pushing down on it as if performing CPR. I slap her cheek sharply, trying to shock her back into life.

'Caty, stop.' Patrick grabs me from behind and pinions me in an arm lock. 'Stop, Caty. Stop.'

I struggle for a bit but he's too strong for me. I succumb. I lean back against him and allow the arm lock to transition into a hug, allow his grip to loosen and his hands to stroke my arms into some sort of submission.

I am defeated.

Our World, Collapsing

Jesus wept, I think. The shortest verse of the Bible from the Gospel of St John. Strange the things that come to mind at the worst possible moments. Jesus wept when he arrived at Lazarus's home and found him already dead. But he performed a miracle. Lazarus rose again.

Where is our miracle? Where is it?

I don't believe this is actually happening.

It doesn't seem possible that Beth, who is still warm to touch, whose heart still beats and whose chest still rises and falls, will not rise from her bed and walk.

Perhaps it is this disbelief that prevents me from weeping – for the time being.

Joe arrives later with Sophie and Alfie, who comes straight over to me, stepping ahead of his parents. 'Aunty Cate,' he says, and there's no bravery. He's crying. He won't look at me.

'Alf.' Sophie puts her hand in the small of his back. 'Ned sends his love,' she says to me. 'Obviously he wishes he could be here.' Ned's been away for the year, backpacking in Asia, seeing the world before starting university just like Beth should have been.

They have moved Beth into a private room for the day.

Alfie can hardly look at her.

He glances briefly to the bed and asks Sophie if he can

go now. I'd probably do the same if I were him. He's fifteen, too young for this.

Evan comes with his mother too. He looks so worried he appears several years younger: an anxious ten-year-old, not the young man who'd been in a relationship with my daughter. He bends down and kisses her and I look away, allowing him this moment of privacy.

When I look up he's walking away from the bed and his mother has her arms open but it's me he turns to and I find myself hugging him, too tightly.

I leave the room when Rachel arrives. She is tearful when she comes out and she holds me the way she must have held Patrick moments earlier. 'I love her very much,' she says.

I nod because words are inadequate now. She takes my hand and gradually lets it go, stifling a sob as she walks away, on her own.

She shouldn't be alone but Patrick must be here, with me and Beth.

Mum's holding Beth's hand, fiddling with her rosary in the other, saying prayer after prayer as her fingers move around the blue glass beads. She is wearing one of her church dresses today, patterned with tiny flowers. And Dad's in a jacket and tie again. Respectful.

'Caty, love,' Dad says, after they've both kissed Beth, but nothing more.

Mum hugs me so tightly I can hardly breathe.

And then it is just the three of us, Beth, Patrick and me. I put my hand on her chest so that I can feel its rise and fall, take her hand and hold her wrist so I can sense her heartbeat drumming against my fingertips. I want to tell her how much I've loved her, what joy she brought to my life, how without her it would have been a shadow of a life, but I can't speak.

Everything I feel and have felt is eclipsed by the reality and the moments that will follow.

Patrick raises her hand to his face and kisses it. I watch him as he holds it against his cheek and runs his fingers down her forearm. I see him mouthing words silently.

And then there's a quiet knock at the door and it opens gently and Dr Tregowan is momentarily caught in a shaft of morning sunlight as she stands there. Her hair shines around her gentle face like a halo. She has the appearance of an angel and she has come to take my angel away.

'When you're ready,' she says.

I bend over Beth, I hold her tight and I kiss her, and when I try to stand up, I feel my legs giving way and Patrick's hands under my armpits as he tries to support me.

He holds me now, but not so tightly that I cannot see Dr Tregowan, and a nurse coming into the room.

I bury my head in Patrick's chest, unable to watch as they wheel her out of the room.

I struggle to breathe, gasping, trying to get air into my body and then I feel my lungs inflate and a sudden rush of cold air enter and I begin to howl. Something somewhere deep inside me has been dislodged: a pain far worse than any I have experienced before is unleashed.

At first it is all-consuming. After a while I am aware that Patrick's body, too, is convulsing in pain, as he emits deep, low animal sounds of distress.

I stretch my arm and put my hand on his back. He turns

and reaches for me and somehow the physical presence of each of us calms the other.

I read something somewhere about the enormous odds every one of us defies to be born. For us to be here depends on a particular sperm fertilizing a particular egg. Over an average lifetime a man produces around five trillion sperm so the odds on one fertilizing one of a woman's hundred thousand eggs are about one in five quadrillion. That's a five with fifteen zeroes on the end. And that's before you calculate the chances of your meeting the person with whom you have a child in the first place.

To have a child, for any one of us to be born, is a miracle. Most people are never going to die because they will never be born. But it doesn't help to know that the miracle my mother's been praying for, and I've been hoping for, has already happened, eighteen years ago when she was born. That we've had our miracle.

What Remains

What is it that remains of someone who has ceased to exist?

Beth's presence is everywhere at home. In her sweat-shirt slung over the back of a chair in the kitchen, in the bottle of nail varnish on the coffee-table in the living room, in the half-drunk coffee on the table in the hall and the pile of clothes in her bedroom.

She is here in all those existent objects but in the non-existent ones too. She's here in the absence of apple juice, which I mentally note I must buy, forgetting that she will not be there for breakfast. She is here in the email about student finance, and she is here in the unspoken conversations I keep half opening my mouth to have.

I find myself struggling to comprehend how she can possibly not be here.

There's a photograph on the mantelpiece, of Patrick and me standing beside our tent in the Serengeti at dusk. We are young and happy, our faces softened by love and the soft shine of stars.

The Serengeti was the biggest, widest landscape I'd ever encountered. Endless plains, hung over with huge skies and thousands of animals moving together, across and below them, travelling thousands of miles over many months in search of food and water. It made me feel very small and yet somehow a part of something much bigger.

It was where I had got pregnant with Beth.

'Where was I when you were there?' Beth had asked me when she was about three, looking at the photograph, still too young for me to explain that she'd been conceived there. 'Why didn't you take me with you on that holiday?'

The idea that before she was born, she had simply not existed was impossible for her to grasp.

'Where was I when you met Daddy?' she would ask.

'You weren't born yet.'

'I know that but where was I?' I can still see her face. Expectant.

'You weren't anywhere. You didn't exist.'

It's an incomprehensible thing to say to a five-year-old.

'But I must have been somewhere. I can't have just not been anywhere.'

And I find myself asking versions of those questions now. Where is she? How is it she has gone and yet I feel her absence more acutely than her presence?

'I'm just going to water the roses,' I tell Patrick, heading out to the garden.

I plan to place small bunches of roses around the crematorium, like the ones I used to arrange in a jam-jar beside her bed, throughout the summer months, an ever-present display of soft pinks, yellows and reds with their gentle, subtle scents. I want her to be surrounded by family and friends and the small touches that were part of her life.

'Are you sure you're up for it?' Sophie asked. 'I'm happy to arrange them if it would help.'

'No.' I was adamant that I would do this.

I also plan to make her a wreath with flowers from the

garden: lavender, soft pink mallow flowers and Beth's favourite Michaelmas daisies. She and Chloe used to make giant daisy chains with them when they were small.

I remember going out one day to find the garden draped with the biggest floral necklace ever, the girls delighted by their efforts.

I want to delight Beth with mine.

I have been tending the garden with renewed care since we left the hospital: weeding, watering, pruning and dead-heading. I want the flowers to be perfect, beautiful. 'Do you think I could ask if one of the florists in town will let me have foam? Or should I order it online?' I ask Patrick, as I watch wreath-making demonstrations on You-Tube, finding it hard to believe that any of this had really happened.

Patrick's presence, at home, in the house he hasn't shared with us for years, heightens the sense of unreality. It's as if we have simply slipped back in time and I half expect seven-year-old Beth to appear, twiddling her hair furiously around her finger the way she used to until she coiled it so tightly one day at school that she stopped the blood supply and the teacher, in a panic, cut it free.

'Another lasagne!' Patrick announces, putting an ochre foil-covered ceramic dish on the kitchen table. 'Is there any room for it?'

I'm by the freezer trying to make space for the variety of pies, flans, stews and lasagnes that people have brought round or left on the doorstep. Friends and neighbours don't wish to bother us but they need to do something. They bring food.

'How many is that now?' Patrick asks.

'At least ten.'

'It's like *Bake Off*. We should judge them.'

I know this is a joke, that Patrick is doing his best, to keep going, to use humour as a way of dealing with it all but I can't find it in myself to raise a smile.

'Mediterranean vegetable with pine nuts.' He squints at a handwritten label stuck to the side of the dish. 'Why so many lasagnes?'

'Because they're easy.' I try to free a bag of frozen fish fillets stuck by the cold to the back of the freezer. 'It's all there: meat, pasta, veg. All you have to do is stick it in the oven. It's the perfect meal for the sick or the grieving.'

'If there's anything I can do,' they say in notes attached to foil trays, Tupperware containers and patterned earthenware dishes.

'We should eat the ones in the fancy dishes first,' I say. 'They'll probably be wanting them back.'

'The woman who brought this said there was no need.' Patrick sits at the table and watches me, as I build a small cairn of frozen food on the floor.

'Who was it?' I feel guilty that I send Patrick to answer the tentative knocks, to deal with whoever it is. His presence is not altogether a surprise to them but still creates a slight awkwardness.

'An older lady.' Patrick describes the bearer of the ochre earthenware dish. 'Silver grey, wispy hair. She said she lives down the road.'

'Joyce?'

'I think so. She had very fine features and lively eyes.'

Patrick has no memory for names but a photographic one for faces and features.

'Beth used to babysit her husband, a few years ago.'

'Babysit?'

'Dementia,' I explain. 'She'd sit with him for an hour or so while Joyce went to the shops. She couldn't really leave him towards the end and he seemed to like Beth – or, at least, he didn't get upset by her presence, the way he did with some of the carers Joyce had tried before.'

'I think she mentioned it. And wasn't there something to do with their children too? Beth said something about them.'

I don't really want to talk about them but Patrick seems determined to elicit something. 'Her son's in prison.'

'That's it. For robbery or something?'

'He broke into a house and stabbed the owner when he woke up and disturbed him.' I tell him enough to stop the questions.

I don't tell Patrick that Joyce's son won't let her visit him in prison any more, and that her daughter no longer speaks to her because she's still there for her killer child, or would be if he let her.

Joyce is a kind, gentle woman, with a tragedy of her own. I can't imagine what it must be like, living on her own, knowing she has two children out in the world but that neither of them wishes to see her. Does she suppose, as I do, that at some point they will reappear?

It seems impossible that Beth is gone for ever, that she is not somewhere on the other side of the Atlantic investigating gravitational lenses. A letter from the college, addressed to her, arrived the day we came back from the hospital. My first thought was to text her, to ask if I should open it.

It seems unbelievable, given the amount of organization Patrick and I are putting into her funeral and the gathering afterwards, that she will not be there, surrounded by her friends and family.

I expect her to walk into the kitchen, kick off her shoes and flop into the armchair by the fridge or start rearranging the garish magnetic letters that have been on it since she was a child, even as her father stands by the window making phone calls that I cannot bring myself to make.

Patrick stands, by the window, where the reception is better. The magpie is back but I ignore it. No point in wishing it the time of day. It does nothing to offset the sorrow they bring.

I find myself watching Patrick. He shifts his weight from one foot to the other, inclines his head, slightly, as if cradling a receiver and runs his hand along the edge of the windowsill absent-mindedly.

He is so like Beth. She used to make exactly the same movements and gestures. They're physically alike too: the bluey-green eyes, the golden skin, the wavy hair. Beth was beautiful and, as I watch Patrick making call after call, I am transfixed by the elements of her I see in him. She is still there in the outline of her father's face and in the way he conducts himself. She's not gone.

Chloe calls around one afternoon, a large tote bag over her shoulder, which she drops on the floor of the hall as I hug her tightly. Neither of us says anything. I know she is devastated by the loss of her friend. I hold her and then offer her tea.

'Kostin was wondering if he could play the cello at her funeral,' she mentions timidly.

'That's very kind of him.' I'm touched by this thoughtfulness. 'Are you sure he's up for it?'

'Yes. He really wants to do something. And a few of us bought this.' Chloe fumbles in the tote bag, which is now on the chair. She produces a large pale blue fabric-covered book, the size of a photo album.

'We thought you could have it at the reception so that everyone could write their memories of her. For you to read afterwards.'

'Oh, Chloe, that's so kind.' I breathe back the tears that have started to form, for Chloe's sake. 'What a lovely idea.'

'I thought about offering to say something but I really don't think I'll be able to, Cate,' Chloe says, her voice cracking.

'It's okay, sweetheart.' I put out my hand and take hers. She squeezes mine in return.

'But this way everyone will have the chance to say some of the things they'd like to say.' She lets go of my hand and traces the grooves of the book's fabric with her fingers, as if caressing the memories of her friend that it does not yet contain.

I wonder if I'll be able to say anything about my beautiful, wonderful, talented daughter. Occasionally I lock myself into the bathroom and I try to practise in front of the mirror. But I'm thrown by the drawn appearance of the woman I see reflected. I don't look like myself. I look like a woman who has lost a child, a condition that cannot be summed up in a single word.

There is no opposite of 'orphan' or 'orphaned', no shorthand for a person who has been a parent but has lost their child or children. It's too terrible to contemplate, too dreadful to allocate a word to it.

Back Now

'We should get out for bit,' Patrick says. 'Do you fancy a drive?'

'Are you okay to drive?'

Patrick doesn't own a car. He picks them up wherever he goes, hiring jeeps to drive across the Kalahari, or VWs to take him up into the mountains of Europe, and once an Ambassador to drive along the coasts of Bangladesh and Bengal. At home in London he uses public transport but is still insured to drive the ageing Vauxhall Nova we bought when we moved down here.

I never took him off the insurance. There were already too many connections severed. I didn't want another and it made no difference to the premium. He drove it to Cornwall in the early days after our separation, when we thought we could bury the resentment we felt towards each other for long enough to reassure Beth that the split would not make a great deal of difference to her.

'We'll still have holidays together,' we'd pronounced.

And we had: a week in a cottage on the north Cornish coast, where I'd slept in a twin room with Beth, and Patrick had the master bedroom to himself. We were polite and stiff with each other, and Beth had cried herself to sleep at night, unable to articulate what was wrong but saying she didn't like it.

I didn't like it either, didn't like the people we had

become, the people who turned every question about what we might do during the day, or even what we would have for dinner, into a stand-off, whose every exchange was laden with subtext. Two people who still loved each other enough to hurt but were too proud to expose themselves further in an attempt to sort out where they'd gone wrong.

'You've still got the bunting up,' Patrick says, holding the passenger door open as I climb in. He smiles wryly now, where once 'the bunting' had been another source of tension.

'How many years is it?'

'Eight, I suppose.' I fasten my seatbelt and wait for Patrick to go round to the driver's side.

I put it into the car for Eleanor Prince's tenth birthday. We were going to Legoland for the day, a half-term treat, I hadn't known it was Eleanor's birthday when Beth asked if she could come with us but it had turned out it was double-figures day for Eleanor – it needed to feel birthdayish.

I'd found the bunting, which I'd won at a school fete, in a drawer. I put it up in the car and never quite got round to taking it down. It had infuriated Patrick. The flags flapped against his head while they simply fluttered above mine, but leaving them up was a small victory in a battle I don't think Patrick was remotely aware I was still having with him.

It seems inappropriate now. Too festive. I will take it down.

Patrick squeezed into the driver's seat and bent down to move the seat back, then adjusted the rear-view mirror. 'Where to?' he asked, turning the key in the ignition and unleashing Jay-Z's 'Anthem To New York' at full volume. Beth had put in the CD when we went last-minute 'America shopping'. It had seemed apt at the time. Now it was another unbearable reminder.

'I don't mind.' I switched off the CD player as Patrick manoeuvred the car out of its space.

I stared out of the window, at the row of seventies yellow-brick box-style houses, with their slightly asymmetrical roofs. They were all almost identical to mine although some were bigger, a planned assortment of two-, three- and four-bed family homes, strung out along the edge of town.

Patrick had hated the house when he first saw it, hated its suburban location, boxy layout, and the particularly garish hue of the brickwork. But it was near the sea, close to a footpath that ran alongside a river that eventually led out into the estuary. The sea was never visible from the house but the wide openness of the skies and the saltiness of the air hinted constantly at its presence. To grow up in a house within reach of the sea was compensation, I said to Patrick, for the fact Beth would never have siblings.

We'd been told there was no reason why I couldn't conceive a second time. It was unexplained infertility. 'Just one of those things,' my mother said, yet I had held it against Patrick, more as the years went by.

But we'd been happy, when we'd first moved here. Patrick set to work on the exterior brickwork before he even began to unpack any of his things, rendering it a milky cream he was happy with, and I embarked on the garden with his help, digging up the newly turfed expanse of grass to create flowerbeds, planting a handful of saplings and giving the potted shrubs that had lived on our London balcony a more permanent home in the soil.

'It's a lovely place to live,' Patrick said to me, perhaps a year after the move. 'I couldn't see it at the time, but it's a wonderful place to bring up our child. It's funny, but I've never really thought how lucky I was to grow up on the coast. I never really missed it in London, but even when we don't go for ages, I like knowing that it's there, just down the road.'

We're heading towards the beach now, in the car. Patrick turns left, joining the ring road. The next exit will take us along the narrow lane that ends at the car park behind the dunes.

He glances at me and I nod because, without being consciously aware of it, this is what the last few days have been leading up to. We have to go there and we have to go there together.

The lane is familiar: the sign that points to the country-house hotel where we sometimes stopped for supper after a day at the beach, the field with the rusty red corrugated-iron barn where a prisoner on the run from the nearby open prison once hid for a week, the intermittent lay-bys that allow larger vehicles to pass on the narrow country lane, and finally the golf course, strung out along the dunes, and the thin strip of blue beyond.

Patrick parks in a space opposite a white van and reads the hand-painted 'Ionuţ's Donuts' on the side.

Ionuţ's doughnuts are small, the size of meatballs, and made with lemon and yoghurt. I used to buy a bag of five when I went to the beach and Beth and I would eat them for pudding with peach sorbet.

The van had first appeared in May. Ionut was from Romania he'd told me when I first stopped to buy something, his name Romanian for John. He'd come with his wife and two sons. She worked at the flower nursery.

They were from Jupiter, he'd told me, and I'd looked it up later and discovered a resort on the Black Sea, numerous creeks fragmenting its coastline. And other resorts nearby, Saturn, Neptune and Venus.

Ionut is there now, leaning on the counter, and I nod as Patrick opens the passenger door for me, but he disappears as I get out and is suddenly outside the van, walking towards us, removing and folding the striped apron he always wears. He does this, I realize, as a sign of respect.

'Hallo.' His voice is arresting but solemn. He holds the folded apron between his hands and bows his head slightly.

'Your daughter,' he begins, looking from me to Patrick. 'I hear about the accident. I am so sorry.'

'Thank you,' I say, touched. 'This is Beth's father.'

Patrick puts out his hand and the Romanian clasps it in both of his, repeating, 'I am so sorry,' holding Patrick's hand for a few moments before letting go and nodding, as if to allow us on our way.

We climb the wooden steps over the dunes and descend the sandy path to the edge of the groyne. The beach is fairly empty. It's a weekday, a school day, the weather cloudy and the air damp.

An older woman walks a red setter across the sand. A younger one carries a toddler on her hip and drags a pushchair backwards across the beach. A couple whose sex is masked by hooded sweatshirts sit on a rug clasping their knees, watching a fisherman dig for worms. A few other figures are visible in the background.

But right in front of us the foreground is dominated by a mound of cellophane-wrapped flowers, some tied to the groyne, others piled beside it. 'Oh, God.' I exhale. 'I hadn't expected this.'

What had I expected when we came here? I had no idea. Answers, perhaps. Or something that made sense of it all, in a way this shrine of incongruous, wilting, garish flowers did not.

I am reminded of the last time I visited my parents, the lamppost at the end of their road bedecked with similar cellophane bouquets. They marked the spot where a young man on a bicycle had been knocked down by a lorry as he pulled out of the junction. We were there for a 'family meal'. Bill and Susan, Joe, me, Laura and families. No Ned, though.

'Of course it's very sad for his family.' Mum stressed the last three words when she told us what had happened. 'But since when did everywhere become a makeshift memorial?' I could tell she disapproved of the floral tributes even before she said, 'People have become so exhibitionist.'

'It all seemed to start when Diana died,' Dad said, but Joe contradicted him.

'There was that tree where Marc Bolan was killed,' he said. 'On Barnes Common. It became a shrine.'

'Marc who?'

'A pop star, Mum!' Joe had used the term Mum uses for any musician who is not a classical violin player, and raised his eyebrows.

'It's all just "look at me mourning",' Mum said, quickening

her pace as we passed the spot where the cyclist had been hit when we went for a walk in the afternoon.

What would she make of this? I wonder. Of the flowers tied to the groyne, just beyond the point where the tide was highest. And piled up at its base. Of the messages attached to them with bits of ribbon, all bearing her granddaughter's name.

'I didn't think,' Patrick begins, half apologetic, as if he were responsible for bringing me here.

'Me neither,' I say.

I haven't stopped to consider that, outside my immediate family, other people are mourning Beth in their different ways. I've been too wrapped up in my own grief to think of her friends and their families. And yet here it is, a conspicuous display of their loss, mounting up where the reach of the tide has pushed the pebbles into a makeshift repository for these flowers.

'A *descanso*,' Patrick says. 'It's what they call them in Mexico. It means an interrupted journey.'

'*Descanso*,' I repeat, my eyes smarting with the impact of its meaning.

'Shall we? Are you up to it?' Patrick bends down and touches one of the cards.

'Yes.' But where to begin?

He crouches in the shingle and I squat beside him, studying the handwriting on a small floral card. '"The best friend anyone could wish for. Will miss you so much. Evie x,"' I read it out loud, surprised by the control in my voice. 'Did you know Evie?' How many of Beth's old friends did Patrick remember? How many of her new ones had he heard about?

'I know the name. I heard Beth talk about her. I don't think I ever met her.'

So many messages from friends who would miss her. So many friends I would miss being a part of our lives. So many names that were unfamiliar to me as well as Patrick.

And it isn't just flowers. There are CDs, books, pictures, postcards, items of clothing and the odd toy. I reach out to touch a scarf wound around the post at the top of the groyne, pinned with a note. It's familiar. I can see Beth pulling it out of a bag. 'I bought this for Jess,' she was saying.

Was it just before Christmas? This memory?

'Do you think she'll like it?'

I look at the note, attached to the scarf. 'You gave me this,' it reads. 'But the warmth of your friendship was the greatest gift anyone could have wished for. Love you always. Jess xxx'.

Beth's friendships had always surprised me in their strength and solidity, their loving declarations. I don't think I had friends like that when I was her age.

'What's with the angry little girl?' Patrick picked up a plush toy.

'It's one of the Moomins. Little My.' Beth and I had read nearly all of the books together and there was the dressing-up for World Book Day. I hadn't known they still resonated. 'To my brave fearless friend, the best listener in the world. Who will I talk to now? I will miss you so much. C xxxx'

'Who's it from?' Pat asked.

'Chloe, I think. She used to say Beth looked like Little

My, when she wore her hair in a topknot.' I feel a brief flash of anger towards Chloe. Why?

'"Saying goodbye to you was the hardest thing I've ever done."' Patrick reads another. '"Life without you in it has already begun to pale. You were the brightest star. Love you always E X."' He looks at me.

'Evan.' I feel a pang for him. Losing your first love is always painful. Losing someone like this must be unbearable. Poor Evan.

'What's this?' Patrick's holding a small silver object with a note attached. He hands it to me.

It's a whistle and the note is written on a luggage label attached to it. 'Sorry to hear you didn't make it. Danny.' The ink has started to bleed and I can't quite make out what it says underneath.

'Lifeguard,' says Patrick.

I close my hand around the metal of his whistle and stare at the note. Danny. Did he bring her out of the sea? The feel of the metal in my hand, this connection to someone who was with her, brings a nano-second of respite from the rawness.

But it's broken.

'Such a terrible tragedy.' A shrill voice cuts through the still of the soft autumnal air. The woman we'd seen earlier with the dog is standing beside us.

I take in the long olive cardigan she is wrapping tighter around her, creating an autumnal palette alongside the russet of her dog.

'A young girl,' the woman says, almost proud to be informative.

I cannot say anything.

'The rip tides here take people by surprise.' Her tone is slightly critical now, her presence intrusive.

Her dog has run off, back to the shoreline, and she takes her phone from her pocket and holds it aloft.

'No,' I say, thinking she will take a photo.

'I'm calling the dog,' she says, plummy, irritating. 'He comes to the light of the phone.'

I don't believe it.

'Can we go?' I say to Patrick. He nods and gives me his hand.

By the time we get back to the car, I'm shaking, a violent uncontrollable shiver that is at odds with the temperature outside.

'Are you okay?'

It's like the tide, the way the grief comes in waves and surges. Sometimes it recedes a little, still high tide but out a bit, then rushes back in, hitting me with all its force.

Patrick holds me, before I begin to cry, as if he can see the gathering tide and is trying to sweep me out of its path, enveloping me in his arms, letting me bury my head in his chest while I sob, oblivious to a mother and child peering curiously at the car as they walk past carrying a bag of Ionut's doughnuts.

'It will get better,' Patrick says, without conviction.

'I just hate the fact that everyone . . .' I jerk my head towards the beach, as if it represents the rest of the world, '. . . all of those people say they're going to miss her. I know they're going to miss her. But it will pass. They'll carry on as before. Their lives will be the same. Mine will never be the same again.'

It is there, sitting in the car a few hundred yards from

the *descanso*, that I begin to redivide my life into two separate halves: the life I'd been leading up to the moment when Beth was wheeled out of the ward, still warm, still breathing, thanks to the ventilator, but pronounced dead, and the life I would have thereafter.

My life after Beth.

15 September 2016

Patrick is standing at the kitchen window, black-suited. Joe is coming to pick us up, to drive us to the crematorium and on to his house where family and friends will gather afterwards.

I am standing in the middle of the room, going through a mental checklist: the flowers are ready, my speech is prepared. It feels as if I've forgotten something, and it slowly dawns on me that it's Beth. I should be calling her, asking if she's ready, chiding her for making us all late.

'Two crows,' Patrick says.

'What?'

'There on the fence. Come and see.' He turns, beckons me towards the window.

I go, stand next to him.

'Oh, God.' I shiver when I see them, two sleek black birds perched on the fence at the bottom of the garden, still, silent, staring right back at us.

'It's okay.' Patrick puts his arm around me.

The two birds begin to shuffle on their wooden perches, then glide down onto a patch of grass just in front of the window. They look up again, seemingly at us, dip their heads in unison, and then they fly away.

The doorbell rings and I hear Joe turning his key in the lock, appearing dark-suited, like a human corvid in the hallway.

'Blimey, it looks like a florist's in here.' He takes in the line of jam-jarred roses lining the hallway. 'You must have stripped your garden bare.' He gives me a hug that says everything his jovial words do not.

'There's a few left,' I respond with levity. It's the easiest way to get through the day.

Afterwards I will remember only moments and I will wonder how I got through them all. My brain creates its own anaesthetic, leaving me only with fragments of a day that is one of the hardest I have ever lived through.

In a moment that reminds me of a wedding, mourners arrive, forming a line, as Patrick and I stand at the doorway to the crematorium, but their greetings are more sombre and our responses devoid of hope.

'It's lovely to see you. Thank you for coming.' I hug a succession of relatives, Beth's school friends, colleagues from work. My words sound trite but they're heartfelt.

Chloe and Evan walking up the aisle together, Chloe catching my eye, nodding towards an empty pew. 'Is it okay to sit here?'

'Of course.' I give them the best smile I can muster.

Patrick, Joe, Dan and my father shouldering the coffin – my dad's leg dragging beside him, his face contorted. Me thinking about how it hurts his leg, knowing that this is not what is reflected in his face.

Kostin, playing Rachmaninoff's 'Vocalize' on the cello, creating stillness in the room, which is packed and, when he finishes, momentarily silent.

Ned's voice, newly imbued with a taste of the world and gravity, as he reads Mary Elizabeth Frye's 'Do Not Stand At My Grave and Weep'.

My mother's, breaking as she recites Psalm 23, 'The Lord Is My Shepherd'.

And Alfie's mobile ringtone, Adele's 'Rolling In The Deep', loud and inappropriate, but a welcome break from the sombre atmosphere. Sophie glaring and admonishing him under her breath while he fumbles to switch it off. Me catching his eye and winking. It's okay, Alf, I think. Everyone needed that.

And then I am standing at the front, behind a lectern in a room filled with family and friends, a piece of paper in front of me.

'I don't know if I'll be able to say everything I want to,' I begin. 'So I've written it down in case I can't go on. Laura, my sister, has said she will read it for me if I can't.' I look at Laura. Her face is rigid and flushed and her eyes are moist. 'It's okay,' I address her directly. 'I've typed it. You won't have to decipher my handwriting.'

People laugh. Laura smiles and dabs at the corner of her eye with a tissue. I am briefly buoyed by the laughter, the goodwill it generates towards me.

'Beth, along with a lot of her friends, was about to leave home,' I say. 'And other people keep saying things like "Our biscuit bill is going to be slashed by seventy per cent," or "We're not going to spend nearly as much on hot water." And I realized that the number of Post-it notes I needed would be greatly reduced.'

There's a small ripple of laughter.

'Beth was a great one for leaving me notes around the house. Sometimes they were to tell me something: that she needed more dinner money or a lift after school, but at others they were just her way of talking to me, even when she wasn't there. She'd stick them inside the biscuit tin, saying something like "Stop snacking and get on with your work!" I found one recently on the top of the bookshelf in the living room. She told me she'd put it there years ago. It read, "I didn't think you'd ever get round to dusting!" And it was, by then, surrounded by dust.'

More laughter.

'I kept some of them over the years – I've got a box file full of square yellow pieces of paper with all sorts of messages. Last week I found a new one. I'd been writing lists of things to do, getting through Post-its like nobody's business, and when I tore off one of the sheets, I saw Beth's handwriting. "Help!" it read. "I'm stuck in a Post-it note factory!"'

There's a lot of laughter then and I find I can laugh too.

'I don't know how long ago she wrote it,' I continue. 'If she meant me to find it after she'd gone away or if she'd thought I'd have got there before, but I can't ask her . . .'

This is when I begin to lose it. My voice cracks and I take a deep breath.

'She had a wonderful sense of humour,' I carry on, and I try to say all the other things I want to say about Beth but it's impossible to put all my thoughts and feelings into words.

'She was kind and clever and funny and beautiful and she made my life so much more than it had been before.' I reach the end of my eulogy. 'Having her was like falling in love several times over, and that feeling never went away.

'And now,' I pause, this time unsure if I can go on, 'I read somewhere,' I say quickly, 'that grief is love with nowhere to go and it's true. I loved Beth. We all did. She was lucky to be surrounded by love but now . . .'

I can't finish. I can't say that now there is nowhere to channel that love, nowhere for it to go.

Later

Language, I was told when studying linguistics, is what holds civilizations together. We set so much store by words, by our ability to use them to explain the world and communicate with other human beings. We believe this ability raises us above other living creatures, yet we do not fully understand the sophisticated way in which bats communicate, using echolocation, starlings organize their murmurations, using some form of telepathy, and even apes, so close to us in genetic make-up, speak to each other in a variety of ways that don't include words.

There are numerous ways to describe the act of procreation and our manifest attitudes to it: love-making, when it's tender and heartfelt, shagging when recreational, rape when it's forced. But there is no word to describe the need to be close to someone alive, warm and breathing, to succumb to a basic biological instinct to numb the pain of bereavement, to cling to life, to the very act that creates it.

People talk about need and that evening Patrick and I need each other. Our bodies need each other's for warmth and comfort, and they need the act of love to forget momentarily. Or perhaps to remember. Or for the release of all the emotions that have been swirling around over the past few weeks.

Patrick holds me, afterwards, until I fall asleep.

And this is when I first sense her presence although that is perhaps too strong a word. It is more an accumulation of abstract entities that together add up to presence: a warmth where it is unexpected, a scattering of light in the darkness, a movement, as if someone is pushing aside the still night air. It is practically nothing and yet it is so vivid that I'm sure it is her. Beth, watching over her parents as we sleep.

Patrick is still there, lying beside me, the following morning when I wake. There is no awkwardness. And no guilt.

Even as I recall Rachel coming out to Joe's car with us as he was about to drive us back here, leaning through the window, telling me I'd been incredible and then, to Patrick, in a whisper, 'I love you.'

The night before had not been to do with either of us, but with Beth and the way we related to her as parents. I doubt I will ever tell anyone because no one would understand. Others would see it as a betrayal of Rachel or a sign of hope for Patrick and myself, when it was neither. It was simply a need.

'Do you want tea?' Patrick sits up and moves to the edge of the bed, reaching for clothes on the floor and shaking his head, the way he does when others might say something but he has decided not to, a gesture that brokers no further discussion, whatever the subject.

The crows return later in the day, just before the taxi arrives to take Patrick to the station and Mum comes to roost on the sofa-bed in the living room for the next few days.

This time I spot them first, perched on the fence closer

together than they were yesterday, their feathers touching, and their presence somehow less ominous.

'The taxi's here,' Patrick calls from the front room.

'I'll just be a few moments,' he says to the driver.

And then we're standing in the hallway, Patrick's bag, packed, just inside the doorway.

'We had her, Cate. At least we had her.' He puts his arms around me and holds me close for a few seconds.

I used to say that to myself, when Patrick left, but in the present tense.

'We have Beth,' I would remind myself, when his absence was haunting me. 'At least we have Beth.'

'I'll be in touch,' he says, pulls away and walks to the waiting cab.

When, I wonder, as he gets in and raises his hand in a wave as it draws out into the road? Now that the person who was part of the equation that connected Patrick and me has gone, when will I see him again?

I shiver in the cold of the morning, button my cardigan, then slip my hands into the pockets and encounter something soft and silky: the hair I'd taken from Beth's hairbrush, moments before my life began to fall apart.

PART TWO
Three months later

The pleasure of remembering had been taken
from me, because there was no longer anyone to
remember with. It felt like losing your
co-rememberer meant losing the memory itself,
as if the things we'd done were less real and
important than they had been hours before.

— John Green, *The Fault in Our Stars*

Advent

'Don't put your hair up,' Beth used to beg, whenever I reached for a beak clip to hold it in place or took elastic off my wrist and scrunched it into a ponytail. 'I like it better when it's down. You never get cross when your hair's down.'

I can almost hear her now, saying, 'Leave it down, Mum,' as I pull it back into a severe bun, which will disguise the fact it is dirty and unbrushed. And my foul mood.

People expect grief to make you nicer, softer, more accepting of the minor irritants, because what does any of it matter?

I find it doesn't work like that. My hair is up and I am furious with the world, with all its minor irritants and practically everyone in it.

I am in the local supermarket looking for dinner, it doesn't really matter what. I may look as if I'm browsing the shelves with intent but really I'm just staring, unseeing, ready to take anything off the shelves and put it into my basket.

The freezer dishes have run out. The steady stream of lasagnes turned to a trickle in the weeks after the funeral and now they have stopped altogether. My appetite is still in abeyance but I know I have to eat. And I will eat. Whatever I decide to put in my basket will be heated up and consumed, without enjoyment, but eaten nevertheless.

It's early December, and the bakery is overflowing with mince pies, the shelves are stacked with festive nuts and celebration biscuits and the chiller cabinets are bulging with smoked-salmon and turkey bakes. I'm not in the mood for any of this celebratory food. So far, all I've picked up is a single tin of cat food.

'Why don't you have the moussaka?' I hear Beth suggest, her voice only audible to me. 'Have it with broad beans. You love them. You need veg, Mum.'

I smile and turn, almost believing I might see her.

But it's someone else. Someone real and corporeal, whose voice is loud and whose appearance obliterates the sense of Beth I am still, sometimes, able to hold on to. This woman is tall and solid. Not large or overweight. Statuesque. She has thick straight hair with blonde highlights.

It dawns on me slowly that she is one of the mothers from Beth's primary-school days. I cannot remember her name but I remember how we met. It was Beth's first day at school and we were waiting outside her classroom, Beth clutching her toy lion, which still went everywhere with her at the time. And then, when the teacher opened the classroom doors Beth had handed it to me. 'Here, Mum,' she'd said, suddenly so big and brave – and understanding. 'I think you might need him to look after you today.'

A rush of pure unadulterated love. And a few tears. This woman, whose child Beth had become friends with, had been beside me, witnessing my tears, asking if it was my first child to start school.

I'd nodded and she'd said something about it being her third and it never getting any easier, and then I'd noticed the distinct curve of her belly and envied her. What was the name of her daughter?

'You're Beth's mother, aren't you?' She can remember.

'Caitlin,' I say.

'Yes, of course. I thought it was you.' She doesn't help me out with her own name.

'I was just talking about you the other day,' she says, too cheerily.

'Yes?' I can only imagine she's heard my news.

'A friend is moving into your road. Are you still there?'

'Yes.' She doesn't seem to have heard.

'And do you still have that wonderful garden?' she asks, and I feel a slight swell of pride, despite myself.

'I haven't had much time for it recently,' I say.

'Oh?' I can see her taking in my appearance: the grey hair, the lines on my forehead, the shadows under my eyes, which I have not disguised with make-up, the straggly nature of my brows and the pallor of my lips.

She is perfectly made up. Too perfectly. Her skin is entirely concealed with foundation, her eyelashes are thick with mascara, her lips lined and filled in with a shade of red that seems too vivid for a woman in her late forties.

'Millie's at Bristol,' she chatters on, 'reading law, which was a surprise to us all, but loving it and doing really well.'

'That's good.' I want her to go.

'And Beth? What's she up to, these days?'

I know I should be mindful of the inevitable discomfort that will stem from my telling someone who does not already know my news, yet increasingly I do not care.

'Beth had a place at Cambridge to read physics and was

about to spend a year on a research placement in America but there was an accident.'

'Oh dear, I'm so sorry. I didn't know. Is she okay?'

'She died,' I say, flinching as the image of Beth lying in hospital comes into my mind, an image that is not Beth, not my girl as I remember her.

Her hand flutters to her mouth, in an exaggerated expression of shock. I notice her nails: long, perfectly manicured, siren red. They are not sympathetic nails. She'd need to be careful with them if she made lasagne.

'I'm sorry,' I say, to Judy, if this is her name. 'But there's no easy way to say it. She drowned a few days before she was due to leave.'

'Oh, you poor thing. I had no idea.' She rests her manicured hand briefly on my shoulder.

I resent it being there. I resent that she thinks about doing her nails, that her life is one in which she concerns herself with manicures.

'That's just awful. Shocking.' She looks tearful, says something about needing to get on, people coming round for dinner, but it was lovely to see me and she's so sorry. Something about Beth being such a lovely girl.

'I don't think she ever liked me much,' I imagine Beth saying, as I put a moussaka in my basket and go to the checkout.

Back home, I put the foil dish into the oven. I open the cat food and fork half into Tiger's bowl. Then I sit at my desk, tucked behind the door in the living room, and switch on my computer, filling the time before the oven pings that its forty minutes at gas mark seven are up.

I have two emails, one of which is from a woman who calls herself 'Medium Theresa' and insists all my problems are about to end, the other from the IT department at work, letting everyone know they will be working on the server during the night and there will be no access to it for a few hours.

I'm still on compassionate leave and can't yet imagine ever being able to go back to the offices of the small business and educational publisher in town. They've been good to me, telling me to take as much time as I need.

I need more and yet I also need something to keep me busy. In the absence of manuscripts needing to be read and checked for accuracy, I have found something else.

I click on my internet browser and scroll through the bookmarked pages: all variations on the same theme. All news stories about people who had been on life support and made miraculous recoveries.

I know the stories well. I've been taunting myself with them nearly every evening, staring at the images that accompany the text, images of happy, living people who, the captions beneath tell me, had been given up for good as dead.

I click on the latest story added to my bookmarked list, and see the familiar face of a teenage boy, staring directly at me from the screen, his mother next to him, arm around his shoulders, her hand gripping him tightly. She is not letting him go.

'Miracle Recovery by Brain Dead Boy' reads the headline and underneath a story of how he was declared dead by three doctors. His parents insisted on a further opinion, just moments before his life-support machine would have been switched off.

The boy. This boy whose face is becoming increasingly familiar to me had been in a medically induced coma following a car crash. Three doctors told his family he would never recover and asked the parents to consider donating his organs.

But they hadn't agreed. They didn't give up on their son. They'd enlisted the help of a private doctor, asked for a neurologist to re-examine him and the neurologist had detected brain waves. Weeks later he was discharged from hospital having made a near full recovery.

He's at university now, training to be an architect, enjoying life, thankful that his parents did not accept the word of the doctors but fought for him.

I read these words again and again.

'I'm so grateful that my parents didn't give up on me.'

Why isn't my daughter staring out from the pages of a newspaper, or the glare of an online article, telling the world how grateful she is her parents did not give up on her?

I ask myself this, again and again.

And the answer is always the same.

Because we did. We were too accepting of what the doctors told us. We did not fight hard enough. We allowed her to die.

All that remains is the urn containing her ashes. A woman from the crematorium had called, a couple of days after the funeral, to tell me we could collect them. But I hadn't felt up to it.

'We can keep them here, if you're not ready,' the woman

had said kindly, as if she sensed from my silence that I was still too raw, that I needed more time. Perhaps she just knew this from experience.

'We can store them for up to five years.' Her tone was reassuring. 'So there's no rush. I'm just phoning to let you know they'll be here whenever you decide to pick them up.'

'Thank you.' I'd been grateful for the way she phrased everything, giving me dispensation to wait. 'I don't think I'm ready at the moment.'

Had she heard the suppressed sob as I said that?

'It often takes a while,' she'd said. 'There's no correct time. Some people collect them within a few days. Some wait until the time feels right. And that can take years.'

'Thank you,' I'd said again. 'I'll talk to her father and we'll let you know.'

'Let's wait until we decide what to do with them,' Patrick said, when we'd discussed it.

I didn't tell either of them that I could still feel Beth's presence, so acutely sometimes, that she almost felt real, that I still often spoke to her, or sat with her, and I worried that if her physical remains were in the house, her intangible ones would disappear.

I don't hear the oven timer's ring, signalling that the moussaka is ready. Or detect that the air, which had been aromatic with the scent of meat and thyme, now smells of chargrilling. It is only when the smoke alarm, which Patrick insisted on having fitted, goes off that I remember my dinner in the oven.

The Following Week

'The Shed' is anything but: not small or womb-like, but a vast converted warehouse in Shoreditch, all rustic rough-hewn wooden dining tables, mismatched cutlery and heavy recycled glasses. It's big and noisy even though when I enter there's only a handful of East End hipsters with requisite goatee beards and sleek Apple products dotted around the cavernous interior.

I remember when Patrick and I used to meet here after work in the early days, in an Irish pub that Pat favoured for its great beer and terrible food. It had a varied menu but all the variations were on mince, grey, chewy mince served as shepherd's pie, burgers, with potatoes or bread.

'Shall we meet for a drink and maybe something really bad to eat at the Irish pub?' he used to suggest.

On paper, it wasn't that enticing but it was Patrick, and I was head over heels in love with him. That he favoured this pub full of old men with pints of Guinness and dreadful food over the trendy wine bars just beginning to spring up on the outskirts of the City was all part of Patrick's charm.

Shoreditch has changed over the years. The Irish pub is now a vegan brasserie. The flat above a kebab shop where Patrick lived with another photographer when I first met him is now an Uber office. And the launderette we used to come to at the weekends is now a co-working space.

I felt a tinge of nostalgia for it all as I walked from the tube. So many happy weekends spent, with the newspapers and a tea in a polystyrene cup, sitting on the benches at the launderette watching Patrick's sheets go round and round, blissfully happy to be sharing domesticity with him.

Patrick suggested meeting here today, because it's close to his flat. 'And there's always plenty of room,' he said on the phone when he called: a sign, I thought, that he was about to go away.

This has been the pattern over the past few months. He calls when he's about to leave the country, as if he's worried I might make some claim on him or his time and he has an excuse ready. 'I'm off to Senegal, Georgia, Scotland. I'll call you when I get back.' Never quite connecting.

But this time he's not going anywhere. He wonders if I'd like to meet. Lunch, perhaps. How do I feel about coming up to London?

Anxious. Like I should. That it would do me good to break the daily routine of simply getting myself through the tasks: dressing, cat feeding, washing, cleaning, a walk, the radio, sitting in Beth's room for hours at a time, unable to disturb the contents as if everything is a fragile artefact.

Her half-packed suitcase is still on the floor, two mismatched dirty socks near the door. If I wash them the barely discernible scent of her feet will be gone. The pile of notebooks is still beside the suitcase, ready for the physics labs of Connecticut, filled with notes I do not understand but devour anyway.

I try to understand it, as if doing so will bring her back.

Dust is building on the surface of her desk, around the leather jewellery box, which once contained a pair of earrings and is now where I store the last strands of hair. The ones I denied the house-martins for their nest.

The rest of the house is spotless. I've cleaned in places I didn't know existed: soaping behind the washbasin in the bathroom, dusting the tops of picture rails, vacuuming the right angle where one stair meets another with a special crevice tool that has never before been used.

I need to be busy, yet I've put off going back to work until after Christmas.

Janey, my boss, remains understanding. 'Whenever you're ready. We all miss you.'

And my family is gently persuasive. 'It might help you to have something to take your mind off things.'

Perhaps, but until the new year frantic cleaning helps. Events elsewhere are beyond me but here, at home, I can create an impression of order and cleanliness. Inside anyway. I haven't been near the garden because gardening has always been a source of pleasure. To plant bulbs, to attend to the winter pruning, is something I enjoy, and that does not feel right.

But, anyway, I'm on the train to London now.

It moves slowly through water meadows, which have earned their name during the past few days of heavy rain. Large pools of water, in place of fields, 'swimming-pools', Beth used to call them when she was little.

I watch them disappear into the distance and remember afternoons spent with Beth, paddling in her yellow Paddington wellies. Me freezing, asking, 'Shall we go home in a minute?' Her ignoring me, oblivious to the cold and damp, happy to wile away hours trekking back and forth in several inches of water, letting it slop over the tops of her boots. Delighted by the wet of it all.

I wonder if Patrick remembers.

I cannot see him when I enter the Shed but am shown to a table by an Eastern European waitress, who asks, 'How many are you?'

'Only two,' I say, but am seated on a sackcloth-cushioned bench at a table for eight and handed a menu.

It's seasonal, full of cranberries and Stilton and walnuts, and ingredients that speak obliquely of Christmas.

'Would you like something to drink?'

'Tea, please.'

'What kind of tea?' The waitress points to it on the menu, a whole page dedicated to it.

There's too much choice. I can no longer make decisions.

'Just normal tea, please.'

'What is normal tea?' She is genuinely perplexed.

'English Breakfast,' I say, where I might say 'builders'.

'Okay. I bring.'

I fiddle with the fabric of the cushions, which are made from old coffee sacks, and wonder at the irony of a material once worn by mourners and penitents now being used to cushion the backsides of London hipsters.

I check my phone in case Patrick has left a message and the Wi-Fi connection flashes up the name of the café and 'Tom Hinks phone'. Already I know the name of one of the hipsters with a beard.

My tea comes in a pot. The milk is in an eggcup. It spills when I pour it.

Eventually, Patrick arrives, his phone to his ear. He

mouths to the waitress, gestures to me and says to whoever he is speaking to 'We'll talk about it later. I have to go now.'

'Sorry.' He puts a hand on my shoulder, bending and kissing my cheek. Solicitous. Kindly. He shrugs off a navy donkey jacket and hangs it over the back of a chair.

'That was Rachel. She says hello.'

I nod.

'Can I sit here?' Patrick slides into the sackcloth-covered bench beside me. Close. Too close. I move away a little.

He empties his pockets onto the table, an old habit: phone, keys, some change, an e-cigarette.

'You're still smoking?'

'It's electronic.' He taps it on the table to prove this.

'Anyway, how are you?' He looks at me, with his photographer's eye, taking in the jeans, grey sweater, the tied-back hair and the lack of make-up.

I sigh as a precursor to some kind of answer, which I never make because the waitress is asking Patrick what he would like to drink and he is ordering a beer and saying we need more time to decide what to eat.

'Sorry I was a bit late,' he says. 'I came from the darkroom.'

A lot of photographers never print a single image, these days, but Patrick still does. He sends digital images to the magazine when he's away, fulfils his brief and completes his commission, but he prints images for himself when he's back.

He reaches into his bag now, taking out a brown A4 envelope.

'These are for you.'

'Oh.' I open the flap, tentatively.

'They're from Finland,' he says. 'I thought you might like to have copies.'

I take out a sheaf of photos, some black-and-white, some coloured: Beth on the veranda of a wooden cabin, barefoot and relaxed, smiling against the backdrop of a lake; Beth lying on her stomach in the grass looking out across a plain where a herd of bison roams; Beth in a restaurant, carving curiously into what looks like a loaf of bread but with a filled centre.

'What's that?'

'*Kalakukko*,' he tells me. 'A kind of fish pie made with rye bread.'

'These are from your trip?' Beth had accompanied Patrick, in late June, just after she'd finished her A levels. He was documenting the reintroduction of European bison a century after they were almost hunted to extinction – 'For their hides and for drinking horns,' Beth told me, when she came back, full of the experience but relating it as if she'd been there on her own.

'Are there any of you together?' I ask Patrick now.

'Yes, keep going,' he says, and I leaf through the images, reaching one of them in a kayak crossing a lake, all broad smiles and so alike that I find myself looking up from the photographs to Patrick now, taking in the contours of his face, the wave of his hair, the intensity of his gaze.

'What?' He shifts under mine.

'You two were so alike.'

'I always think she was so like you.'

'She looked more like you.'

'But her mannerisms, her way of speaking, her diligence, they were all yours.' He touches my arm briefly as he speaks.

I pick up my cup and hold it to my lips but I have already drained it.

Patrick puts the photographs back into the envelope, as the waitress approaches and asks if we are ready to order.

We both have different memories of her. Patrick's photographs allow a glimpse of his.

'Thank you, for these,' I say, defying the seasonal menu by ordering fish and reaching into my bag for something I want to show him.

'What's this?' Patrick picks up the object I have placed on the table between us.

'It's the lifeguard's whistle. The one he left at the beach with all the cards and flowers. Don't you remember?'

'I do now. Yes.' He looks at me, curious.

'Danny. That was his name. I went to see him.'

'When?'

'After her funeral.'

'You never told me.' Patrick is turning the whistle over in his hands.

'I wanted to know what happened. I wanted to hear from someone who was there. I couldn't bear to think of her, alone, when she came out of the water.'

'I wish you'd told me. I'd have liked to come with you.'

'Would you?'

'Of course,' he says, a little tetchily.

And, in my heart, I know that this is true.

Too late, I realized that Patrick had tried to support me through the hardest times and that I, blaming him for a tragedy that was nothing compared to the one we face now, had pushed him away, refused to need him when he had needed to be needed.

But I need him now.

'So what did he say?' He relaxes a little, unclenching his hand so the silver sheen of the whistle becomes visible again.

'He said he was really shocked when he heard she'd died. He thought he'd saved her. Imagine that, Patrick, thinking you'd done your job, thinking you'd saved someone's life, working so hard to save it and then hearing that it had all been in vain.'

Patrick says nothing but his hand tightens around the whistle again.

'I've been thinking and doing a bit of research,' I say, delving into my bag again and producing an envelope of my own.

'I don't understand,' he says, looking at the sheaf of newspaper cuttings and articles.

I say nothing but watch as he skims the content.

'Jesus, Caty, why've you been digging up all of this?' His tone is accusing.

'Because we let her down,' I retaliate.

'What do you mean exactly?' The next diner is a few feet away from us but Patrick's slightly raised voice causes him to glance up and in our direction.

'Look,' I say, quietly, nodding towards the printed sheets in his hand. 'All those stories of people who made a recovery.'

'But they're not Beth.'

He puts them on the table and rubs his eyes. 'They're completely different people in completely different situations.'

'But they're not,' I insist. 'They were all in the same

situation. All the parents were told their children had no chance of recovery yet they didn't give up. They fought for their children and now they're back at home with them.'

'So you're saying you don't believe the doctors – all the different doctors – who told us that there was nothing they could do?'

'That's not the point,' I say, because, deep down, I did believe them, even though I didn't want to.

'Then what is the point?' Patrick looks at me and I can see the tiredness written all over his face. He's done in. He doesn't want to fight. He hasn't the energy.

But I do. Being angry is the one thing that is stopping me falling entirely to pieces.

'We shouldn't have given up so easily,' I repeat.

The waitress arrives with a large earthenware dish containing pork belly for Patrick and a copper fish kettle with a sliver of sea bream for me. What happened to plates and jugs? It's the most appetizing-looking thing I've had to eat for weeks but I'm not hungry.

I toy with it a little, in silence, after the waitress has gone. 'I just can't help wondering if there was something more we could have done,' I say to Patrick.

'Don't think I haven't thought the same thing,' he says. 'But you can't keep torturing yourself.'

I can.

I look away. I take another mouthful of fish.

'Do you see Beth's friends at all?' He changes the subject.

'Sometimes, yes. Jess had some books of hers that she brought back, and Chloe's been round.' I thought back to her visit. Nadia had called to say Chloe was back from uni for a few days and would like to see me. Could they drop round for a cuppa?

I missed Chloe. I missed Beth's friends and the house being full of them.

But Chloe, sitting at the kitchen table refusing the cake that Nadia had brought with her, only magnified Beth's absence.

'How are you getting on at uni?' I'd asked. 'What are your halls like?'

I'd come out with plenty of serviceable questions and Chloe muttered vaguely satisfactory replies. But all I could think was: It should be Beth. It should be Beth with stories to tell about the world opening up to her. It shouldn't be Chloe, only half engaged with hers.

'She's finding it really hard,' Nadia said, when Chloe went to the bathroom.

And that was when I realized that it wasn't only Beth who was gone but also a better part of me: the part that could empathize with others, the part that might have felt for an eighteen-year-old trying to make new friends in a new place when she was grieving for her oldest friend, trying to get over the trauma of seeing her resuscitated on the beach and flown to a hospital from which she emerged in a coffin.

I could only think what my mother had articulated in the days after Beth's death: 'It should have been me, Caty.'

I hadn't responded but I'd silently agreed. Or Chloe, who was the weaker swimmer. Chloe, who was safely reading on the beach while Beth struggled to breathe.

I can't seem to forgive Chloe for being there when it

happened. And I can't forgive her or any of Beth's other friends for simply having lives to live.

I don't tell Patrick that I stalk them on Facebook, see their shiny happy faces, holding pints at freshers' parties or cocktails on foreign beaches, and it's all I can to do stop myself messaging them, asking them how they find it so easy to move on?

Evan, too. He has no shame about uploading photos of him on a train with a carriage full of girls, his arms slung casually around two, a smile on his face.

'Do they talk about her?' Patrick asks.

'Not really.'

I push my plate away and nod when the waitress returns and asks, 'You finish?'

'I miss her too,' Patrick says, almost an accusation.

'I know.'

'Can I come down before Christmas?'

'If you want to.' I'd like to see him but I'm reluctant.

'I'd just like to be in the house again.'

'Okay.'

'Are you sure?'

'Yes. If you want to,' I repeat, as the waitress places a dessert menu in front of me.

We pass on pudding. We say goodbye awkwardly and I head home.

Back Home

In my bed at night, lying awake listening to the croaking of mating toads and the courting call of nightingales, is where I feel Beth's presence most keenly. I lie still and I can sometimes almost feel her beside me, the way she used to climb into bed when she was little, seeking me out after waking from a nightmare.

Tonight I am the one having the nightmare.

I am in the car with Beth, except the car is a taxi. Beth is sitting in the driver's seat and I am in the back, separated from her by the glass screen. The car is being driven into an automatic car wash.

Beth looks around through the glass divide between us and smiles, as the water-soaked brushes begin rolling down the windscreen. But there is no windscreen and her smile is short-lived. The brushes roll towards her, pushing against her face, pushing up against the screen that separates us.

I try to open it but it's locked. I can see the fear on her face as the water-laden brushes roll further into the car. I can see her utter distress. The awful sense of being engulfed by water.

And I keep trying to force open the screen but it won't budge. I am powerless to do anything except watch Beth's face up against it, gasping for air.

And then the horn of the car begins to sound and I

wake up and realize it is not the horn but the doorbell, buzzing, loud and insistent.

I look at the clock beside my bed and it's one a.m. Who is ringing at this hour? Perhaps it's a taxi been sent to the wrong house. I bury myself in the duvet and hope it will go away but the ringing continues and knocking.

I get up, put on my dressing-gown and, pulling the curtains aside a little, I look nervously out of the window.

I wonder if it's a burglar, although it's ridiculous to ring the bell, and I think that normally I might be scared but I'm not, because the thing I didn't even know I was more afraid of than anything else has already happened and I doubt I will ever be scared of anything again.

I can see the outline of a figure on the doorstep, moving unevenly, as if drunk.

'It's a drunk,' I say out loud, as if the empty room needs an explanation for this early-hour disturbance. I'm about to knock on the window, wave him away, but then I recognize him. It's Alfie, my nephew, and he is almost certainly drunk but what's he doing here?

I hurry downstairs and open the door.

'I'm really sorry,' Alfie says, teeth chattering. 'I didn't mean to wake you.'

'It's okay. You didn't,' I lie, concern replacing any other emotions. 'You'd better come in.'

'Thanks,' he says, stumbling so that he almost falls as he steps over the threshold, and would have done if I hadn't caught him and the slight whiff of vomit.

'Have you been out with friends?' I ask. 'Was there a party?'

'A gathering,' he says, regaining his balance and moving away from me.

'Ah,' I say, although I'm never quite sure what the difference is.

'A gathering is just having a few drinks at someone's house,' Beth used to tell me.

That sounded like a party, but apparently it's down to numbers. Somewhere around thirty a gathering becomes a party.

I presume Alfie's gathering was in town where most of the kids at his school live. Joe is forever complaining about having to act as a chauffeur because the bus service to the beach, where they live, doesn't run at night.

'I was supposed to be getting a taxi home,' Alfie answers my unasked question, 'but I was sick and the driver said he wouldn't take me. I'm sorry. I didn't know where else to go.'

'It's fine. Don't worry. Are you feeling okay now?'

He nods, embarrassed. 'Yeah, but I'm cold.'

'I'll make up the bed for you. Do you want a shower?'

'Yeah, I guess.'

He follows me upstairs and I take a clean towel from the cupboard on the landing.

'If you want to leave anything that needs washing outside, I'll find you something to wear tonight.'

'Thank you,' he says, looking green in the bright light of the bathroom.

'If you feel sick again use the bin.'

Alfie nods. 'Is it okay if I stay?' His voice is plaintive.

'Of course.'

'Thanks, Aunty Cate,' he says, crossing his arms and pulling the sweatshirt he's wearing over his head to reveal a skinny teenage torso. 'I think this is the only thing that needs washing.'

'Just stick it on the floor by the top of the stairs. I'll find you something to wear in bed.'

I go to my room and fetch a pair of tracksuit bottoms that I bought when I briefly took up running. They're fairly unisex, and I find a T-shirt that might as well be and leave them both outside the bathroom door. 'Alf?' I say through it.

'Yes.'

'I ought to call your mum and dad if they're expecting you back.'

'Oh, God,' he groans in reply. 'They're going to be livid.'

'They'll just want to know you're safe,' I say. 'I'll think of something to tell them.'

I text Joe, after I've put Alfie's sweatshirt to soak in the sink and made up the sofa-bed. *Hi, Joe, it's Cate. Forgot to let you know that Alfie texted earlier and asked if he could stay here tonight. Something to do with losing the taxi money!*

I lied but it would save Alfie a little embarrassment.

He's here now and in bed. Another lie. *Sorry I forgot that I was supposed to text you earlier.*

Thanks, Cate. His reply came back quickly, saving me having to call them. *Was just beginning to worry about him and knew nothing of this plan to stay with you. Hope you're okay with that?*

Yes. It's fine, I replied.

If you're sure. Thanks then. Tell him to call in the morning and one of us will come and pick him up.

Will do!

I hear Alfie coming downstairs as I send it. He looks clean and snuggly in his makeshift pyjamas, better than he did half an hour ago.

'I told your dad you'd arranged to stay earlier and I'd forgotten to let him know you were back.'

'I cannot thank you enough,' he says, shaking his head, as if his own predicament is a mystery to him.

I smile. 'Do you want anything to eat?'

'God, no!'

This time I laugh. 'Do you just want to go to bed then? It's all made up.'

'Yeah. I'm really sorry I woke you.'

'I'm glad you did,' I say, giving him a hug before he goes into the living room. 'I was having a nightmare.'

I've almost forgotten it, and when I get back into bed it's not Beth's ethereal presence I'm aware of but Alfie's corporeal form, in the room directly below me. I fall into a more restful sleep.

The Morning After

'Hi! Do you want some breakfast?' I deliberately don't ask Alfie how he's feeling when he appears in the kitchen reasonably early the following morning.

I'm taking his top out of the machine and putting it on the radiator when he comes in.

'Please,' he says. 'I'm starving.' And then, noticing what I'm doing, 'Oh, God, thanks.'

I leave the sweatshirt to dry. 'What were you drinking?'

'Sirroc,' he says, or it sounds like that.

I'm none the wiser. 'What's that?'

'Supermarket vodka.' He grimaces. 'I drank nearly a whole bottle, I think.'

'Jesus, Alfie, no wonder you were sick. I presumed you'd had a few beers.'

'I know,' he says, going over to the kettle and putting it on. 'But the boys I was with kind of egged me on.' He lifts the kettle off its stand and goes to the sink to fill it, busying himself with the task, avoiding looking at me and my concern.

'They made you drink a whole bottle?' I know this is what kids get up to, but when it's your fifteen-year-old nephew whose skinny fifteen-year-old body is still developing and whose fragile fifteen-year-old brain is still growing it's not what you want to hear.

'They didn't make me but just, you know, everyone

else was.' He turns around, kettle in hand, looking apologetic. 'I know it was stupid, Cate. I'm sorry.'

'I'm not cross,' I tell him, opening the fridge. 'I just don't want you to end up dead because of some stupid drinking game.'

It's the sort of thing I would have said half jokingly. I intended to say it half jokingly but the word 'dead' stuck in my throat. It made the rest of the sentence serious. It stops Alfie in his tracks. 'I'm really sorry, Cate,' he says, turning, his face anxious and pleading. 'I didn't mean to scare you.'

'It's fine. You didn't. Do you want bacon and sausages? And eggs? Scrambled or fried?' I'm all questions.

'Yes, please,' he says.

'Which?'

'All of it?'

'Even scrambled eggs and fried eggs?'

'Maybe just fried!'

We sit down to a massive fry-up. I've not eaten anything much for ages and I find that getting up in the middle of the night has made me ravenous.

'So where was the gathering last night? Was it friends from your class at school?' I ask, a bit auntish but curious too. I miss young people.

'Not a particular friend. Someone from my English class.'

Alfie's taking his GCSEs this year.

'I'm in the bottom set,' he adds. 'So it's kind of full of losers but I have to get on with them.'

Poor Alfie. He's really talented at art and good at maths and music, but struggles with essay subjects, causing some concern to his parents. I think he'll be okay.

Alfie, whose name means 'advised by elves', is a genuinely sweet child and wise, in many ways, beyond his years.

'Are you still friends with Jude?' I ask, referring to one of his friends I've met on more than one occasion.

'Not really. He's cool now.'

'What do you mean?'

'Oh, you know. Obsessed with being cool, hangs out with all the other people who hardly speak any more because obviously that's not cool!'

I smile at his description but feel for him, remembering myself as a teenager, how friends could disappear, swept away on a tide of coolness.

'I wasn't that keen on going to the party,' Alfie says, as if acknowledging some of this in his own life. 'But I was asked and it's kind of weird at home now without Ned.' He pushes a piece of sausage onto his fork. 'And when it's just me with Mum and Dad they keep asking me questions.'

'About?'

'Oh, you know. Just stuff. How was school today? What are you up to? How was the party? They're so annoying.'

I laugh. 'That's parents for you!'

'Exactly!'

'Well, you can always stay here if you need to,' I say, without really thinking.

Of course I didn't mind him turning up last night. And if it makes it easier for him to stay after parties, I suppose he can sleep in the living room again. I don't want anyone sleeping in Beth's room.

But I don't imagine staying with his grieving aunt is really an offer Alfie's going to be keen to take up.

'Thanks,' he says, as if it is. 'I guess I'll have to keep drinking vodka and pitching up in the middle of the night, then.'

'We can sort out an alternative arrangement, if you like,' I say, laughing for the first time in I don't know how long. 'Do you want me to give you a lift home after breakfast? I'm going to see Laura later but I could drop you off first.'

'I can get the bus,' Alfie says. 'Or walk even.'

'You won't be back before dark.' It's a good nine miles from here and he arrived in flimsy canvas shoes, which I also wiped clean.

'I could do with a bit of fresh air,' he says, grimacing slightly as if the breakfast is beginning to kick in.

'You could take Beth's bike,' I say, a sudden impulse that came from nowhere.

'That's an idea,' he says. 'But I'm happy to get the bus.'

'It's just sitting in the shed,' I say, trying to keep my tone even, to make Beth's bike sitting in the shed feel like the most normal thing in the world, trying to erase the memory of her setting off on it and Martin bringing it home in the back of his car, later that week.

'It might need a bit of oil,' I say. 'And the tyres could probably do with some air. Oh, and I think it's locked. It's a combination. The password is 1984.'

'That's a rubbish password,' Alfie says. 'Half the classrooms at school have that as their door code.'

'Really?' It's the door code at work too.

'Yes,' he says, as he heads out into the garden. 'The ones that aren't 1234.'

'It's a good bike,' he says, wheeling it out of the shed a little later.

'Patrick gave it to her for her last birthday,' I tell him. 'She'd suddenly grown out of her last one.'

'Yeah, I've grown out of mine,' he says. 'I was going to have Ned's but he's taken it to uni with him.'

'Then you can keep Beth's,' I tell him.

'Really?' he says. 'Don't you want to hold on to it?'

'I've got my own bike,' I tell him. 'And I hardly ever use that.'

'I know,' he says. 'But . . .'

'I'd rather you got some use out of it, Alfie,' I say, but as he pedals off and I stand in the street watching his departing back and the hand he raises without turning to wave goodbye, I find myself swallowing hard.

It's only a bike, I tell myself.

Beth was nearly six when she learnt to ride one. I can still remember the day. Do all parents remember when their child first learnt to ride a bike? It's one of those milestones like learning to walk and losing a tooth.

Patrick had bought her that bike too, for a birthday present, only then it was from both of us. The one Alfie had ridden off on was a present from him.

We'd taken her to the park, ready to do the thing that parents do: run behind her holding the back of the saddle for hours, maybe days on end until finally the child got their balance and pedalled off on their own.

But Beth hadn't liked that method at all. 'I'm going to do it how you do it,' she said. 'No one pushes you.'

'They did when I was your age. Joe taught me how to ride a bike like that.'

'I'm going to teach myself,' she insisted.

Instead of running back and forth across the grass holding the back of her saddle, Patrick got us both a drink and a sandwich from the café, and we sat on the bench watching Beth, twisting the pedal up with her foot and pushing it down only to wobble and fall almost immediately.

'Are you okay?' I called the first few times, but she ignored me, picking herself and the bike up and trying again.

'She's a determined little so-and-so,' Patrick said, watching her fall repeatedly after just a few spins.

'I wonder who she gets that from!' We said it at the same time, then muttered about not being determined ourselves.

'She gets it from you,' I said. 'Look at how successful you are. You've forged the exact career you wanted for yourself. You love it and you're good at it.' I said it with pride.

'And look at you,' Patrick said, turning to me, as if we were new lovers still unable to take our eyes off each other.

I resisted the urge to look away from the sudden intensity of his gaze. 'You've given me the best things in my life, your love and our Beth.'

I bit back the urge to ask where that had come from and leant in to kiss him, but the moment was punctured by shouts from Beth.

'Mum! Dad! Look! I'm doing it! I'm riding it! I can do it!' She wobbled towards us and rode straight past, stopping only after a good thirty-metre run and jumping straight up again, smiling from ear to ear. 'I did it!'

She could do anything if she set her mind to it.

She could have done anything, I think, as I close the shed and go back inside, getting ready to drive across the county for lunch with my younger sister.

Fifteen Shopping Days
Until Christmas

Have a lovely time with Laura.

There's a text from Mum when I look at my phone as I stop for petrol. She's learnt in the past few months to tap out a few predictive words on her seventeen-year-old Nokia. She's been through an entire ten pounds' worth of credit and topped it up.

'I like to be able to keep in touch,' she says, when we joke about it, as if she's kept up with technology all along.

I read this latest message as I join the queue of shoppers in the service station, their baskets full with croissants, crisps, Scotch eggs, magazines and flapjacks, and garishly Christmassy poinsettias because garages are also part-supermarket and garden centre.

Nobody but me appears to be buying petrol. The man in front of me has a litre bottle of Coke in one hand and a small boy tugging at the other.

'This and a Premium Wash.' He puts the Coke on the counter and fumbles for a note in his pocket as the boy jumps with excitement.

'Yeah! I love car washes!'

My pulse quickens, as the image from my previous night's dream comes back to me but I force a smile at the boy as he does a little skip on the spot.

I sit in the car and reply to Mum. *Thanks. Looking forward to seeing her. Hope you and Dad having a lovely weekend X*

Upbeat. Positive. Letting them know they don't need to worry about me, although I know Mum does, probably all the time.

'So you think they won't like it?' Laura asks, as we sit at a table tucked behind a wardrobe in a strange café-cum-furniture-shop, eating soup from two Victorian-style blue floral-patterned mini tureens, complete with handles and lids. We can buy them when we've finished eating, if we wish. It's a bit like one of the junkyards Mum used to take us to when we were kids and Dad was away. We never bought anything. They were simply outings.

Everything here is for sale, even someone's family silver, with which I spoon my spinach and nutmeg soup. It's monogrammed with an F. I wonder, vaguely, who the Fs are and why their silver spoons are up for grabs.

Laura and I have been shopping. She wanted my opinion on a fireside kneeler she's thinking of getting Dad for Christmas. She insisted I drove over to visit the workshop of the carpenter who makes them, to give an opinion, but I know the subtext.

Cate needs to get out of the house, needs to be kept busy, at least until she starts to ease herself back into work after Christmas.

'I don't know. It seemed a bit gadgety and you know what they're like about stuff.' I shiver slightly despite the soup.

Laura chose this table as it was out of the way but it's in a slightly damp and chilly corner.

'You're probably right.' She doesn't seem bothered by

my lack of enthusiasm for her proposed Christmas gift. 'I'll find something else.'

'I can't quite believe it's nearly Christmas. I've no idea what to get for anyone.' I haven't done any Christmas shopping: not one impulse purchase or online order. It's not just Mum and Dad who 'don't need any more stuff'. No one does. I can't think what to get my siblings or nephews, even though we'll spend Christmas together. The only thoughts I have about it are versions of 'Beth might like that'; 'I might get Beth this for Christmas'; 'I wonder if she'd like this or prefer something else.'

Even as I was giving her bicycle to Alfie this morning, I noticed that the bell didn't work and thought about getting her a new one for her stocking.

'There's something I'd like to do for you, for Christmas, in lieu of a present,' Laura says.

'What's that?'

'I'd like to spend a few days helping you sort out the garden. Do all the winter pruning and things you normally do in the autumn. I know you've not been able to face it but perhaps if we did it together . . .'

'That's kind of you. But it can wait until the spring.'

'I could do with a bit of post-Christmas exercise,' Laura says. 'And it might help take my mind off things.'

I mishear her. I think she says it might help me.

'I'm going back to work part time,' I remind her. 'And I said I'd help Alfie with his essays. He's struggling a bit.'

'Yes, Joe said. They're a bit worried about him. Have you seen them recently?'

'Alfie came to stay last night.' I keep the details to myself.

'Did he? That's nice.'

136

Laura plays with her soup, swirling the silver spoon with its monogrammed F around the cooling remains. 'Actually, Cate, I didn't just want to go Christmas shopping today. There's something I need to tell you.'

My stomach tightens in a selfish knot and I look away, trying to compose my features because I'm guessing that what Laura has to tell me might be good news – good news that I will struggle to deal with just now.

I'll have to force myself to be happy for her instead of feeling sorry for myself.

'What is it?' I try hard to sound excited.

'I didn't want to tell you, not with everything that was going on,' she looks up at me and away again, 'but Dan and I had another round of IVF. We decided it was the last one. We can't afford to try again.'

'And?' is all I can manage.

I don't like myself for it but I'm really not sure that if Laura tells me she's pregnant I'll be able to summon the appropriate enthusiastic response. I know how that sounds. Irrational. Selfish. And the rest. Laura and Dan have been trying to have children for years. They've had four attempts at IVF, two on the NHS, two they paid for themselves. This would be their fifth and, it seems, final attempt. If Laura is pregnant it ought to be the best news ever but I'm not sure I can bear it. I'm not sure I can stand my little sister having a baby when mine has been taken from me.

I feel my chest tightening, the weight pressing down on it. Breathe, I tell myself. Don't forget to breathe. And the image of Beth struggling in the water comes back to me. She's drowning and I'm drowning too.

Be bigger than this, Cate.

'I'm not pregnant,' Laura says. 'I failed again.'

She's fiddling in her bag and takes out a photograph, a grainy image like the one I have of Beth from her first scan.

'They gave us a photograph of the embryos.' She shows me, struggling now with her own grief. 'As if the fact they can fuse them is enough and who cares whether they ever get as far as implanting them in my womb?'

'I'm sorry, Laura.' I reach across the table.

She takes my hand. 'You're shaking.'

'You won't try again?'

'No.' She shakes her head. 'It's too hard. Having your expectations dashed. I can't keep putting myself through it. Or Dan. It's taking its toll on us.'

'I know.' I feel a pang of genuine sympathy for her now. I do understand.

After Beth, when Patrick and I tried for another baby there appeared to be no reason why it never happened. 'Unexplained secondary infertility', the doctors called it.

'Just one of those things,' Mum had said, urging me to be grateful for the child I had, and I was, but it was still hard not to mourn the child I couldn't have. How much harder must it be for Laura?

'Have you thought of adoption?'

'We've talked about it but it's too soon. I need to grieve first.'

I nod and she lets go of my hand.

'I know it's not the same as what you're going through,' Laura says, apologetic now as if she shouldn't have used the word 'grieve'.

'It's hard, Laura. It's really hard. I do understand.'

'When I look at the photo of the embryo, I know it's only a few cells but it seemed to contain so much hope, so many possibilities. I would have loved that baby, Cate.'

'"Grief is the price we pay for love."' I say this more to myself than to Laura but she hears me.

'Is that Shakespeare?'

'No. It's the Queen!'

'The Queen?'

'Yes, I saw it on a fridge magnet in the corner shop!'

The owner of my local corner shop, a kind and gentle man, called Ajit, who runs the Friendly Stores, suddenly decided that, as well as bread and milk and papers, pesto and quinoa, his customers also needed magnetic aphorisms with accompanying scenic views. There's a clutch of them on the counter.

'It's not the mountain we conquer but ourselves': a quote from Edmund Hillary, over a backdrop of snowy peaks. 'No man steps in the same river twice': Heraclitus, looped in italic font around a meandering waterway, and 'Grief is the price we pay for love', the writing set against a background of cherry blossom, 'Queen Elizabeth II'.

'And are you sure fridge magnets are a reliable source?' Laura asks me now.

'I looked it up. It was part of a speech she wrote for the British ambassador to Washington to read at a service of remembrance for the British victims of the Twin Tower attacks.'

'That's rather lovely,' Laura muses.

'It makes sense, but it doesn't really help, does it?'

'I guess you just have to keep loving the people you do still have,' Laura says. She takes my hand again and squeezes it.

Five Days Before Christmas

'How are you doing?' Patrick kisses me affectionately on the cheek when I answer the door to him. He puts a couple of bags down in the hall when I usher him inside and gives me a hug.

'You're losing weight,' he says, stepping back as if my thinness offends him.

But he's concerned. 'You need to eat, Caty.'

I shrug. What does he expect? That I'll be going out for dinner every night or cooking my way through Jamie Oliver?

Maybe I should. Maybe it would give me a purpose. Maybe I could write a book about it: *How Cooking Through Jamie Oliver Helped Me Get Over the Death of My Daughter*. I'd go through the books page by page, recipe by recipe, until I'd done them all. If nothing else, it might help me maintain my weight, which, as Patrick, Joyce and numerous others have pointed out, seems to keep dropping. The last time I really ate was when Alfie was here for breakfast. I do eat but not enough, it seems, not however many calories a woman my age must consume if she is not to be consumed by grief.

Maybe by the time I'd finished eating Jamie Oliver, enough time would have passed for its healing to be done.

Because that's the other thing people say: 'Give it time.'

How much? How long do I have to wait before the

pain, the anger, the guilt, the bloody heart-wrenching-ripping-right-through-me misery lifts?

Einstein was right. The idea of time moving on is an illusion. It's not going anywhere. It's hovering, keeping me trapped in a moment I only half want to be out of. Or maybe time's like a piece of elastic. It can be stretched to give the illusion of distance between the here and now and the moment Beth died, but it always pings back, taking me with it.

Today is the day on which every year since Beth was born we have bought our Christmas tree. The first year, when she was only a few months old, Patrick's father had come to stay with us. He'd arrived, on his birthday, by train from Scarborough, tired by the journey but happy to be here and to see his granddaughter again. Patrick's only remaining parent had met her just once before, when we'd been up to visit him in late October. Terry lived in sheltered housing and we'd stayed in a B-and-B but I'd found it hard, travelling with a new baby, and our visit had been brief.

This time he'd stay with us for a week, and Patrick had dragged a tree back from the local pub where a Bangladeshi family had set up a stall just before Terry arrived. I'd made a cake and we wished him a happy birthday over tea, and Patrick had given him a framed photograph he'd taken when we'd visited him of him holding Beth in front of him, his head tilted slightly to one side.

I remembered the moment. He'd been dancing with her, doing a quick foxtrot around the living room of his flat, succeeding in stopping her crying when, moments earlier, my soothing had not.

'That's lovely,' he'd said, after opening the gift. 'I'll put that on the mantelpiece when I get home.'

After tea, Terry had sat on the sofa in the living room, quietly watching as I tried to get Beth to 'help' decorate it: lifting her up, manipulating her fingers around the shiny baubles in an attempt to get them onto the branches, even though she was happier sitting on the floor and licking them.

When it was finished, I switched off the living-room lights and turned on the tree's, which twinkled. Beth had chuckled and clapped her hands.

And Patrick had looked at his dad, a little concerned, and asked if he was okay. His face was slightly contorted when I looked at him and I was worried too, but then I saw he was trying to blink back tears. 'It's so lovely seeing you with a family of your own,' he said to Patrick. 'I can't tell you how happy it makes me.'

Patrick hadn't appeared to know what to say so I'd said something about how lovely it was to have him with us.

'I mean it,' he'd said, as if we were trying to stop him saying something it was really important for him to say. 'Seeing Pat settled with you and this lovely girl is the best birthday present I think I've ever had.'

And because it was Beth's first Christmas and we'd bought the tree on Terry's birthday, that became the day we bought it in subsequent years, establishing a tradition that we maintained even when Patrick and I were no longer together, and even after Terry died.

It was the day we always all spent together over the festive period. Patrick would come down from London and we'd drive to collect a tree from the garden centre, decorate it together, and when Beth stood on a chair to put on the top the cardboard angel she'd made in primary school, we wished Granddad Terry a happy birthday.

It was almost always still a happy day, as if Terry had somehow blessed it with his sentiments, allowing us to carry on being happy together just before Christmas for many years to come.

The only vaguely Christmassy thing this year is the plywood wreath Alfie made in his DT class and gave to me when he came for his first essay-writing session. That, and the handful of cards I have opened and placed on a shelf in the kitchen; a couple from friends, wishing me a Christmas that is 'not too hard' rather than a happy one, one from Janey, my boss, wishing me 'well at this difficult time of year', no mention of my return to work, which I've suggested could be mid-January.

And there's one from Chloe: a photographic image showing reindeer migration from above, the sort of picture that Patrick might have taken. Inside, her familiar handwriting: 'I'll be thinking of you over Christmas. I know you'll be missing Beth. I miss her too. Chloe x'

'I brought you this,' Patrick says, following me into the kitchen and setting a large jute bag on the table. 'I know we decided against a tree but it didn't seem right to let the day pass without anything.'

I peer inside and see a willow basket containing an arrangement of spruce sprays, berries, red roses, white carnations and eucalyptus.

'I thought it was Christmassy without being too much,' Patrick says nervously, worried I may not like it.

'It's beautiful. Thank you.'

I leave it in the centre of the table, thinking I might move it into the living room later.

'I almost bought a poinsettia,' Patrick says, 'but then I remembered you ranting on about how garish they are.'

I manage a small laugh. 'I just don't think they work in this country,' I remind him. 'They're Mexican Christmas plants. They seem out of place here.'

'I know.' He smiled. 'I thought this was more in keeping with the kind of arrangement you used to make with things from the garden.' He looks around the room, as if expecting to find one now.

'I haven't done much gardening,' I tell him and he nods, as if he understands. I'm grateful to him for this too.

'And something to put under it.' He produces a small wrapped package, the shape of a CD, from his pocket.

'Oh, thank you,' I say. 'I didn't get you anything.'

'I didn't expect anything. It's just something I thought you might like.'

'Thank you.' I feel a little awkward with Patrick here. 'Coffee? And what's with the beard?' He has a week's worth of growth on his chin and is wearing a big cable-knit sweater. The effect is Nordic fisherman and unfamiliar.

'It didn't seem . . .' He shrugs, just as I did when he asked if I'd lost more weight. 'And yes, please, to coffee.'

Patrick sits down in his seat. There are four chairs around the kitchen table and, for as long as they've been there, they've been assigned to each of us. Mine is closest to the cooker and the sink, Beth's on my right, a legacy of the spoon-feeding years, Patrick's to her right, and opposite me, on the other side, a spare seat for guests.

I boil water, spoon coffee into the cafetière and take mugs from the cupboard above Beth's timeline.

Patrick gets up again and gets the remains of a bottle of milk out of the fridge, pausing to inspect the interior.

'I'll make something to eat in a bit,' I say.

'What with?' He looks at the empty shelves before closing the door and staring at the configuration of plastic letters.

PLASMA NUTINI. Beth had rearranged them in the summer.

'I have tins,' I tell Patrick. 'And other stuff. I could make Beth's tomato tuna bean bake.' A dish she invented: a tin of tuna, a tin of borlotti beans, a jar of tomato sauce and a packet of crisps crushed and sprinkled across the top, then baked. The kind of dish a teenager, who often has to make her own meals, might come up with. A surprisingly tasty one.

'That thing with the crisps?' Patrick asks, as I join him with coffee. 'That was a good invention.'

It's a little thing, but it matters that he remembers. I smile as I sit down and Pat takes my hand. 'And Marmot-egg,' he adds. 'Remember that?'

'Of course.' Mashed potato with Marmite and a poached egg on top. 'Genius! I'd forgotten about that.'

'She used to make it when she stayed with us.' Patrick smiled as if at the memory.

'How's Rachel?'

'Okay.' Patrick is noncommittal. 'She sends her love.'

'Work?'

It feels weird having Patrick here, more awkward than when I met him in London. That was neutral. This has become my space.

We lapse into a silence.

'Have you thought about Beth's ashes?' Patrick breaks it. I shake my head.

He drains his coffee and puts the mug on the table. 'Can I go up to her room? Can I just go and sit there for a while?'

'Yes. Of course.'

'Will you come with me?' Patrick asks.

I go first and Patrick follows, lingering – looking at the photos on the stairs as he climbs them. I open the door of her bedroom and allow him in first, pausing on the threshold as he goes to stand in the middle of the floor, looking around slowly, taking in the untouched jumble of clothes, the books piled on her desk, the posters on the wall, before he sits on the bed and pats the space beside him. I sit and he puts his arm around me.

We stay there. I'm not sure how long for. It may be a few moments. It may be half an hour or longer. We are silent and the silence is companionable, our communing with the dead unspoken, the presence of each other unremarkable but right.

I can almost feel Beth's head on my shoulder.

When tingling sets in I shift my position, moving away from him. 'I should go and find something for us to eat. Stay here, if you want.'

'I might, just a bit longer,' Patrick says, and I go back to the kitchen and begin preparing Beth's tuna bean bake. Tiger appears, pushing into the kitchen through the cat flap, as I combine the ingredients in a dish and put it into the oven to heat, while I scour the cupboard for crisps.

'What are you doing for Christmas?' Patrick asks, when he comes down.

'I'm spending it with Joe and Sophie and the rest of the family.'

'That's good,' he says.

'And you'll be with Rachel,' I say.

'Yes, we'll be at the flat, but I'm going away again soon after. To Madagascar.'

'Madagascar?' I think back to several evenings and afternoons sitting on the sofa beside Beth, watching the Disney film. What I know about wildlife in Madagascar stems from watching it time and again. 'To photograph lemurs?' I know they're endemic to the island. I know also that their name derives from the Latin *lemures*, meaning ghosts or spirits. How apt.

'No, bark spiders,' Patrick says. 'Darwin's bark spiders were identified a few years ago and there's still a lot about them that's not understood.'

'Yes?'

'They can make the biggest and strongest webs in the world, spanning rivers as wide as eighty-two feet, Spider-Man-like size and strength, but scientists have no idea how they make them so big.'

Patrick becomes animated. His voice and face take on a liveliness that was not there before. He's excited about the trip, eagerly anticipating it. He has something to look forward to.

I resent this. I'm angry with him for his ability to move beyond dwelling. I'm dreading my own return to work.

And it begins: accusations and recriminations at first, about how easy he seems to find it to move on, which

147

build into a full-blown row, raised voices, things said that both of us would later regret.

Into this atmosphere I hurl the empty tuna can, its razor-sharp lid hanging by a tiny thread. It catches Patrick just below his eye, puncturing the skin, unleashing a flow of blood so great that it immediately stems the tide of our argument.

'Jesus Christ.' Patrick grimaces and screws up his eye, grappling blindly with outstretched arm for something to hold against it.

I reach for the dishcloth. 'I'm sorry. I'm sorry. Did it get your eye?' I fold the cloth and hold it against his eye. 'I'm so sorry. Can you open it?'

He does so slowly, but there's too much blood everywhere.

'Hold this. I'll get something to wash it with.'

I fill a bowl with cold water and grab a box of tissues. 'Here, let me.' I wash the area around his eye and Patrick winces as I dab around the cut below his eyelid. He blinks and opens his eye as I soak up the blood. 'Can you see okay?'

'Yes.' He lifts a finger to his face, feeling the damage. 'It's just a cut. And it missed my eye.'

'But it's a deep one.' I take a dry tissue now and hold it there, watching as it rapidly turns from white to a brilliant red. And another. And another, until eventually the flow subsides.

Tiger, I notice, has been sitting on Beth's chair all the while, watching us in the unflinching way cats have. He gets up now, yawns, as if we bore him, and heads back out into the garden as I repeat, 'I'm sorry.'

'I'm sorry too.'

'I'm so angry.' I admit it to myself, properly for the first time. 'I'm just so fucking angry all the time and there's no one to be angry with.'

A Step Back in Time

I used to wonder if things would have been different if we'd had another child. Would two children have forced Patrick to find work closer to home? Did he jump at opportunities to work abroad because he couldn't handle the sadness my unexplained secondary infertility caused me and was powerless to do anything about it?

Patrick was away on Beth's eighth birthday. By this time that hardly needed stating. People no longer bothered to ask, 'Will Patrick be there?' They were more likely to register surprise if he was.

Beth had asked in the morning, when she came into our bed and sat on his side opening her presents, 'Will Daddy call later?'

'Of course. As long as there's mobile coverage.' I'd added that just in case.

Patrick was in Albania or Northern Greece, crisscrossing the border in pursuit of the 350 remaining bears that live in the mountains between the two countries, their existence threatened by deforestation, poaching and traffic.

'He's going on a bear hunt.' I poached the lines from the children's book, telling her he'd 'catch a big one' but he wasn't scared.

She was. 'I don't want Daddy to get eaten by a bear.'

'It's okay, sweetheart. They're not grizzly bears. They

don't eat people,' I reassured her, but I wasn't happy about it either. I wasn't that happy by then.

It's a mistake, my mother had said to me, to equate love with happiness. So why, I wondered, did we build our lives around it? I still loved Patrick but I resented spending so much time on my own while he roamed the world, untouched by fatherhood, and was tired of explaining to Beth why he wouldn't be there for the next occasion or milestone or event that her friends' fathers turned up to.

'Chloe's dad doesn't have a job,' she told me, after coming home from her friend's house one day.

'He does, sweetheart. He works for a marketing company.'

'He doesn't,' she insisted. 'He's always at home with Chloe and Meg and Nadia.'

Her party was at 'the trampoline farm'. That was how farmers had diversified in the south. Growing things and keeping livestock was no longer enough. That one, a short two-mile drive outside the city, had trampolines. About twenty of them. Beth and her friends bounced together on huge circular trampolines, or opposite each other on long rectangular ones, or rolled around under some that were covered with canvas, giant bouncy tents, which you could sleep in, if you wanted: the trampoline farm didn't close at six.

I prepared the party food, while they bounced and laughed and shrieked. There were twelve children, including Beth. Sophie and Joe were on holiday with Ned and Alfie, so it was all girls.

There was a new girl, Jenny, in Beth's class. Beth was very taken with her – at least, she was very taken with her hair. 'It's so straight and shiny,' she told me, more than once, tugging at the ends of her own as if its wave was a source of annoyance.

Jenny's father brought her to the party. I'd already guessed that the girl in the butterfly T-shirt with the dead-straight shoulder-length blonde hair must be her.

'Can I help with anything?' her father asked. 'I was planning to hang around so if I can do anything . . .'

He'd looked a bit uncertain, then added, 'But I've brought a book if you'd rather I didn't get in your way.' He brandished a copy of Dave Egger's *The Circle*.

'Thanks. You could help with this.' I was unwrapping sandwiches. 'I was just going to put these onto plates. I love that book, by the way.'

His name was Mathew. They were new to the area. Jenny's older sister was blind and they had moved here for the secondary school, which had an excellent special-needs unit. Jenny seemed to be settling in.

'It was nice of Beth to invite her to the party,' Mathew said.

'She really likes her. She talks about her a lot.' I glanced over to where they were bouncing, Jenny's hair defying gravity in the way it still hung neatly in the bob while Beth's flew up and down with every giant leap into the air.

'It's not always easy for her. Becca's needs always come first.'

'It can't be easy for any of you,' I said.

Mathew arranged the sandwiches on a serving plate in an impressive swirl. 'It's not quite how we pictured having kids, but then it never is. Is it?'

'No,' I said, with a little too much feeling. 'What do you

do?' I pushed Patrick and his absence from my mind. 'And Jenny's mum?'

'Emma's a solicitor. Contract law. She works for a big firm in London and commutes.'

'And you?'

'I'm a scriptwriter,' he said. 'Mostly corporate stuff and a bit of TV but it's had to take a back seat.'

'So you're the main carer?'

'Yes. Hence my winning ways with sandwiches and sausage rolls.' He'd constructed a makeshift tower with the latter, a fitting centrepiece to the array of sandwiches, bowls of crisps and obligatory carrot and cucumber sticks.

I laughed.

He had an easy way around the girls, who appeared hot and hungry at the end of their session.

'Put your hand up if you want lemonade,' Mathew said, going round the table with a bottle, while I did the Ribena.

'Move up a little so – What's your name? Jess? Move up so Jess can squeeze in on the bench.'

We'd established a good routine, refilling glasses, proffering sausage rolls, wiping spills with primary-coloured napkins, escorting girls across the yard to the toilets. We worked well together, so well that when one of the other mothers arrived, early, to pick up her daughter, she assumed he was Patrick.

'I'm sorry to have to drag Meg away but this orthodontist appointment's been in the diary for ages,' she said to me, turning to take in my helper. 'Hello. It's lovely to meet you at last.' She extended a hand to Mathew, who shook it.

'And you.' He looked a little confused.

'So, are you just back from somewhere exotic?' The penny began to drop, for me, if not for Mathew.

'This is Mathew.' I jumped in with proper introductions. 'Jenny's father. They moved down from London at Easter.'

'Sorry,' she said, a little later, when Mathew had gone back out into the yard with Jenny. 'I thought he was the famous Patrick.'

'Patrick's in Albania,' I told her, trying not to show that her comment had upset me far more than it should.

'I'll go and extract Meg,' she said, as if she realized anyway.

Meg's departure briefly interrupted the game Beth and her friends were playing, leaving them temporarily a girl short.

'Can you be the egg now, Mum?' she asked me.

Their game, Crack the Egg, required a player to sit in the middle of the trampoline, holding on to their knees while the others bounced around them, attempting to make them 'crack' or let go of their knees.

'Well, I don't want to leave Jenny's dad on his own,' I said, looking back towards the picnic area but finding that Mathew had come over to the trampolines.

'He could play too,' Beth insisted.

'Yes, he's a really good cracker.' Jenny seconded her.

I looked at Mathew, who smiled and shrugged, and we climbed up to join the three remaining girls on the trampoline.

'Mum's the egg,' Beth said bossily, as I assumed my curled-up position in their midst.

'Right! Let's see how tough she is to crack!' Mathew

said, beginning to bounce with a vigour that caused me to crack almost immediately and made the girls dissolve into fits of laughter.

'I didn't have you down as quite so competitive,' I said to him, as I got up and Jenny declared him the new egg.

But I felt a sense of childish retaliation come over me and was determined to bounce him into cracking equally quickly, if possible.

'You're bouncing too hard, Mum,' Beth complained. 'You're making me almost fall over.'

'We've got to crack him,' I replied, giving it my all.

And I fell, as Mathew cracked, onto the trampoline beside him in a literal heap of laughter, which turned to slight embarrassment as I caught his eye and he held my gaze a fraction of a second too long.

'Right. I'd better go and finish tidying up the tea things,' I said, getting up. 'The other parents will be here soon.'

'I had such a good day, Mum,' Beth said, when I put her to bed later that evening. 'But I wish Dad had been able to call.'

'I know, sweetheart. I'm sure he's been trying. He must be somewhere there's no reception.' I didn't allow her to see that I was angry with Patrick for failing to call all day.

I'd been checking my phone ever since we got home, expecting at least a message from him, but there was nothing.

'If he calls soon and you're still awake I'll bring the phone up.'

'Okay,' she said sleepily.

My phone beeped and I took it out of my pocket, my

anger dissipating as I anticipated how happy Beth would be to hear from her father.

'Is it Dad?' Already she was all smiley anticipation and wide awake again.

It wasn't. A number came up and not a name.

'It's not Dad,' I said, disappointed, as I opened the message. *Hi. It's Mathew, Jenny's father. Just wanted to thank you for the party today. Jenny had a great time* ☺

'It's from Jenny's dad,' I said to Beth. 'He says she had a great time.'

'Oh, good.' Placated a little by the news that her new straight-haired friend enjoyed herself, Beth was sleepy again.

'Good night, sweetheart.'

'Night, bestest Mum,' she mumbled into the duvet.

My phone beeped again as I closed her bedroom door. Another text from Mathew. *And so did I! Mx*

I smiled to myself as I went downstairs, trying to compose an appropriate reply in my head. *I could tell!* I type. *It was good to meet you and thanks for your help* x

Christmas

I text Patrick first thing on Christmas Day: *I hope today is not too hard. Thinking of you. Cx* I send it early in the morning as I lie awake, waiting for the rest of Joe's house to stir, trying to ignore the pain in my chest.

The first thing I hear is the sound of teenagers rendered childish again by the day, awake at the crack of dawn, excited by the stockings at the ends of their beds and the novelty of sharing a room.

The pain in my chest becomes so acute that I struggle to sit up: it's as if someone's sitting on it, pushing down on my heart. But my stomach is churning too. I think I might be sick. I have to get up and go to the bathroom. I try to breathe. Force myself to take deep breaths. And I try to block out the noise of Beth's cousins bunked up together in the room next to mine, eagerly anticipating the day ahead, excited still by Christmas. By life.

Joe and Sophie insisted we all stay with them, all wake up together, even though I could have driven over for the day. Cue Mum telling us all how angelic Sophie is. 'You think she'd want a rest at Christmas, given how hard she works all year.'

'But I enjoy entertaining,' she says, when I try to protest, try to secure myself a stay-at-home-alone card. 'We must all spend Christmas together. Especially this year.'

So I must make a supreme effort to be brave, not to

let my anger and grief get the better of me, to appreciate the efforts being made by those around me. To perform a hopeful charade, like the one Beth and I used to play every year when, after waking and opening her stocking, she would put everything back, bring it into my room and remove the contents again, as if she was seeing them for the first time, as if I had not bought them in the first place.

Last year, when she plucked out the swimming goggles 'Santa' had brought her, with a triumphant 'Anti-fog goggles! He must have known I lost mine last week!' I'd replied with a 'Gosh, how clever of him,' and watched as she proceeded to show me the pyjamas – 'The exact ones I wanted!' – and asked her where they came from.

'Do you think we'll still be doing this when you're at uni and you come home for Christmas?' I had asked her when all the contents of her stocking were strewn on my bed.

'What?'

'You coming into my bed, pretending you still don't know who filled your stocking and me expectantly waiting to see what's in it?'

'If it means I keep getting a stocking,' she'd replied, 'I'm happy to keep it all up!'

For the last few years Beth had done a stocking for me, too, and I had also pretended it was from Santa.

I can hear Ned and Alfie opening theirs in their room. Through the wall I catch snatches of 'Look' and 'What is it?' and 'Oh, I wanted this.'

I force myself up, push against the weight of Beth's absence and hurry down the landing to the bathroom, where I'm sick.

Happy Christmas, Cate.

I splash water on my face, open the bathroom window and gulp in the cold December air. Then I knock on the door of Alfie's room.

Dan and Laura are sleeping in Ned's room, next door to the bathroom. I'm in the spare room. Sophie and Joe have given up their room for Mum and Dad. 'They need an en-suite,' Sophie insisted. 'The boys like sharing at Christmas so they can wake and open their stockings together. We can use the garden room.' Joe's out there, but when I went down for a glass of water in the night, I spotted Sophie on the sofa in the living room half-covered by a red snowflake-patterned blanket. She looked Christmassy, except she was sleeping alone on the sofa in the living room.

'Yup,' Ned says, in response to my knock.

He's sitting on the edge of Alfie's bed in a T-shirt and checked pyjama bottoms. Alfie is propped up against the pillow, hair sticking out all over the place. He smiles his big smile as I open the door.

'Did Father Christmas come?' I say, with as much sparkle as I can muster.

Alfie looks at Ned and says in a mock-whisper and with a deliberately obvious wink, 'Don't tell her he doesn't exist. He did!' he says to me.

'Can I see what he brought you?'

'Yes. Shove up, Ned.' He orders his elder brother to make room for me on the edge of his bed and points to the spoils that are strewn across the blanket. 'Lots of art materials. Paint. Brushes. Deodorant. Shower gel. Socks. Mum – I mean Santa – has been very practical this year.'

'Yeah. He gave me a student cookbook, lots of spices

and a potato peeler. He obviously doesn't think I eat properly at uni.'

I laugh as wholeheartedly as I can muster.

Alfie looks at me, suddenly serious, as if he can see the effort it took. 'Happy Christmas, Aunty Cate,' he says, leaning across the bed to give me a hug.

'Yes. Happy Christmas, Cate,' Ned said, putting his hand a little awkwardly on my shoulder.

When I go back to my room someone has placed a small striped stocking on the end of my bed. I pick it up and put it on the bed beside me as I climb back in, wondering who it's from, suspecting that whoever put it there will appear to watch me open it.

'Happy Christmas.' Laura comes into my room a few moments later, wearing Ned's tartan dressing-gown, carrying coffee.

'Thanks.' I sit up in the huge bed, and retrieve some of the pillows and cushions I'd flung on the floor the night before.

'Can I get in?'

I pull back the duvet and she climbs into the space next to me, the way she used to when we were kids and our beds were next to each other. 'Is this from you?' I indicate the stocking.

'No. Father Christmas.' She smiles knowingly. 'Are you going to open it?'

I feel the outline first, then delve inside: there's a packet of seeds, 'edible flowers', a bottle of relaxing bath milk, a box of Lindor, my favourite chocolates, and a book of poems for nature lovers.

I'm touched. 'Thank you, Laura.' I kiss her cheek.

'Dan thinks they're silly,' she says, leaning back on the pillows beside mine. 'But I wanted to make one for someone.'

The unsaid is out there.

'Loz?' She looks so small, in Ned's oversized dressing-gown against the pillows, which are large and plump. Sophie and Joe have great bedding, all Siberian goose feathers and hundreds of thread-count sheets. 'It's just so, well, it all revolves around kids, doesn't it?'

Life's not fair. It's Mum who says this and sometimes I find myself about to say it too. It's a family tic, ready to trot off the tongue, but not always appropriate. And not now.

When I was younger, if I'd thought about which of us would have the large family, it would have been Laura. She was always maternal, tending my cast-off dolls in a way I never had, rescuing small animals that'd been abandoned or hit by cars, as she continues to do throughout her life.

That was how she'd met Dan.

She'd found a badger that had been hit by a car, injured but still alive. Instead of leaving it or calling the RSPCA, she'd heaved it into the boot of the car and driven to the vet. 'One of the other partners buzzed me to say there was a very pretty girl with a badger in Reception and I should take a look,' Dan jokes, when anyone asks how they met. 'I was amazed that she'd brought it in. They can bite and claw you and they're heavy, yet this diminutive woman was there holding it wrapped in a car blanket. I took one look at her and thought, There's a woman I'd like to know better.'

They'd married a couple of years later. The way they met was unconventional but they were perfectly suited and yet, inexplicably, infertile. Laura's thirty-seven now. Nearly all her friends have children.

'Come here.' I put my arm out and move over in the bed.

Laura snuggles up, the way Beth used to, the way Laura had when she was still a child and I was in my teens. 'You would have been the most brilliant mother, Laura,' I tell her. The pain in my chest has been replaced with a more vicarious sense of loss for my little sister.

We perform all the rituals: a brunch of smoked salmon and scrambled eggs, a walk across the fields to the church in the village, then changing into a dress before the annual present-opening ceremony, which seems more modest this year, the pile of gifts smaller than usual.

I don't want anything except the thing that has been taken from me, yet I force myself to repeat, 'Oh, thank you, how lovely,' several times. A pair of gardening gloves with printed reindeer. Very festive. Useful too, if I hadn't abandoned the garden. A book. A scented candle. An Eric Ravilious calendar, from Laura, which is filled with lovely images and big spaces, which I imagine will remain empty, most of them. 'My offer with the garden still stands xx', Laura has written on the tag she attached to her gift.

Joe and Sophie give me vouchers, several, for the Treatment Rooms. 'We thought maybe you'd like to have a few massages or something,' Joe says a little awkwardly.

It's a generous gift. Thoughtful. 'That's really kind of you.'

'Or your nails or something before you go back to work,' Sophie says, as if she knows I don't feel ready to be pampered.

'What did you get Sophie, Joe?' Mum shouts, above the noise of everyone, forcing Joe to shout back.

'We didn't get each other presents this year. We need some work done on the roof.'

'Oh.' My mother, who doesn't want 'stuff', nevertheless looks miffed on behalf of one or other of them – maybe both. Their presents to each other are usually so extravagant: weeks away, cashmere knitwear and cases of wine. One year Joe bought Sophie a new car, a convertible, like the one she'd coveted that belonged to a fellow doctor.

I wonder if the sensible restraint is somehow for my benefit.

Mum hands a parcel to Alfie.

'Great, just what I always wanted!' He's unwrapped a small box.

'What is it, Alf?' Joe asks.

'It's a knitting kit. I told Gran I needed to learn cos I want to do textiles at college when I go.' He holds up the box. 'I'm going to knit myself a beanie.'

Everyone laughs and Mum looks a little put out. 'He did say he wanted to learn to knit.'

'It's brilliant, Gran. Thank you.' He gets up and goes over to kiss her, then comes to where I'm sitting and plonks himself on the sofa beside me, wrinkling his nose slightly at the candle, which is emitting a sandalwood smell, on the coffee-table.

'I don't know if you'll like this.' He hands me a brown card envelope addressed to him. Amazon packaging.

'Nicely wrapped!' I smile.

It does help being here, with Joe's kids. It's still hard but not as hard as I imagined.

'Yeah.' He gives me a grudging grin and watches closely as I open it, draw out the handmade A5 comic, take in its title, the hand-drawn images, and the words, and begin to well up.

He made it himself, sketched the cover, drew and coloured the individual frames and told the tale.

'I'd started it already,' he says, his voice rising, flustered by my reaction. 'I was going to give it to her but I thought you might like it. I'm sorry. If it's a terrible idea.'

'I love it,' I say, through the lump in my throat. 'I love it, Alfie.'

'What is it?' Sophie comes over, bottle of Prosecco in her hand, ready to refill my glass.

'It's kind of a book,' Alfie says.

'He made it.' I show it to Sophie.

'*The Elephants of Mount Elgon*,' she reads. 'Where's that?'

'Uganda.'

Beth went there the summer before last, with Patrick, to the oldest solitary volcanic mountain in East Africa. I'd read about how its slopes were riddled with caves carved out by moving lava. How elephants walk as whole families into the pitch darkness in search of salt seams, which they mine with their tusks, a dietary supplement they need for their plant-rich diet.

'We had the time of our lives,' Patrick reassured me, and Alfie's pictorial account of the one she'd given him seemed to bear this out.

He'd told it in his own way, with a sequence of drawings.

'Did she talk to you a lot about this trip, Alfie?' I ask.

'Yeah,' he says, embarrassed by the attention directed towards him. 'And it's kind of a nice story, the way the elephants dig for salt. I thought it would make a good strip and I was going to give it to her.'

'It's amazing, Alf.' I find myself smiling, genuinely this time, marvelling at the way he's captured Beth, with just a few lines, Patrick too. 'You've got a real talent.'

'Thanks,' he says.

During dinner, when Joe tells him he can pull the wishbone, he wipes it with his mistletoe-patterned paper napkin and offers me the other end. I take it and start pulling because I know this is the best way to let the other person win, and I don't want to win because the one thing I wish for is never going to come true.

'Thanks,' Alfie says, as if he knows I lost deliberately. 'I need a wish.'

After lunch, it begins to snow. It doesn't last long but there's enough to create a thin layer of white outside the window.

Joe lights a fire in the sitting room and announces, 'Time for *It's a Wonderful Life.*'

It's another family tradition, watching the film after lunch, or sleeping in a chair in front of it, the way Mum and Dad do.

'Or we could watch something different,' he adds quickly, beginning to flick through the pile of DVDs stacked beside the TV.

'No. Let's watch it. It's still my favourite film.' I try not to think too hard, as we watch. I try to concentrate on the flickering images on the screen and the presence of Alfie beside me on the sofa. I try not to let my mind drift to the dark place where it has spent too much time over the past few months. I try to take comfort — when Clarence tells

George he's received a great gift, the chance to see what the world would be like without him – from the fact that I had Beth in the first place.

'We had her.' It's Patrick's voice I hear clearly now, repeating the words he spoke when he left the day after her funeral.

'I'm just going to phone Mum.' Sophie gets up as the credits roll and I slip away to check my phone, which has remained beside my bed all day.

I catch snippets of her conversation, coming from the kitchen.

'Well, yes, it helps having everyone here for Christmas. How are things there?' I pause, eavesdropping, realizing it's her sister she's speaking to. Her sister lives in Scotland but has spent Christmas in Lincoln with their mother.

'And Mum?' I hear Sophie say and her voice is more audible as if perhaps she knows someone is listening.

I head upstairs to my bedroom, where my phone is lying on the bedside table.

It is hard, Patrick has replied. *I wish I could do something to make it easier xxx*

And I can no longer hold it together, no longer put on a brave face for the sake of those making such an effort around me, no longer hold back the tears.

Melting Snow

The snow has almost gone by the time Laura drives me home. Only the odd patch remains, glinting in the winter sunshine.

Laura and Dan drove over separately because Dan was the vet on call for his surgery on Boxing Day, and in the early hours of 26 December there'd been an emergency.

'Did Sophie and Joe seem okay to you?' Laura asks, as we travel along the lanes leading from their house to the main road.

'Yes.' I'm thinking about going home to an empty house, half wanting to be alone after all the Christmas company and half dreading it.

'Are you sure you don't want to come to ours for a couple of days?' Laura asks, pulling up outside the house.

'It's kind of you . . .' I begin.

'But you need some time to yourself.' Laura finishes my sentence for me.

'Is that ungrateful?'

'No. It's understandable. Christmas was pretty full on.' She leans and gives me as much of a hug as her seatbelt allows. 'But the offer's there if you change your mind over the next few days.'

She waits in the car, while I put my bags down and search for my keys, unlocking the door and turning to wave goodbye, now that she knows I'm safely in.

Tiger appears almost immediately, brushing up against me as if he's starving, even though Joyce has been in to feed him. There's a note from her on the table next to the festive foliage that Patrick brought and the wrapped CD I'd left beside it. 'Tiger fed at 5 p.m. I tried to put the heating on to warm the place up a bit but I couldn't work it out! Hope you're managing, my dear. Joyce.'

I go to put the heating on, Tiger still brushing around my ankles. Then I make myself a cup of tea and take it into the living room with Patrick's gift. I open it, anticipating a CD he'd picked up on his travels somewhere: Mongolian throat singers or Indian snake charmers. Most of Patrick's own music collection is made up of things he's encountered while working abroad.

But it's a compilation he's put together himself, eighteen tracks, one from every year of our daughter's life, each of them in some way pertinent to her – to us. It's a lovely gift, like getting a mix tape from a first love, which in a way it is. Patrick was my first great love. Beth my next. I go to the CD player and put it on. Then I smile and weep as I listen to the tracks that bring back so many memories.

The last is Pharrell Williams's 'Happy', a positive, upbeat, melancholy-defying song, yet poignant too – a reminder from Patrick of all the happy times we had shared, the three of us.

Tipping Points

It doesn't take much to tip the balance. Someone pays you more attention than they should. Another doesn't pay you as much as you hoped they would. Therein lies attraction and dissatisfaction. And the speed at which it escalates surprises you.

Patrick always seemed to be away. Mathew always seemed to be around. For coffee after the school drop-off. To pick Jenny up, when she'd come back to play. I didn't count the number of playground chats, the number of 'Are you walking in my direction?'s, the coffees in cafés near the school or cups of tea that morphed into glasses of wine when I went to pick Beth up from his house or he came to collect Jenny from ours.

For our friendship to go any further threatened all sorts of things: his marriage, mine, Beth and Jenny's friendship.

I knew all of this. And I ignored it.

A gasket on a coach saved me from myself. One of the purple coaches with the word 'legendary' emblazoned along the spine of a dragon that made Beth ask, 'If dragons don't exist why is there a word for them?' The logo was suggestive of adventure, and Beth and Jenny were off to a safari park.

It was the last week of the summer term, fifteen months after the trampoline farm party. Fifteen months, during which Patrick had been away for nearly seven and I'd spent increasing amounts of my spare time with Mathew. Too much time.

The safari park was an end-of-term treat. Some of the parents were going too. They needed adults to help. I should have volunteered.

I hadn't.

I'd arranged to meet Mathew in a hotel twenty minutes down the coast road. An anonymous hotel, aimed at long-distance drivers, where we would be unlikely to bump into anyone we knew. Where we would not be at home, surrounded by reminders of our real lives and responsibilities. Where, if it weren't for the gasket blowing, I might not have caught myself, not have looked into the future and seen the damage I was about to cause.

The call from the school came just as I was parking in the hotel car park. The coach had broken down. The children had been sitting by the side of the motorway for nearly two hours. The legendary coach company could not find a replacement and the problem could not be fixed. The dragon-emblazoned vehicle was breathing real smoke and not going anywhere. Could we pick up our children?

I said I was on my way.

There was a message from Mathew on my phone when I arrived at the coach. And another: *Just got the call from school. Guess you're driving up. Might see you there. Why didn't you call?*

I texted him: *Yes. I went to rescue stranded kids.*

And I came to my senses.

I ignored him for a few days but eventually he forced me into a coffee shop and I told him I was sorry for all sorts of things but we had to stop before anyone was hurt.

And when Patrick returned from China, I confessed to the thing that almost threatened our relationship.

Why?

Because I wanted him to know how unhappy I'd been. And I wanted him to know that I loved him but something needed to change, because who knew what might happen next time?

'I was lonely,' I said to him. 'I miss you when you're away. I wanted company. I wanted to be with someone but it wasn't Mathew I wanted to be with. It was you. I didn't go through with it.'

'But you thought about it,' Patrick said, too quietly. His lack of emotion wrongfooted me. 'What would have happened if the coach hadn't blown up?'

'It didn't blow up.'

'Don't dodge the issue.'

'I'm not. I'm trying to confront it. The issue is not Mathew, it's us. I don't want to go on like this, with you being away so much, with people, friends not even knowing who Beth's father is.'

'I didn't realize,' Patrick's voice was barely audible now, 'quite how bad things had got.'

He remained quiet. Too quiet. For too long. Days. Days in which I felt alternately riddled with guilt and furious with him for keeping up the silent treatment, for making it all worse.

New Year

Six months after I first met Patrick, he'd asked what I was doing for New Year. I didn't have firm plans. A colleague was having a party. My flatmate had suggested we have one.

'Would you like to come to Somerset with me?' Patrick had asked. 'I've found this converted hayloft in Babcary.'

I had no idea where that was.

'It will be quiet,' he said nervously, as if this might not appeal. 'Just us, but we can go for walks and sit in front of the fire and you can tell me stories.'

'It sounds wonderful.'

It had been.

And on New Year's Eve Patrick had cooked a stew in our hayloft and brought it to me as I sat on the floor in front of the fire with a big glass of red wine.

'Would you like to go out after?' he'd asked.

And I'd said okay. I was happy to stay where I was but thinking he wanted to drop into the local pub and equally happy to do whatever he wanted.

'You'll need to wrap up warm,' he'd said.

'Why? Where are we going?'

'You'll see.' He'd been mysterious and not had anything to drink.

He'd driven me to the base of Glastonbury Tor, pulled a large rucksack from the back of our hire car and held my hand tightly as we climbed to the top of the ancient peak where we had a 360-degree view of fireworks being let off in various towns and villages below.

'What's in the rucksack?' I kept asking a tight-lipped Patrick.

Only after the fireworks had died down and the handful of other people who'd had the same idea had left did he tell me.

'I've got a tent and a sleeping bag. You might be too cold but we could stay here and watch the sun rise together.'

I clung to Patrick for warmth as we slept on and off until dawn, when Patrick unzipped the door of the tent so we could watch the light filtering over the mist-filled valley from the snug confines of our shared sleeping bag.

'Have you done this before?' I'd asked him.

'Not with anyone special,' he replied, and I glowed with warmth inside.

It was a gift, for him to tell me that, and there was more.

'I love you, Cate.'

It was the first time he had told me, and as the weak wintry sun began to rise on the new year, I felt I had everything I wanted.

This New Year Alfie is staying, a pre-planned sleepover after a proper party.

'It's a girl in my art class,' he'd told me earlier, when Joe dropped him off. 'She's a bit crazy but really nice.'

'Bottles-of-vodka crazy?' I asked him.

'No. Purple hair, weird clothes, no boundaries, over-friendly,' Alfie enlightened me. 'She'll probably have invited loads of random people she met at the bus stop.'

'Sounds like it's going to be quite a party,' I said, starting to worry about what trouble Alfie might end up in this time.

'I think her parents are going to be there,' he tried to reassure me, but I still spend the evening worrying about him and hoping he'll get back safely.

Joe had asked if I fancied going with them to watch the fireworks in town but I told him I'd rather stay at home, watching Jools Holland, and trying not to think too much about going back to work in a week's time.

Alfie texted me just after midnight. *Happy New Year, Cate! There's a boy here who lives near you. His parents are picking him up and he'll give me a lift so you don't need to wait up. Still got my key!*

I'd given him the spare key, Beth's key, earlier, but had said I'd wait up, in part because it gave me a strange sense of purpose.

But I was tired. I made up the sofa-bed for him and went up to my own, listening out for Alfie and falling asleep when I heard the key turn in the front door, then the triple thud of him closing it behind him and taking off his shoes.

I wake in the morning to find him sprawled across the sofa, still dressed, the duvet slipping onto the floor, his face utterly sweet and childlike in repose, despite the shadow of moustache that has only just begun to etch his top lip.

There's something about a sleeping child. Something that catches you. I can't help moving closer, adjusting the duvet so it covers him again.

And Alfie opens his eyes and closes them again, in a

way that suggests he's still asleep and hasn't even registered my presence. But he's put out his hand too, grabs mine and holds it for a moment, then shifts his position, turning towards the back of the sofa, snuggling down beneath the bedding and tucking his hand back into his chest.

The pang I feel is almost unbearable.

'Breakfast?' I'd asked when he emerged around midday, looking bleary and a little the worse for wear.

'Urgh. Maybe just a coffee.' He slumped on Beth's chair and started reading the back of the cereal packet I'd put on the table.

'Breakfast is one of the most important meals of the day.' He looked up at me. 'That's not very persuasive.'

'It is important.'

'Yeah, but one of the most important meals of the day. There's only three to choose from. That's basically saying it's a meal.'

I laughed. 'And you say you're not good at English.'

'But that's not English. English is all "Why did George kill Lennie in *Of Mice and Men*?" and "How does Charlotte Brontë use the weather to foreshadow events?" I don't think she does. I just think she makes it rain a lot cos it rains a lot in Yorkshire.'

I laughed again. 'English literature, maybe. But you're good with English language.'

'It ought to say something like "Make breakfast the most important meal of the day" or "Treat it as . . . "' Alfie was still intent on the cereal packet.

'You ought to go into copywriting, then,' I said. 'And

are you tempted to eat any of it or are you just going to deconstruct the wording on the packet?'

'I'm going to treat it as the most important thing I put into the temple which is my body all day,' he said, pulling the bowl I'd put out towards him.

After Alfie has gone, I sit inert on the sofa, staring out of the window at the cloudy January afternoon. I'm wearing my coat – it's cold and I seem to have inherited my parents' belief that you can't put the heating on if there's just one of you in the house, no matter how cold it is. The cat is in my lap, like a hot-water bottle.

The radio is on, switched to the local channel, and people are phoning in to talk about New Year's resolutions.

'So Gene is on the line from Selsey,' the presenter is saying. 'What's your resolution, Gene?'

'My resolution is a bit of a selfish one,' Gene says. 'I'm not giving up booze or anything like that.'

The presenter titters.

'I've always wanted to see the Himalayas,' Gene says, 'and I've never been able to afford it but I'm getting on a bit now so I've decided to cash in the value of my home and go.'

'Well, that sounds like a positive plan,' the presenter says, and I begin to tune out and think.

I need a positive plan. I need to start moving on. Somehow. Going back to work will at least get me out of the house, force me to spend time with colleagues and think about other things.

'I'm going to take up hooping,' a woman on the radio is saying.

'What's that when it's at home?' asks the presenter.

'Hula-hooping,' she says. 'It's supposed to be amazing exercise especially if you've got a bit of a muffin top, like me.'

I need to do something physical, I think, as the presenter assures Ms Hula-hooper that he doesn't think she has a muffin top. I look out of the window at the garden. It needs tending and I know that the longer I leave it the worse it will get. But I can't quite face it now.

Instead I go upstairs and root around in the back of my wardrobe, looking for the running shoes I bought years ago, in another New Year fit of good intention. I only used them once or twice.

I pull on a T-shirt and tracksuit bottoms, slip my foot into a trainer and feel something in it. A leaf?

I put my hand in. Touch paper. Pull it out. A yellow Post-it note. Beth's handwriting. 'Going running? Seriously Mum???'

How long ago did she put it there?

Christ. Fuck. Jesus. Her handwriting. Her humour. It takes my breath away. Deep inhale. Don't let it get to you. Put the note beside my bed.

Go downstairs. Grab my iPod and head out of the house. I run down the street, towards the ring road, towards the sea.

Patrick's eighteen-year playlist keeps me going. 'Don't Stop Me Now'. I'm not having a good time but it keeps me going along the riverbank, envisaging Beth bouncing on her bed in Disney princess pyjamas.

I slow my pace a little as I jog along, listening to Shaggy's 'Darling Angel', watching Patrick holding baby Beth and rocking her in time to the music.

Who am I kidding? I'm not going to run very far. I cross a bridge, looping back and heading home on the other side of the river. One of the songs Beth and I used to sing together comes on. Gorillaz, 'Clint Eastwood'. I, with my terrible inability to remember lyrics, could just about sing along to the chorus, and Beth would happily rap the rest. I can almost hear her now as I carry on running, despite how much it hurts. My lungs are struggling. My legs are aching. But it's good. I feel as if I'm starting to purge myself of some of the anger and guilt that have been consuming me over the past few months.

PART THREE

Six months on

Existence is a strange bargain. Life owes us little;
we owe it everything. The only true happiness
comes from squandering ourselves for a purpose.

— William Cowper

Trying to Move On

It was Laura who suggested I 'see someone' after I'd done something so stupid that I instantly regretted it but could not undo it.

I confessed to Laura when she dropped in on her way to visit Mum and Dad. She'd brought food and was putting her offerings in the fridge; her back was turned to me, making it easier for me to say what I had to say out loud.

I half hoped she'd tell me it was okay. That it wasn't that bad.

She didn't.

Earlier that day I'd logged on to Facebook, because it's one of the only places where Beth is still alive. She's still there, born in 1998, attended the local secondary school, 'in a relationship'. Her timeline may have stood still but it's still active. Occasionally someone will tag her in a photo, as if she's still around to remember the particular gathering or outing.

Patrick had suggested we delete it but neither of us knew how to. Alfie said it was almost impossible, 'like trying to kill a cockroach', but Ned had deleted his in order to assume a more enigmatic personality at university. 'I can show you but you'll need her password.'

I didn't know it. Until that morning when it suddenly came to me. I remember her telling me. Strokkurgeyser, the name of a geyser because she'd been to see it with Patrick on a trip to Iceland, just before she'd signed up for social media. Strokkurgeyser: I'd tapped it in earlier and found myself privy to the posts of my dead daughter's friends.

Some appeared on my own timeline when I looked. Chloe in the kitchen of her halls of residence, with new friends, Kostin playing cello at Birmingham City Hall, Jess in a bar surrounded by friends, new friends, as all of Beth's friends had begun to make.

And here, on Beth's timeline, rather than my own, was a picture of Evan, Beth's former boyfriend, on a beach in India, his arm round a beautiful girl in a bit of a bikini, smiling happily at the camera.

He left after Christmas to travel in the Far East and appears to be enjoying himself.

This photo has attracted a string of comments. So many comments.

Who's the beauty?
   Monica. Met her in Goa. She's from Naples!!
Nice one!
Ciao, bella!
You look happy!
   I am!

Why was I even on the site? And why did I let it get to me? What right did I have to stalk the boy who'd been through a kind of heartbreak beyond the normal teenage kind? Why did I resent his happiness when he had every right to it?

If I'd waited. If I'd logged out, put my computer to sleep, fed the cat, gone for a run, done anything before waking it up again, maybe I'd have stopped myself.

But I didn't.

I sent Evan a message, a direct message: *It didn't take you long to forget, did it?* I wrote. It would look as if it was from Beth.

As soon as I'd sent it, I regretted it.

I'd sent another, explaining, apologizing. But it was out there.

'He'll understand,' Laura says.

'Do you think so?'

'No.' She shakes her head and we both laugh.

'He'll either be spooked or really pissed off.'

Poor kid, I feel for him now, receiving weird messages from a madwoman when all he was trying to do was move on with his life.

'Are you going to see if he's replied?' Laura asks.

'I don't know if I can bear to look. I feel so stupid. God, I'm turning into this awful bitter person.'

'You've every reason to feel that way. But it might help to talk to someone who understands these things.' Laura started seeing someone after her last round of IVF failed.

'Maybe. At this rate, I'm not going to have anyone else left to talk to. But what is there to say?'

'It might help you move on,' Laura says.

'But I don't want to move on. I'm not ready to start forgetting her.'

'Oh, Catkin,' Laura says sadly, 'no one is suggesting you're going to forget her. But it might make it hurt less, the remembering. You might be able to find a way to keep her memory alive without it causing you so much pain.'

I'm beginning to struggle, though, to recall her with the vividness that I used to.

I can no longer sense her when I go into her room, or summon up a clear impression of her or the sound of her voice.

I'm relying on prompts: photographs, and the one voicemail message that remains on my phone, which I've listened to over and over. My contract provider keeps offering me an upgrade: a new phone, free and so much better and faster than the one I have.

But it won't have the one thing on it that I want. The message from Beth, two days before her death: 'Hi, Mum. It's me. Is it okay if Jess stays tonight? Her parents are in London. She's here now so . . .'

That's it. Not really asking, just letting me know what the plan is. Tantalizingly brief in hindsight. I've listened to it so many times. I'm thankful for the wonder of digital technology. Another type of recording would have stretched or warped by now, become distorted through the sheer number of plays.

'Hi, Mum. It's me. Is it okay if Jess stays tonight? Her parents are in London. She's here now so . . .'

I play the words through in my head. But it's no good.

I take out the memory book that Chloe had asked friends to write in after her funeral. I read their words, saying how good a friend she was, recalling the times they shared that I had not.

I know some of them off by heart: the message from

184

Evan, saying he remembered her putting her hand up to answer a question in their physics class and he'd looked at her and listened to her explaining something and thought, I didn't know girls like that existed.

But she's slipping away.

No scent of her in the clothes hanging in her wardrobe, no real sense of her in the disturbance of the books on her desk, which are exactly as she left them. Even those few strands of hair, saved from her hairbrush and stored carefully in a leather earring box, appear to be losing their sheen. I'm haunted by the fact that I'm increasingly not haunted by her.

Back to Work

'This is pretty.' Emma, a new colleague at work, picks up the clay dish on my desk that is a repository for loose change and paperclips.

'Thank you,' I say, moving it closer to me, away from the edge of the desk where it might easily fall and break when she puts it down again.

'I love the design. Is it from Italy?'

I work in an open-plan office. Emma sits opposite me. She joined the company while I was on compassionate leave. Perhaps it's because she didn't know me before that she doesn't give me the kid-glove treatment others do. She's just made me a coffee and put it down beside the dish.

'No, my daughter made it in an art class at school,' I tell her, and she doesn't grimace in apology the way others do when the subject of Beth comes up.

'It's really lovely,' she says. 'How old was she when she made it?'

'Seven or eight, I think.'

'Wow, that's impressive. She had a real eye for design,' Emma says, without the tone of apology everyone else seems to adopt if they stray into Beth territory.

Going back to work was surreal, a bit like returning after Beth was born. Then I had felt utterly changed by motherhood but my colleagues, most of them, behaved as if I'd been on holiday, asking vague questions about 'the baby', unsure even of her sex. This was different, of course. I've known most of my colleagues for longer.

I was offered a lot of tea on my first day and every cup was served with a sympathetic smile. Janey, my boss, hugged me when I arrived in the navy dress I've not worn for months, looking like a woman who works in a small editorial office, even if I didn't feel like one any more.

But I was surprised by how quickly I began to readjust, it was almost as if I'd not been away, and the rhythm of office life was vaguely comforting.

Emma is bright and energetic. She goes running at lunchtimes, arriving back at her desk glowing and often carrying some sort of green shake. And she's organized, more adept at using technology than I fear I will ever be.

She's working on several books at once and has created a program to help her track the progress of each. She tacks a printout that details the work she needs to do each day on the wall beside her desk and has offered, when I've marvelled at its ingenuity, to set up something similar for me.

'Perhaps when I'm back up to speed,' I tell her, not wanting to hide that I've been given a lighter workload to start off with, a book on creating a garden from scratch and another beginner's guide: *A Year to Becoming a Pianist*. I must get my head around the author's instructions on how to develop a pianist's muscle memory through practice of scales, arpeggios, chords and harmonies, so that by the time I come to play an ambitious piece I have an instinctive feel for many of its sequences.

But it doesn't really interest me.

I'm bored with this job. It used to suit me because it was local and fitted around my childcare but now I feel like I'm treading water, filling my time in a way that is vaguely productive but not nearly as productive as Emma. I suspect she views me as one of the many tasks she must give her attention to.

Perhaps Janey assigned Project Try to Keep Cate's Spirits Up to her, along with the nine or ten titles she's working on.

She certainly asks more often than anyone else if I fancy joining her for lunch, a run or a drink after work. I decline with increasing regularity.

'Are you up to anything this evening?' she asks, as I'm getting ready to leave the office.

'I've got my nephew coming to stay,' I tell her.

'Oh, how sweet,' she says. 'How old is he?'

'Sixteen.' It's strange the way people expect nephews and nieces to be perpetual small children. 'He's got a weekend job in a burger bar and he sometimes stays with me if his shifts finish late.' The odd Friday or Saturday. He still sleeps on the sofa-bed in the living room. It's nice having the company at weekends.

'Which burger bar?'

'Bert's,' I tell her. 'Near the station.'

'Maybe we should go there after work sometime,' she suggests.

It's a late-night takeaway, not a gourmet burger bar. I guess Emma doesn't know this. 'To be honest, Alfie's accounts of it haven't done much to tempt me.' He describes it as a refuge for the drunk and homeless with fast food on the side. And seems to love working there.

'Oh.' Emma looks momentarily stumped. 'Well, do you fancy a quick drink somewhere nicer before you go home?'

'Actually,' I tell her, 'I've got an appointment I have to get to.'

'Another time then,' she says.

I suspect she doesn't believe the bit about the appointment, but it's true.

Starting to Talk

The counsellor's office is just behind the cathedral, a two-storey mid-terrace sandstone building, marked out as non-residential by a trio of doorplates: J G Funeral Advice, Spire Housing, and E. Ewing, counselling and psychotherapy.

I pause briefly, taking in the surroundings: the cobbled courtyard that leads to the east wing of the cathedral, surrounded by similar yellow-stone diocesan buildings. I guess E. Ewing counselling is handy if people don't find the answers they're looking for in God's house.

My counsellor is Emily Ewing, whose name is vaguely familiar. I realize why when I'm on her couch, and say, '*Dallas*,' as it comes to me.

'I'm sorry?' Emily Ewing is older than me, a striking woman with a silver-grey bun. She wears a pale grey spotted shirt and wide-legged grey trousers. She exudes professionalism and experience.

'Your name,' I explain, secretly pleased to have wrong-footed her because I feel nervous. I'm about to expose myself to a stranger. 'I thought I knew it from somewhere but I was thinking of Ellie Ewing, from *Dallas*.'

She looks mystified.

'The TV series. J R's mother.'

'Ah, I never saw it.' She smiles and opens a large sage green Moleskine notebook, which actually matches the paint on the walls, and picks up a pen.

'So, is it okay if I call you Caitlin?' she asks and I nod, looking around. Her office reminds me of Sophie and Joe's living room: oak bookcases, Persian rugs and a couple of mismatched armchairs, but smaller and without the sweep of their garden beyond. Potted plants on the windowsill. Begonia. Cyclamen. African violets. All flowering. All looking cared for. Two boxes of tissues on the low table between Emily and myself, as if one might not be enough.

And an orchid, white flowers holding themselves on slender stems and its leaves a healthy pale green. It's hard to keep orchids alive. They need just the right amount of care and Emily appears to know how to give it.

I relax a little as she reaches out to turn the plant slightly, adjusting it, the way I used to reach out to smooth a stray strand of Beth's hair, almost unaware.

'It's good to meet you, Caitlin,' she says, and asks me to tell her a little more about myself than I had when I telephoned to make the appointment.

I fill her in. Beth's death. And since. Wading through life.

She asks me to tell her about Beth. 'It's often hard to think about someone we've loved a great deal without finding it painful,' she says. 'But memories can be a comfort too. Could you maybe describe to me something you did with Beth? It doesn't have to be anything significant. It could be something as simple as doing the chores at home.'

I tell her how we used to garden together, that even when she was tiny she liked to potter around outside, picking up snails and examining the stripes of their shells with awe, helping me dead-head flowers and plant bulbs.

And how we would often dance in the kitchen, when we were stacking or unloading the dishwasher. I tell her that sometimes when she'd been out with her friends and I was already in bed by the time she came home, she would climb in next to me, tell me about her evening and snuggle, like a child.

'It's okay to enjoy these memories, Caitlin.' Emily seems to know exactly what I am, and have been, thinking. 'And to savour the good bits of your life. You don't have to feel guilty for sometimes feeling okay.'

'I find it hard,' I tell her. 'I can't seem to separate anything from what happened.' I try to explain: that it doesn't seem right to be getting on with life, my sense of failure for not having been able to protect her.

'Love is impossible,' she says. 'It makes you want to protect the object of your affection from the realities of the world and in that you can only fail. Everyone does.'

I think about this and say nothing.

'Tell me,' Emily says. 'Supposing you had come to see me a week before Beth's accident. Supposing I had asked you to describe your job as a mother. What would you have told me?'

'I don't know.'

'Think about it.' Emily folds her hands on the notebook in front of her and looks at the space just in front of them. Waiting.

'I suppose I might have said that it was, well, obviously to feed and clothe and look after her and instil some values into her. But more, if I'd seen you then, I suppose I would have said it was to get her to the point where she was ready to forge her own way in the world?' I phrase

192

this as a question and look at Emily to see if she approves of my answer.

'And do you think you'd done that?' She asks another question.

'I suppose,' I say grudgingly, looking out of the window at the spire of the cathedral stretching up into today's clear blue sky.

Emily makes a note in her book and looks up as the clock emits an almost imperceptible buzz. It's enough to make it move, slightly, on the oak surface of the table: to indicate that my hour is almost up.

'You're doing very well, Caitlin,' she says. 'You just need to keep in mind that this is normal, that it will get better and that you can be kind to yourself in the meantime.'

I nod hesitantly.

'Okay.' I start to gather up my things and stand up.

Emily begins speaking again as I sling my bag over my shoulder.

'Grief,' she delivers a tiny nugget, 'is a remembrance of moments of shared joy. You just need to find a way to ensure it doesn't eclipse those moments, and you have to stop blaming yourself for what happened.'

'Thank you,' I say to Emily, feeling better – not a great deal but as if a slight weight has lifted.

'Well done, Mum.' I hear Beth, a surprisingly clear voice inside my head, as I leave Emily's office and walk through the cloisters to the cathedral café.

I ask for a pot of tea and slice of lemon drizzle cake at the counter and carry it to a table in the garden outside, recalling the countless times I had arranged to meet Beth here over the years.

I remember the first time she and Chloe were allowed to go shopping by themselves. Beth must have been nine or ten at the time, excited and trepidatious. I left them at the car park, checking they had their money and mobile phones, and arranging to meet here in the cathedral café in a couple of hours' time.

How slowly the time passed for me and how quickly for them before they appeared, Chloe laden with carrier bags from H&M, Primark and Boots, a pre-teen's booty, and Beth, slightly in awe of Chloe's ability to shop but not really interested, telling me she'd bought a packet of pens from the stationery shop.

Funny girl, I think, as I finish my tea.

And then I register Beth in a way I have not for a while. An inexplicable presence.

I was a good mother, I say to myself, with more confidence than I could say it to Emily, and I think I can feel Beth acknowledging this.

Thank you, sweetheart.

A pigeon hops over and stands hopefully close to my feet and I scatter what's left of my cake, knowing how just a few crumbs can sustain a bird for a surprisingly long time.

As I leave the café, the sound of choral singing draws me into the cathedral. The choir is rehearsing for evensong and the building is almost empty, except for a few tourists looking at the medieval carved reliefs and the remains of the Roman mosaic floor.

A girl who, from behind, looks just like Chloe is asking an official where the John Piper tapestry is. I walk towards them.

'There, behind the altar,' she says, gesturing towards

the vibrant multicoloured cloth. I see the girl's face now in profile and that it isn't Chloe at all.

'The animals are representations of the four gospel writers,' the woman is saying to her, as I walk towards the centre of the church and take a pew.

There is an otherworldly purity in the voices of the choristers. Time seems to pause, as the sound rises slowly towards the vaulted arches of the ceiling. The singing is excruciatingly beautiful and I sit for longer than I intended, listening to the harmony of human voices and watching the evening sunlight as it dapples the wood panelling of the pews with the muted shades of the stained-glass windows through which it filters.

I can't even begin to describe what I feel in those moments when time stands still. It's like a poem that has not yet been written.

Small Steps

Hello, Caty. It's Mum. She texts me a few days later when I'm at work. Mum has become adept at texting over the past nine months but still has not quite grasped the inherent concepts of the medium. She doesn't realize her name comes up on the screen, so it's not necessary for her to identify herself. And it's not a letter either.

I'm just writing now because your father's going to visit Dennis next Wednesday and I wondered if I might come and see you. Lots of love, Mum x

She's the same when she leaves an answerphone message, treating the machine as if it's an actual person.

What sort of time? I reply.

I was thinking about midday.

That's fine. I work from home on Wednesday. Mum knows this. *And I'll make lunch. Please don't bring anything.*

But I know she will. She hates to arrive anywhere empty-handed.

And she never rings the bell either, I think, when at midday on Wednesday I hear a tentative knock. She hates doorbells: 'They give you such a jolt.'

She's clutching several carrier bags containing the food offerings I had told her not to bring.

'Oh, and I was at the garden centre at the weekend and I bought you these.' She hands me a packet of bulbs.

'Acidanthera,' Mum says, although I can see for myself. 'They're so lovely, don't you think?'

'Yes, they are.' Abyssinian gladioli, star-shaped white flowers with a dark blotch of violet at their centre. They smell lovely, too, but I've never had any in my garden.

I used to help Mum in the garden when I was a kid and Dad was away. I suppose it's where my love of gardening came from.

'So what have you been up to, love?' Mum asks, sitting down while I make her tea.

I tell her a bit about work, how the piano manual is almost finished and the *Instant Garden* book is coming together. I mention I've been running.

'That's good.' She nods vigorously although I know she thinks running is a peculiar form of exercise.

'And Alfie's been to stay a few times, after his new job.'

'Joe told me. He said it's been a real help, you having him. A real help,' she repeats, as if letting Alfie kip on the sofa-bed is a big deal. It's not really. I like him being around occasionally, and if it saves him the trouble of getting back home late at night, it's fine.

'And I've been to see a counsellor,' I tell her. 'A woman who specializes in bereavement.'

I know my mother is slightly suspicious of counsellors, too. 'Why pay a professional when you could talk to a friend or your priest?' I've heard her say.

'Well, I'm glad if it helps,' she says. 'To get things off your chest.'

'It's early days,' I say, bringing the tea to the table and sitting down at right angles to her.

Mum clears her throat and I glance at her, ready to ask if she needs water. She has a faraway look on her face, as if she's not really aware of me at all but talking to herself, reciting a speech she's rehearsed. She seems frail and anxious.

'Mum?' I'm filled with a sudden fear that perhaps something's wrong with her or Dad.

But that is not what it is.

'You know I spoke to her the day she died,' Mum says, staring into the distance, refusing to look at me.

'Beth?'

She nods.

'Really? When?'

'When she was at the beach.' Mum glances in my direction, then looks away again. 'I spoke to her on her mobile.'

'You did?' This seems so unlikely and Mum is clearly uneasy when she tells me. 'Why?'

'Because I was going to miss her when she went away, too,' she says, a little crossly, as if I'd never stopped to think about this.

I don't respond, not immediately. There's something else and I'm not sure what it is.

'She asked if she could call me back,' Mum tells me. 'She said she was just about to go for another swim and would I mind if she called me back?'

'So you spoke to her, just before . . . ?'

My mother was the last person Beth spoke to. I think I understand her unease now, her refusal to look at me. But then she starts speaking again.

'I keep asking myself why I didn't just talk to her for a bit longer then. I didn't want a great long chat. Just a few minutes. If I'd delayed her swim, maybe just for a few moments . . .'

'Don't, Mum,' I say vehemently. 'Don't. It doesn't help.'

She gazes at me now, tearfully, appealing to me to try to understand.

And I do.

'Mum, please. You couldn't have done anything to change what happened.' And as I say that I catch myself, hear myself telling Mum not to do exactly what I've been doing for the past few months: blaming myself for not having had the power to prevent Beth's death.

'There's no point talking like this. Beth's death was an accident, an awful, tragic accident.' It's a relief to hear myself say that and to find that I finally accept it. 'You can't do anything more than you already do, Mum. You're here for us,' I tell her. 'Me and Joe and Laura. You've always been here for us. That's enough.'

'Oh, Caty,' she says, really tearful now.

I stand up and go to her, put my arms around her and give her a hug.

She cries then, really lets go, gasping, 'I'm sorry,' between sobs.

'It's okay, Mum.' I'm surprised to find myself comforting her, that I want to and I have the right words.

Brief Moments

The following Saturday I wake to the sound of music. Alfie is already up, making toast in the kitchen. He's switched the radio to a local station and Lou Bega's 'Mambo No.5' is playing. I find myself semi-shimmying into the kitchen.

The song was released when Beth was a baby. I used to hold her in my arms and dance around the kitchen in our London flat to it, watching her smile and squeal with delight.

Alfie pulls his phone out of the back pocket of his jeans, as I sashay into the kitchen, momentarily absorbed in the memory. 'Caught on camera,' he says, with a triumphant grin.

'Oh, God, no! Let me see.' I step beside him.

'No.' He moves his phone away.

'Go on, let me see.' I try to grab it from him but he keeps switching hands and eventually holds it above his head, forcing me to jump to try to reach it.

'Alfie, please!' I jump again and land slightly awkwardly, wincing as I go down on my ankle.

'Are you okay?' The mood has changed and the song is ending, the presenter talking.

'Yes, I'm fine.' My eyes are smarting.

'Are you sure?' Alfie is touchingly concerned.

'Yes. I'm sure.' I manage a smile. It's not my ankle that hurts.

'I'll delete the photo. I was only messing,' he says.

'I know. It's not that,' I tell him.

'I know,' he says, and gives me a hug.

When he's left, I decide to go for a run.

Running is a bargain everyone makes with themselves surely. No one can really enjoy it. Push yourself and you'll reap the rewards. You'll be fitter, thinner, more mentally alert and, in my case, it will stop you dwelling, briefly, on the thing that's always there, in the back of your mind and sometimes hammering painfully in the front.

I run down the street, through the underpass beneath the ring road, onto the footpath beside the canal until eventually it reaches the estuary and the sea beyond. It's becoming easier now, running. It still hurts but it hurts less. Not enough. Not quite enough to obliterate the dark thoughts that I can't quite shake.

I turn around, head home, and push myself harder, faster.

'Good run?' calls Joyce, who is just back from somewhere and getting out of her car.

I rasp a yes and stop, breathing heavily as she locks the car.

'I met your nephew earlier this morning.'

'Really?'

'Yes. He was just setting off on his bike and I was putting some boxes into the boot. He asked if I needed help. A very kind young man.'

'Yes. He is.'

'And kind of you too, to have him to stay.' She echoes what Mum said and looks at me keenly as if gauging how I feel, having a teenager about the house again.

'It's only every now and then.'

'I was wondering about getting a lodger,' Joyce says. 'It seems a bit wrong, rattling around in that house by myself.'

I don't agree, but I want to ask her how she bears not seeing her children. I feel like writing to her son and telling him to let his mother visit, and I want to phone the daughter and ask how she will feel if something happens to her mother and she loses her without ever being reconciled.

'Hence the boxes.' Joyce gestures to the back of her car. 'I've been trying to sort the place out a bit, taking a few things to the charity shop. Your nephew helped me with some of the heavier ones. What a delightful boy.'

'He has his moments,' I say, feeling more appreciative of him for having had this conversation with Joyce.

'Well,' Joyce says, as if something has been decided between us, 'I'd better be getting on.'

At home I shower and change and put away the sofa-bed.

Beth's room is still hers. The only person to have slept there during the past nine months is me, during the long nights when her absence loomed so large that I couldn't rest in my own bed and went to lie surrounded by her things, kidding myself that her unwashed sheets still carried a trace of her scent.

Am I ready to sort it out, tidy up a little, and let Alfie sleep there?

Surely I can bring myself to change the bed, put on a fresh duvet cover and place a clean towel over the chair by her desk? Could I let Alfie sleep in her room? Would that be a good thing to do?

I make a start later that afternoon. Nothing too drastic,

just tidying up, putting away the clothes that are still strewn around the floor, moving the toiletries from her suitcase into the bathroom and sifting through some of the papers on her desk: old physics notes and lists of things she'd needed to do before going to America.

> Borrow Jess's backpack
> Sort travel insurance
> Order dollars
> Adapter?
> Meet Chloe
> Buy cake and eat it!

It makes me smile but it might make me cry so I look at the sheet of paper underneath it: a list of email addresses and phone numbers in handwriting that's vaguely familiar: Rachel's.

Hey, Sweetie,

Here's a few friends you might want to get in touch with when you're away.
I've told them you might.
Rach xx

And I don't know what it is about this list or the tone of the brief message but I feel my chest tighten and a brief stab of pain. It's a reminder that Patrick has Rachel. No matter how hard he has found the past months, he has had someone to share them with.

I've been doing what Emily Ewing told me to do: trying to let myself enjoy memories of Beth but it's still hard. Sometimes I feel it would be so much easier if there was someone to share them with. Someone who loved Beth every bit as much as I did. Someone who may experience the exact same bittersweet sensation when they look at Beth's list and read, 'Buy cake and eat it!'

I decide to call Patrick. He doesn't answer his mobile so I call the flat. I don't normally call the flat.

Rachel answers.

'Hello?' she says, before I have said anything.

I almost put the phone down. It's not Rachel I want to speak to. 'Hello.'

'Cate?'

'Yes.'

'How are you?' Her voice exudes concern.

'Oh, you know,' I say. 'Muddling on.'

'So British!' she says. 'I know it must be really hard.'

'I have good days and bad days,' I tell her. 'Is Patrick there? I tried his mobile a few times.'

'No,' she says. 'I'm sorry. He's not.'

'Is he away?'

'Yes.'

I expected the answer to be yes. It's so often the answer.

'He's in Asia at the moment,' she says. 'And it's not so easy to get hold of him there.'

'Okay. I'll try his mobile again.'

'Can I give him a message?' Rachel asks.

'Um. No, it's okay.' What would it be? 'But thank you. When's he back?'

'I'm not absolutely sure.'

Rachel sounds different today. Strained. Uncertain. Hesitant, where usually she is so forthright.

'I'll tell him you called. Was there anything particular you needed to discuss with him?'

She's reverted to brisk and business-like and her tone seems to demand a more solid answer than 'No, nothing in particular.'

'I was thinking about collecting Beth's ashes,' I say, although I hadn't planned to.

'I'll tell him,' Rachel says, and it dawns on me, when I thank her and put the phone down, that deciding what to do with Beth's ashes is the last thing left for Patrick and me to do together.

Perhaps that's why I've been stalling.

Because burying or scattering Beth's ashes feels like an act of finality, closing the door, not just on Beth's brief life but on us, me and Patrick, the man and woman in a relationship for which there is no word, the parents of a child they no longer have.

After the Almost Affair

After the dalliance that never went beyond the dallying stage, three things changed: the way I felt about Mathew; the way I felt about Patrick; and the way he appeared to feel about me.

In his mind it was more than a brief flirtation: it was an emotional attachment too far, an affair stopped by fate and circumstances, not because I'd wanted it to end.

Patrick's absences were clouded now with a sense of foreboding.

Since we'd moved to the coast, there were times when he needed to overnight in London before an early flight. Sometimes he'd stay with a friend, others at a budget hotel.

But no matter how late his return flight, he'd always come straight home. Until after.

The first time he texted just before midnight when I was expecting a message to say he was on his way home. *Just in. Going to stay over in London this eve. Px*

It didn't seem to bother Beth that he wasn't there in the morning, as I'd promised. Her social life was beginning to concern her more than the whereabouts of her parents.

'Don't forget I'm going to Jenny's house after school today.'

'Oh, yes.' I'd have to face Mathew when I went to pick her up. Mathew, who had changed so entirely in my eyes it was hard to believe I would ever have considered driving to a hotel to meet him in the middle of the day. He was no longer the man to whom I had been briefly attracted but a man alongside whom Patrick shone, where previously I'd lost sight of him.

Patrick stayed in London for a further three nights. 'I booked into a B-and-B near Heathrow,' he'd said, as if that was the way it had always been. 'I was too tired to start getting trains and taxis in the middle of the night.' And then he'd been to stay with a friend: 'I needed to get stuff to the lab, and a photographer from America was in town. I wanted to catch up.'

'Who was that?' I'd turned a little cold thinking it might be another woman.

'Jeff McCarthy,' he'd said. 'An American I met in Rangoon a few years ago. He's got an exhibition on in Bethnal Green. I wanted to see it and spend a bit of time with him.'

It became a pattern, his trips being extended by a few days in London, at the beginning and the end. Things were still strained when he was at home, and I found myself welcoming the extra days without him.

Eventually, instead of wishing it would simply go away, we had to confront the situation: the unhappy thing our relationship had become.

It was early summer, almost a year after I'd confessed to Patrick how close I had come to cheating on him. He had been home for a long stretch in May. The weather was warm and optimistic, and the garden was bursting with life. The apple tree was blossoming, the clematis I'd planted against the side of the house a few years ago was almost covering an entire wall with vibrant blue blooms, and the tiny patch of strawberries I'd made room for in the centre of a flowerbed was beginning to produce fruit.

The time, too, felt ripe for a new beginning and Patrick and I had been making an effort to be nice to each other, to do things together, to reconnect.

'It's Melanie's fiftieth birthday party this Friday. Sophie and Joe said they'd have Beth to stay so we don't need a babysitter.' I'd given Patrick the date and mentioned it several times in passing but I suspected he'd make an excuse and I'd primed myself not to mind if he did.

But instead he had smiled. 'I'm looking forward to it.'

Melanie and Chris lived on the edge of town in a converted barn with a vast garden. Huge sliding glass doors ran the entire length of their living room, opening out onto a terrace. The night was balmy and relaxed. Patrick was smart in a lightweight suit he rarely wore. He was tanned from a recent trip to South Africa. His loose curls glowed golden in the evening sun as they brushed his collar.

'You look lovely,' he said, when I put on a grey silk dress that I reserved for special occasions.

'You too,' I replied, seeing him, once more, in the same light I had when I'd first met him. He was handsome, gentle, softly spoken and charming to everyone I introduced him to at the party.

'I can see why you've kept him to yourself so long,' one of the other mothers said to me. 'He's totally gorgeous.'

I smiled, feeling myself flush when he circled back towards me and touched my arm, asking if I wanted another drink, finding myself newly in love with him when the music was turned up and people began dancing on the terrace outside. Patrick took my hand and led me into their midst.

We hadn't danced together for years. Patrick was a good dancer. He moved naturally, unselfconsciously, and that evening he was looking at me, taking me in, as if for the first time.

I couldn't wait to get home.

'Thank you,' I said, when we went up to our room.

Once inside, he drew me to him, began unzipping my dress, slowly, looking at me, the way he had on the dance floor, as if I was someone new and lovely and he wanted to savour the moments that were about to unfold.

I thought this was the beginning of a new beginning.

The three of us spent the following day at the beach and when Beth was in bed, tired from her sleepover and all the fresh air, Patrick and I sat down to dinner: omelette, salad and a glass of wine.

'Cheers,' I said, picking up mine, feeling buoyant – and confident we were over the worst. 'To us!' I chinked my glass against Patrick's.

No 'Cheers'. No 'To us'.

'What is it?'

'I've been doing a lot of thinking. There isn't really any easy way to say this.' He shifted in his seat, looked away from me and down at his hands, pushed his plate aside. 'I think we should separate.'

Other People's Lives . . .

'You can't come in dressed like that!' Alfie is wiping a Formica table near the door of Bert's Burgers when I go in after work on Friday with Emma. We're going to see a film but decided to get something to eat first. I've told Emma that Bert's is not the most salubrious venue in town but it's on the way from the office to the cinema, Alfie is doing an early-evening shift and, rather than dissuading her with my repeated 'It's not actually that nice', I seem to have piqued her curiosity.

'Like what?' I ask Alfie, a little mystified and wondering if he means Emma or me. 'This is Emma, who I work with.' I introduce my young colleague, who looks lovely, as always, in a blue-green linen jumpsuit. It's the sort of thing that if I wore it I might look as if I were about to fix a car but Emma looks relaxed and professional.

'Like you're going out somewhere!' Alfie says, spritzing the table with something that immediately gets up my nose.

'These are my work clothes.' I look down at my dull navy ensemble. 'And we're going to the cinema but we thought we'd grab something to eat first.'

'I'd better wipe the seat as well, then,' he says, glancing towards the counter where an older man, who looks as if he ought to have a cigarette hanging from his mouth but does not, is propping it up. 'If you're planning to sit down in here.'

I look around. There are only a couple of tables where you can sit, both close to the door.

'We like to sit the attractive people by the door, to tempt customers in!' Alfie says, gesturing for us to sit down.

A man appears to be asleep at the one Alfie is not wiping. His arms are resting on it, his head on them, and there is no movement.

'Declan.' Alfie nods towards him, still speaking quietly. 'One of the regulars.'

'Well, let's see what we're going to eat,' Emma says, looking at the burger menu lit up in neon above the counter.

Given her lunchbox habits, I'm surprised she eats anything that doesn't have health-enriching, gut-enhancing properties, but she orders a 'Bert-Mac'n'chips' and I go for 'Vert-veg burger with garnish'.

The garnish, when I am served it on a paper plate, appears to be shredded gherkin.

'Enjoy!' Alfie says, with relish, opening the door to a man on crutches, who looks old but might be younger than I am. 'All right, Jim?' he says, and the man's face lights up as he smiles a very gappy smile.

'Not so bad, mate. Not so bad,' he replies, limping gingerly towards the counter, giving Emma and me a slightly surprised look as he passes.

'I knew your outfits wouldn't go unnoticed,' Alfie whispers to us, before he ducks under the counter, ready to serve Jim, Diego and Alice, and the trickle of other waifs and strays who come in while we're eating.

Alfie was right when he described the burger bar as more of a hostel for the homeless. Some of the customers take a seat without ordering. Others go for the cuppa, which costs 50p. No one asks us for change but everyone looks as if they could do with some.

Declan stirs and stares at us and starts coughing. Alfie brings him a Coke and Declan fumbles in his pockets, but Alfie tells him not to bother. 'It's on me,' he says, so quietly that I suspect he doesn't want me to hear.

'Good lad,' Declan says, sipping the Coke as if the process of drinking is painful.

'Blimey,' Emma says, when we've finished, said goodbye to Alfie and we're back outside again. 'You come out of there feeling you've been lucky in life.'

'I suppose,' I reply, without really thinking.

It was a noncommittal answer that Emma appears to find provocative. 'Come on, Cate,' she says gently, but with a hint of 'Pull yourself together,' in her voice.

'No, of course you're right.' I suppress the inner voice that's saying I would gladly swap places with any of the Bert's Burgers regulars if it would bring Beth back. I would.

Earlier in the week Janey had asked me in for a meeting. 'Just a catch-up to make sure you're getting on okay,' she'd said, but I worried it was more than that, that my non-weight-pulling had been noticed, that my colleagues were fed-up with carrying the can on my behalf.

'I know Mark Catton's really pleased with the way his gardening book is turning out,' she'd said. 'I gather you had a meeting last week and he said your suggestions were brilliant.'

'Oh, well, I'm glad they met with his approval.'

I needn't have worried – not about the work – but I was getting my knuckles rapped for other reasons.

'How are you getting on with Emma?' Janey had asked after a brief preamble about how I was finding being back at work and how she hoped the workload was manageable.

'Fine,' I'd replied, noncommittal but beginning to suspect again that Emma's persistent asking if I wanted a coffee or drink was an assigned task. 'She's very friendly.'

Was there an edge to my voice as I said this?

'I guess because she's trying to make friends,' Janey replied, and I'd wondered if there was an edge to hers. 'She doesn't really know anyone here.'

'No?' This surprised me. Emma looked like the sort of person who would have lots of friends. I imagined her life was full of them.

'No,' Janey said. 'I don't think she knows anyone down here and she doesn't really have time outside work to meet anyone.'

'No?' I said again, realizing that although we shared an office, and although Emma chatted away and asked me things, I hadn't asked her anything much about herself. I knew she'd left a job as an editorial assistant with a publishing house in London and moved south but I'd no idea why.

'I think her life outside work pretty much revolves around her mother,' Janey said, and I'd wanted to reply, 'Yes, of course,' as if I knew all about her mother, but it would have been a fraudulent response and I was already feeling put on the spot.

'Is her mother not well?' Emma couldn't be more than about twenty-seven so I suspected her mother was not in the elderly-parent category.

'Her back was badly injured in a car crash,' Janey said, looking at me in a way that I could only describe as pitying.

And it wasn't the kind of pitying look I was used to receiving, the one that said, 'Poor Cate, she lost her only child.'

It was a new kind of pitying look, one that said, 'Have you become so self-obsessed that you've been sharing an office with someone for the past couple of months and don't know anything about what they're having to deal with?'

'How badly is she injured?' I asked.

'Well, she ended up unable to walk and apparently it's going to be a long process getting her there. She's still in hospital for the time being, and when she comes out she'll be in a wheelchair for a long time.'

'That's awful.' I was shocked, at the news and at myself.

'It's why Emma moved down here. Her mother was on her own and Emma's an only child. It can't be easy for her, starting a new job and dealing with all of that without a local support network.'

'No, it can't be easy at all,' I said, feeling terrible for her.

I left the office reminded of something Emily Ewing had said in my last session with her. I'd told her about Alfie staying and she had attached more significance to it than I did.

'That's excellent.' She'd made a note and said something about us not only being here for ourselves but for others.

And when I'd gone back to our office I'd looked online to see what was on at the cinema and asked Emma if she fancied seeing the latest rom-com with me.

'I'd love to,' she said.

*

And here we are, leaving the cinema just after nine p.m., neither of us saying what we thought of the film. Instead, we're talking about going to the toilet before we leave and how Emma is going to get home. Eventually, when we're outside, Emma says, 'God, that was a terrible film, wasn't it?'

I laugh. 'Appalling! I'm sorry, it wasn't quite what I was expecting.'

The film was about two people who met while walking their dogs. The dogs had a romance of their own, which mirrored that of their owners. There was a lot of bottom-sniffing and sofa-rubbing and ultimately dog-coupling that someone somewhere must have thought hilarious and might have appealed to a five-year-old.

'I'm sorry,' I say to Emma. 'I should have read the reviews.'

'Don't worry,' she says. 'I've had a really good evening.'

'You're easily entertained then!'

'It was nice to get out.'

'We should do it again,' I say. 'If you can bear it.'

'We could try to see something good next time.' She smiles and I leave her at the bus stop.

. . . And Other People's Problems

Do you fancy a walk? Joe had texted me early on Sunday morning. *I need to get out for a bit.*

I had no plan other than to go for a run and a vague notion that I might tackle the garden, do a bit of the pruning and tidying that was long overdue, but I hadn't seen Joe on his own for ages.

We're on the Downs now, striding along the old causeway, through fields bouncing with spring lambs. There's a farm just off this lane, which leads to the fort, where I used to take Beth to bottle-feed the lambs. I can picture her, small in a yellow anorak, trying to keep her balance as an eager lamb tugged at the teat.

'Thanks for having Alfie,' Joe says.

'He's no trouble.'

'He seems to enjoy the job,' Joe says. 'And it's good for him to be out of the house at the moment.'

A sheep looks up momentarily from where it grazes, two aerosolled lambs tripping beside it, then carries on eating.

I look at Joe. 'Is everything okay?'

'Oh, you know,' he says, as if I should.

'Do I?'

'To be honest, Sophie and I are going through a really difficult time at the moment.'

'Really? But you and Sophie have always seemed so close.'

'We were,' he says.

'Then what's gone wrong?'

'The simple answer is I guess we lost sight of each other,' he says, bending to pluck a blade of grass and tearing small strips off it as he walks on. 'You know how it is. Family life takes over and work gets in the way. I suppose it was when Ned left that the cracks started to appear.' He drops the grass and bends to pick another blade. 'Ned was always such a presence in the house. Alfie's that much quieter and happy to get on with things on his own. With Ned gone, I suppose we caught sight of what it would be like when neither of them was at home any more.'

'And that wasn't good?'

'Like I said, we seem to have lost sight of each other.'

'But you still love Sophie,' I say. 'Don't you?'

'I do, but it's not that simple.' Joe quickens his pace a little. 'I had an affair.'

He's walking a little ahead, as if he expects me to be angry or shocked but I'm neither.

'It happens.' I'm not going to be judgemental.

'It was stupid of me,' Joe says. 'It was someone I met through work and it didn't last long.'

'And Sophie found out?'

'Yes.' He's slowed down again, now he's made his confession.

'How?'

'I told her,' Joe says. 'It was just after Beth died.' He turns away so I can't see his face when he says it but he looks ashamed when he turns back to me. 'It's probably hard for you to hear this, and I'm sorry, but that's what brought me to my senses. I couldn't begin to imagine what you were going through and I knew that if anything like that happened to either of the boys I couldn't go through it without Sophie.'

'I can understand that,' I say, wondering if Joe can have any inkling how well I can understand it.

'But I handled it all wrong.' Joe shakes his head. 'I thought telling Sophie was the right thing to do, to be honest with her. I had no idea how much it would hurt her or that she'd find it so hard to forgive me.' –

'And do you think she can?' I ask, thinking back to Patrick's reaction when I told him about Mathew.

'She's trying,' Joe says. 'She's been trying really hard.'

'I'm sure you'll work it out,' I say.

I can't imagine Sophie and Joe not being together, yet I never imagined Patrick and I would split up when we did.

'We'll see,' Joe says.

And then, as if the matter is closed, he points to a hang-glider in quiet, circled flight not far above our heads.

'Look at him,' he says. 'I guess that's what Patrick's off doing now.'

'Patrick? Have you spoken to him?'

I forget, sometimes, that Joe and Patrick still talk and have no idea how often they do. 'Where is he?' I look at the glider, as if whoever is suspended above us is also in on Patrick's whereabouts.

'In Nepal.' Joe starts walking again.

'He's in Nepal?' I feel an unexpected stab of something. I knew he was in Asia, but not Nepal. 'What's he doing there? Why's he gliding?'

'Filming golden eagles,' Joe says. 'Mimicking their flight paths to get closer or something.'

We'd seen golden eagles on the trip where I met him, soaring high above the peak of Kanchenjunga. It had felt like a big thing, spotting them, something we'd shared as we began to fall in love. It feels weird that he didn't tell me, that he's gone back without my knowing.

And without me. We used to say we'd go back, one day. We talked about taking Beth there.

'I'm sorry,' Joe says, as if he knows exactly what I'm thinking. 'That's where you met, isn't it?'

I nod.

'You still miss him, don't you?' Joe says, and I can feel his eyes on me as we keep walking but I stare straight ahead as I answer.

'Yes.'

The glider is now circling the crest of the hill and I don't tell him that I miss Patrick more now than at almost any other time since we separated.

Things Turning Out Otherwise

A few months after Patrick and I separated, one of his pictures won a category in the Natural History Museum's Wildlife Photographer of the Year competition. He'd taken Beth when she was staying with him to see the exhibition and she'd come back full of it.

'There's a panda, an actual real stuffed panda, when you go in,' she told me. 'It's really sad and it doesn't look real but it's just amazing that it's there.'

I know the panda. I remember being just as taken with it as a child.

'And Daddy's picture is in this special room and there were lots of people sitting on a bench, looking at it.' She was bursting with pride. 'They'd bought tickets and everything to go and sit and stare at his photograph.'

'That's brilliant,' I'd responded, feeling a touch of vicarious pride too, and regret that I was only on the fringes of his world now, that he hadn't told me he had a winning picture.

I'd texted to congratulate him later that evening and he'd replied: *Would you like to see it? I could meet you there when you bring Beth up next weekend?*

The museum was busy when we got there and began to make our way along a corridor lined with wildlife photographs: antelope leaping in the air as a crocodile emerged from the water they'd been drinking, a shipping container full of pangolins bound for dinner tables in China, two March hares boxing on the Yorkshire Moors.

The corridor led into a room where there were four larger photographs, one on each wall, and a square bench in the middle where people were sitting.

'That one's Daddy's,' Beth said excitedly, and I looked at the picture of an orangutan and its offspring. It was an arresting image, winner of the animal behaviour category, because it was a close-up showing just the hand of an adult male, holding the pale, hairless, almost human hand of its baby. It was captioned 'Father and Daughter' and there was something indescribably moving about the moment it captured. I stood looking at it and knew that Patrick was watching me as my eyes filled.

I could see Beth, in my peripheral vision, squeezing into a space among the people on the bench, looking about to gauge their reactions.

And then I felt Patrick take my hand and press it.

It was a brief moment. He'd let go by the time I was telling him it was a beautiful, heart-warming picture. But it was long enough to give me hope that there might still be a chance of reconciliation.

Meeting Up

It's a week now since Patrick called after getting back from Nepal and I glance at him sideways, as he focuses on the road, the familiar profile, clean-shaven again this time, but sad, sadder than before.

'It's the next left,' I point to the sign as we approach the roundabout. It's a brown sign: 'Cathedral, Museum, Crematorium'.

There are only a couple of vehicles in the car park, when Patrick backs into a space and turns off the engine. 'Are you sure about this?'

'Yes. I can't leave her here any more.'

He nods, and briefly takes my hand, then letting go and opening the door.

I take a deep breath before we go inside. It's ten months since we were last here for Beth's funeral, a day I never thought I would get through yet somehow I did. And somehow I have also got through the intervening time. Time has moved on.

A few minutes later we're back in the car and I am holding Beth on my lap, the remains of her in a small pewter urn that reminds me of my dad's beer tankard.

'Drive carefully,' I urge Patrick, cradling the urn, acutely aware that if he brakes suddenly I might let it slip and slide from my lap.

'I will.' He drives slowly, keeping his foot even on the accelerator.

I'm reminded of how he drove us home from hospital when Beth was born. It feels the same, too, when we get back and Patrick opens the passenger door so I can carry the urn the few yards to the house.

I find myself adopting the voice I used to talk to her as a baby too. 'Home now,' I say gently, still holding the vessel tight. 'Home now, lovely girl.'

'Do you fancy a walk or anything?' Patrick asked later, when we'd sat long enough with Beth's urn, feeling as if we'd achieved a lot simply by having picked it up.

We're down by the river now.

'Look,' Patrick says quietly, pausing on the path, nodding towards the banks on the other side. 'Over there.' He puts his hands on my shoulders and turns me a little. 'A heron.'

'Oh, yes. I see.' It's standing on a log just by a reed bed, still, watching.

'Beautiful birds,' Patrick says, as it moves its head to watch us watching it.

I'd half forgotten what it's like to walk with Patrick: he never gets lost in his thoughts but is always attuned to the world around him.

Does it help? Has it helped him cope?

The heron shifts a little on its log.

'Oh, I think it's lost a leg.' Patrick is watching it intently. 'Yes. Look. It's not moving quite right and you see the stump of the other.'

'Oh, yes.' I see it now.

'Do you remember my trip to Iraq?' Patrick asks.

I do. How could I forget? I wonder what has prompted the memory now.

I was livid with Patrick, at the time, for taking the job and only telling me about it when it was too late to cancel – or when he said it was too late, anyway. I worried for his safety. And I remember that when he came back he talked about wildlife, mentioned the names of common garden birds in the same breath as he uttered place names that were familiar to me through the news: sparrows that drowned the sound of rush-hour traffic in Kirkuk, pigeons in Basra and starlings over the Tigris. Patrick had photographed them, huge murmurations of birds, forming image after image in the sky above one of the country's two main rivers, murmurations like mushroom clouds and even one that resembled a toppled statue of Saddam Hussein.

It hadn't been entirely safe. Nowhere is.

'My assistant there had lost his leg,' Patrick says to me now, and the reason for his bringing the trip up becomes apparent. 'Not in the war,' he adds, answering my unspoken presumption. 'He had meningitis as a child. It had been amputated below the knee.'

A moorhen swims to the edge of the river where we're sitting and looks up at us, as if wanting to hear this story too.

'It still caused him pain, though,' Patrick says. 'I used to hear him through the walls during the night, screaming as if he was having a nightmare, but he told me it hadn't hurt that much before it was amputated. Its absence hurt more.'

'It does. Far more,' I say, as another moorhen appears, and the two swim off together.

Patrick says nothing more. He's watching the birds.

'I know it's agony for you too,' I say. 'You don't show it as much but it's there. I know it's there.' I don't mean to push him. I mean to acknowledge the thing that Emily Ewing made me aware of in my last session: my own lack of empathy for Patrick.

I'd told her about not being able to have more children and how I'd blamed Patrick for not feeling the loss as keenly as I had.

'How can you be sure that he didn't?' she had asked me, and I had no answer.

I understood better now that people grieved in different ways, sometimes too different to be able to help each other.

'Of course it's there,' Patrick says now. 'It's almost unbearable, Cate. It's not always all-consuming, the pain, but it never stops.'

'What can we do?' I ask him.

He shakes his head. He has no answer.

We sit for a while longer, watching the river.

'Shall we go on?' Patrick asks, and we stand to follow the moorhens as they swim upstream.

'Do you want to stop for a drink at the pub? Maybe we could get something to eat too.'

'Okay.' I glance at my watch. 'If you've got time. Rachel's not expecting you for dinner?'

'No.' Patrick gives that brief shake of his head and bites his lips, as if to prevent himself saying more.

'Okay, then.' I can't bring myself to tell him I'd love that.

When we get there, Patrick orders fish and chips and urges me to have the steak. 'My treat,' he insists. 'What do you want to drink?'

'I'll have a small glass of red wine.'

I sit at a table by the window, overlooking the river.

'We came here after she got her A-level results,' I tell Patrick, when he joins me with our drinks. 'To celebrate. Martin, Nadia and Chloe came too.'

'She told me.' Patrick sits down and looks out across the river.

'She was such a hard worker,' I say. 'I used to worry about her sometimes. I wasn't half as studious at her age.'

'Neither was I,' Pat said. 'This generation are different. More focused. At least, some of them are.'

'I almost wished she'd go off the rails a bit when she got to uni,' I confess now.

Anything as long as it was in her future.

Afterwards I walk to the station with Patrick.

'You don't have to,' he'd said.

'I want to.'

'That would be nice, then.' He linked his arm through mine. 'Will you let me know if you have any ideas about what to do with her ashes?' he asked.

'Of course. And you. Thanks for coming down, for coming with me today. It's been . . .' How to phrase what I was feeling?

'What?'

'It's been good to talk.'

'Yes.'

We're outside the station now.

'Patrick,' I say.

'Yes.'

It's hard but I need to say it. 'What I said before, about persuading me to turn off the life support, I didn't mean any of it.'

'It's okay,' he says gently.

'But it's not. It wasn't. I was angry. I felt guilty. I didn't mean to throw it all at you. I'm sorry.'

'You don't have to apologize,' he says.

There's sadness in the way he says it, in his eyes when he looks at me.

It prompts me to keep going, trying to articulate what I'm feeling, even though I am not really sure what it is and am struggling to find the right words. In the end they seem to tumble out, almost of their own accord. 'I never stopped loving you, you know,' I say.

It's not the way I used to say it when he first started seeing Rachel, when I understood how much I wanted him back. It's more just a statement of something I realized while we were talking. We had a child together. How could I not? When I look at him, he's tearful, shakes his head, and I get a horrible sense of déjà vu.

He turns and walks towards the station.

If You Could Turn Back Time

When you separate from the person you have a child with, the child or children become spies and counter-spies. I used to wonder if Beth was aware of this, when I asked her what she'd been doing with Patrick. Did she know I was checking up on him, not simply wanting to hear about their trips to the wood, walks by the canal or meals in places Beth regarded as impossibly exotic?

'I ate raw fish!' She was so proud when she told me. 'It wasn't cooked at all and everything in the restaurant went round and round. We just reached out and took stuff.'

'And what did you drink?'

Sometimes Beth appeared to be weighing up her answer, perhaps worrying she'd get her father into trouble if the answer was Coke. At others I felt she was trying to punish me.

'Dad's mashed potato is much better than yours. It never has any bits of skin and he puts cream in.'

His 'better' mashed potatoes rankled but it was the casual mention of women's names that really hurt.

'Abbie told me that in the old days people had to sit still for several hours if they wanted their photographs taken. They used to photograph babies when they were dead.'

The morbid fact should have elicited a response but I was more interested in the imparter. 'Abbie?'

'Daddy's friend.'

Panic. Cold sweating, heart racing, punched-in-the-stomach-style panic.

'I think she works with him.'

'Oh, really?' Faux-levity. 'Where did you meet her?'

'She was at the cinema.'

'Did she go with you or was she just there?'

'She was just there but she sat next to us.'

Beth's spying skills needed sharpening up.

I didn't want Patrick to see anyone else. I wanted him to want to come back. I was too proud to beg him. I thought he'd come to the decision on his own. He'd miss me. He'd miss the ease of having a home where he saw his daughter rather than having to plan to see her. He'd realize the separation was a huge mistake and that neither of us was happier with it. I had dared to hope that this had started to happen.

Until Beth tripped in late on the Sunday evening with her hair plaited in an unfamiliar way.

'Do you want to come in?' I'd asked Patrick, putting my hand up to my own hair, which I'd brushed when he texted to say they'd be with me in five.

'I can't. I need to get back. The next train's at half past.'

He'd dashed off, leaving me telling Beth that her hair looked nice.

'Rachel showed me how to do it,' she'd said.

And I knew.

It was too late.

He'd fallen for someone else.

I walk home after our trip to the crematorium feeling numbed by the way we parted. I'd hoped for something more from Patrick, if only a word of acknowledgement that he still felt something for me, if only as the mother of his child. All I got was that sad shake of the head.

Beth's ashes are in their urn on the table in the living room and I hold it on my lap, wishing there was a way of going back.

But you can't go back. You can't recapture the moments when you first met and fell in love with someone. You can't recall the joy of holding your firstborn child in your arms and falling in love with them. You can only go on, embracing the new stages, hoping life brings you fresh joy, while trying to hold on to little bits of the past — memories.

I need something now to hold on to.

Beth's physics teacher put a talk she did, not long before Beth died, on YouTube. He asked me if I wanted it taken down, after, but I said no. I like watching it.

It was part of her scholarship deal. In exchange for her fully funded placement at Stamford, she had to give a talk to students at a couple of local schools, to encourage others on the path she had chosen.

I take my laptop into the living room and open it.

An alert tells me I have a Facebook message. From Evan. He's sent it to my account. Not Beth's.

Dear Cate [he 's formal, like Mum with her texts]
I'm sorry it's taken me a while to respond to your messages. To be honest, I was a bit shocked, initially, and didn't know what to say.

I didn't realize you would see my posts. I guess they were insensitive. And I know it must look as if I don't think about Beth but I do, often. I find it hard to think about her, but I do, and I'm sorry if you thought I'd just moved on and forgotten about her.

I'm back at home now. Off to uni soon. Maybe I can come and see you before I go or when I'm home next?
Yours, Evan

It took courage to write, and I reply, thanking him, telling him it would be lovely to see him at some point.

I go to YouTube, search for Beth's talk and play it, allowing myself to linger once more in a time that is long past.

Beth is explaining time travel to the assembled youngsters. This, she thinks, is something that might engage them with physics. She stands on the dais with a small toy aeroplane in her hand, a globe on the desk beside her.

'Imagine you're in a plane flying westward around the equator,' she says, spinning the globe with one hand and moving the plane in the opposite direction. She stops the globe with her hand and traces a finger around its circumference. 'This line around the earth is the equator.' She looks up at the kids and away quickly, as if it's easier to pretend they aren't there. 'And these lines crossing it are called meridians.' She taps the poles at either end of the globe. 'They measure longitude, and each degree of longitude is divided into sixty minutes.'

I smile encouragement, as I did at the time.

'So, if it's midday here in London . . .' She puts her finger over much of south-east England.

I remember only half listening as she explained how it would be an hour earlier in the Cape Verde islands just off the coast of Africa and an hour later in Nigeria and France.

I suspect all parents have these moments, when they're so transfixed by the wonder of their children that they don't give their full attention to what they're doing or saying.

'At the equator,' Beth is tapping the globe again and I try to refocus on what she's saying, 'these time zones are just over a thousand miles apart and so, if I fly my plane west, back in time, at a thousand miles an hour, then by the time I reach the next time zone an hour will have passed on my watch but it would still be the same time.'

She picks up an orange, uses it to be the earth and flies the plane around it. 'What the people in this plane are doing,' she says, 'is staying in the same position on the earth relative to the sun. So they are experiencing the same time because we measure time by when the sun rises and sets.'

She has the kids' attention. No shifting in seats or fiddling with phones as she explains that if the plane could stay in the air for days, or even weeks, travelling at the same speed, then time would appear to stand still, and that if the plane went faster than the speed at which the earth rotates then you would effectively be travelling back in time.

'The important thing,' she says, 'is you would have to keep moving faster than the speed of the earth. If you could outrun the speed of the earth, the setting sun would rise again.'

The children clap. Their teacher begins to thank her but he switches off his recording device at the same time.

I go back. I watch the same clip again and again, cradling her ashes, clasping them to my chest. The pain isn't as acute as the stabbing, take-your-breath-away pain I felt immediately after her death: it's more of a weight and slight breathlessness.

'If you could outrun the speed of the earth, the setting sun would rise again.'

But I cannot. I'm always time-travelling but I can only go in one direction, getting up each morning and going to bed each night, moving inevitably forward.

PART FOUR
Eleven months later

Grief can take care of itself but to get the full value of joy you must have someone to share it with.

— Mark Twain

Searching for Something

'Tiger! Tiger!' I'm in the garden, calling for the cat, when the doorbell rings.

'He's a dirty stop-out,' Beth used to say, when the sound of dry food against enamel bowl failed to rouse Tiger from whichever spot he'd chosen to settle in for the night.

He didn't materialize this morning when I went downstairs and shook the bowl, which was still full from yesterday.

'Tiger!' I call, vaguely concerned. Has he not been home in the past twenty-four hours? Or is it longer? I can't actually remember when I last saw him.

'Tiger!' I call again, remorseful.

It's raining, a thin mist of gentle rain, and I don't have a coat, yet I'm determined to find him.

But someone's at the door. Not the postman. It's too early. I ignore it, thinking it's a cold caller, and keep searching.

'Where are you? You must be around somewhere.'

The garden is very overgrown still, despite my occasional attempts to tackle it.

'Are you in the shed? Did you get stuck in there?' I open the door but there's a voice from the other side of the garden wall.

'Who are you talking to?' It's Laura.

Of course. Laura's coming round.

I'd forgotten, momentarily.

'I'm looking for the cat,' I say, over the wall. 'I'll come and let you in.

'I haven't seen him for a few days.' I gesture towards the garden as I usher Laura into the kitchen and put the kettle on, glancing up at Beth's 'Careful Cat' story, tacked to the cupboard where I keep the coffee. Not such a careful cat after all, I think.

'It looks easy to get lost in there.' She peers out of the back door, screwing up her eyes, as if the state of the garden offends her.

'Coffee?'

Laura said, on the phone, that she had something to tell me. 'Have you got decaff?'

'I have, actually. I got some for Alfie.'

He only recently started drinking coffee, a teenage rite of passage, but he's not yet immune to the effects of too much caffeine or completely addicted to it.

'Have you heard from them at all?' Laura asks.

Joe, Sophie, Ned and Alfie are in Italy for a fortnight on a family holiday or, as Joe and Sophie have both separately referred to it, 'possibly our last family holiday'. In part because Ned took some persuading. 'We're going to the Italian lakes because some of Ned's friends are going to be there and he wants to meet up with them.' In part, because there is always a point when family holidays stop happening. 'I don't suppose Alfie will want to keep going away with the oldies much longer either.' And, in part, because Sophie and Joe are still circling each other and the subject of their marriage warily.

'But we can still do the family stuff,' Joe had told me. 'It's the us-as-a-couple stuff that's harder.'

238

'Alfie sent me a few pictures from Milan,' I tell Laura now. 'They went to see *The Last Supper* and he was unimpressed.' I grab my phone to show Laura his message. A photo of the iconic painting and Alfie's text: *This is a photo of a postcard because you are NOT ALLOWED to take them of 'the most realistic painting in the world' even though it's not that realistic at all. They're all sitting on the same side of the table!*

Laura laughed. 'He's a funny kid.'

'He is. He's very bright, even if he's not that academic.'

But I suspect some of this assertion, based on the one Alfie often makes himself, is not entirely true. His GCSE results come out later this week. I've been tasked with picking them up and relaying them to him while he's on holiday. I'm feeling both anxious and hopeful.

'And you've not heard anything from Joe?' Laura asks, and I know the subtext.

'No,' I say, and it remains unspoken that we both hope they're getting on okay – having a good time.

'Actually, I've got a bit of news of my own,' Laura says, as I set the coffee pot on the table.

'I know. You've been weirdly mysterious about it, flagging up that you've got something to tell me and not giving me any clues!' I sit down. I pour the coffee and wait. Expectant.

'I just wanted to tell you in person,' she says, stalling as she reaches for the milk jug and gives the task of pouring it into her drink more attention that it deserves.

'Dan and I,' she begins, faltering, 'we've, well, I told you we're not going to try IVF again.' She takes a sip of her coffee. 'But it's left us kind of, I don't know quite how to explain, but feeling stuck. Does that make sense?'

My stomach tightens. Not them too. Surely not. She and Dan are good together. Right for each other, just as I always thought Sophie and Joe were, as I once thought Patrick was for me.

'We talked about babies right from the start. Everything was half in anticipation of having one, having some, one day: the house, the job, and all the trying and the IVF and now, well, I guess we both feel we're not quite sure what we're working all hours for.'

I relax a little. 'So what are you planning?'

'We just want to do something different for a bit,' she says. 'There's a volunteer vet programme that Dan's been looking into and he's found a placement on a conservation project for a few months, starting mid-September, and then we thought we'd spend the rest of the year travelling.'

'Wow! That's a great opportunity. But what about your jobs? Can you leave at such short notice?'

'To be honest,' she says, slightly shamefaced, 'we'd been thinking about it for a while and we've both been given a sabbatical. I just didn't want to tell you until it was definite.'

'It sounds really exciting,' I say, a little perplexed by their keeping it all under wraps. 'So where's the placement?'

'It's in Indonesia.'

'Oh.' The penny drops. They're not going to be just down the road any more.

'Dan's going to be based in a national park there until Christmas, and after that we thought we'd travel around the Far East. I've always wanted to,' Laura says, although I've never heard her say this before.

I'll really miss her but I know it's selfish to think like

that. 'What will you do initially, when Dan's working?' I try to ask the right questions.

'I'll have time to paint. And getting to know the place will take time. It'll be an adventure.'

'And where will you stay?'

'There's accommodation at the park and other people there too.'

'That sounds brilliant,' I say, but I'm thinking that Laura will be on the other side of the world and I'll miss her.

'I'm excited about it,' she says. 'I need, we both need, something else. I need to make a positive move with my life, Cate, and this feels like one.'

'Does Mum know?'

'Yes. I've told her.' She looks at me and I suspect she knows exactly what I'm thinking. 'I'm really sorry, Cate. I feel as if I'm abandoning you. But it's an opportunity for us and we need a change.'

'It sounds great. I wish I could do something like that.'

'Why don't you come out and join us somewhere?'

'I don't know,' I say. I hadn't really meant what I'd just said. I didn't want to go anywhere. The idea of travelling didn't inspire me. I wanted to be here, in the home I'd shared with Beth.

'Maybe,' I add, half-heartedly.

After Laura has gone I carry on looking for the cat, in places where I know he cannot possibly be. In places where Beth used to hide as a child, telling me with childish mispronunciation to count to 'infinity and a wand' before coming to find her, as if the cat and I are engaged in an elaborate game of hide and seek. It gives me something to do.

'Tiger,' I say, pleading gently, as I look in the cupboard under the stairs.

'Tiger! Are you in there?' I open the blanket box in the living room that is a repository for board games: Monopoly, Trivial Pursuit, Cluedo, Articulate and Scrabble at the top and most recently used.

'Here, Tiger? Are you under there? Are you coming out?' I'm bargaining with him now, as I peer under Beth's bed. 'C'mon, Tiger. Okay. I admit it. I'm lonely without you. Come back now.'

I don't see him.

But I do see a fingerprint, a cut-out photocopy of a fingerprint, stuck with Blu-tack to the inside of the bed's leg.

I peel it off and stand up. Another memory.

It must have been there for years.

I remember that day clearly. It was raining too hard even to take a walk around the block and Beth had Chloe round to play. They must have been seven or eight at the time. And bored.

The crime scene was my idea. I downloaded images of fingerprints from the internet and printed them out, sticking them around the house for the girls to gather as they tried to work out how someone had broken into the house and why.

'I know! I know! I know!' Chloe had pulled the fingerprints off the back door, which I had unlocked, allowing access to the mystery intruder. 'He came in through the cat flap!'

And Beth had solved the crime, better placed than her friend to know I'd hidden a couple of rings that had belonged to my grandmother in a drawer that was now open, the underwear it also contained clearly disturbed. 'They've taken the gold rings.'

'You didn't look under your bed,' I say quietly now to absent Beth, as I peel off the fingerprint and hold it carefully, this fresh reminder of a forgotten rainy, but happy, day.

Doing Something

When I walk down the street later, Joyce is in her front garden, tending a cluster of wallflowers: beautiful magenta blooms that make me wonder why the term 'wallflower' was used for someone who doesn't get to dance.

'Hello,' she says, as I pass on the opposite side of the road, and eases herself up from her half-kneeling position, ready to exchange a few words.

I cross the road. 'You haven't seen our cat, have you?'

She looks at the flowerbed that runs the length of her mini demarcation wall, as if Tiger might well be there, camouflaged behind the saffron-coloured flowers. 'No,' she replies. 'Is he missing?'

'I haven't seen him for a few days. But I'm sure he's around somewhere.' I'm not so sure but I don't want Joyce to judge me, don't want her to think that I've not been looking after the cat or the garden, which I know she will have noticed has gone to seed.

'I'll keep an eye open.' She pushes a strand of hair away from her face with a muddied hand, streaking her forehead. 'How are you managing?' she asks kindly, one of the few neighbours who regularly acknowledges that grief does not go away.

It's like seasickness, or it sounds like it from the way Dad used to talk about it. He suffered, despite a lifetime in the Merchant Navy. 'You get used to it,' he'd say. 'But it never really goes away.'

'Oh, you know,' I tell Joyce, who only half knows what it's like to lose a child. Her children are still out there in the world. She can still hope that the loss is only temporary.

'David's up for parole,' she says, as if she knows what I'm thinking.

'Oh. That's good.' For her, perhaps, though not for the family of the woman he killed. 'And does that mean you'll get to see him?'

'He hasn't been in touch. His probation officer says he has a good chance of getting it, though.' She wipes her hands on the sides of her trousers this time. 'But apparently he still doesn't want contact.'

'I'm sorry,' I say. It's a bittersweet piece of news. 'But there'll be more of a chance that you might see him?' I mean to sound positive but it comes out hesitant, a question not an assertion.

She doesn't reply.

'Your garden's looking nice.' I wave at the neatly tended bed, moving on to easier things and wishing I'd not neglected mine for so long. It was my creation. I used to feel a swell of pride when people told me it was looking nice. Now I just feel their concern that I've let it go.

'I'm expecting a visit from a social worker,' Joyce tells me.

'Oh?'

She looks beyond me now, as if talking to herself but aware of her audience. 'You watch the news and there's all

245

these terrible things going on in the world, and you try to tell yourself that at least you're not starving in Africa or under fire in the Middle East, but it doesn't always help.'

'No,' I agree.

'It might not be as bad as war or famine but loneliness is still hard.' Her eyes are misting now. I put out my hand and stroke the side of her arm. Poor Joyce. I feel for her.

She smiles weakly, and lays her hand over mine briefly before taking a step back, ready to pull herself together. 'Anyway,' she pushes her hair back from her forehead again, 'I was thinking about getting a lodger but I've decided to register for fostering. I've got this big house, two spare rooms and no children or grandchildren coming to visit. There's all these refugees and children whose own parents don't seem to want them, and I'm not so old I can't cook and clean and give them somewhere to live for a while.'

'Really? That's an amazing thing to do.'

It's a positive step. Again, I think, What could I do, apart from having my nephew to stay from time to time, that might have a positive impact on someone else's life?

'I don't know if they'll think I'm suitable, but we'll see.'

'I'm sure they will,' I say warmly, although of course there's the worry with her son, especially if he comes out of prison. 'But you might want to wash your face before the social worker arrives.' The mud she's rubbed into it absent-mindedly makes her look like an army sergeant on patrol and camouflaged.

She touches it again, questioningly.

'It's a bit muddy.'

'Oh.' She puts her hand to her cheek and rubs it. 'Could

it pass for foundation?' She smiles and I laugh. 'I'd best go in and tidy myself up a bit, then.' She gestures towards the house. 'I'll let you know if I see your cat anywhere, Caitlin.'

Results

I haven't been inside a school since Beth left hers and it feels strange to be walking up the drive to Alfie's, with small groups of fifteen- and sixteen-year-olds all anxiously anticipating the exam results they've come to collect. I can see some of them looking at me, wondering why this old person is in their midst, guessing I must be the parent of someone who, for whatever reason, cannot pick up the results themselves.

'Is this the right way to the sports hall?' I ask two girls I've been following up the drive as they branch along a smaller path to the left of the main building. I presume it must be since all the kids seem to be heading that way.

'Yes.' The taller of the two smiles. 'You can go through the main building but you can get to it this way too.'

'Thank you.' I drop back a little, not wanting to intrude on their big day, but the girl I spoke to hovers on the path.

'Are you picking someone's results up?'

'Yes. My nephew's. He's away on holiday,' I say.

'Who's your nephew?' asks the other girl.

It's a big school, nearly fifteen hundred students and around three hundred in each year. I don't expect that either of them will know Alfie but it turns out they do.

'Oh, Alfie's in my art class,' the taller girl says. 'He's really good. He'll definitely get the highest grade.'

'I hope he does well,' I say, anxious on Alfie's behalf,

not so much about his art but his other subjects. He wants to do A levels at the local sixth-form college – art and graphic design, maybe photography as well, but he needs to get fives in English and maths and he's not confident that he will.

'I'm Nancy,' says the girl, confident and friendly. 'And this is Sasha.'

'Are you the aunt he sometimes stays with?' Sasha asks.

'Yes.' I've obviously asked directions of two girls who know him reasonably well. 'Are you friends of his?'

'We're in the same friendship group,' she says, as if it's an important distinction.

We're at the entrance to the sports hall now and there's a bit of a bottleneck getting in.

'Do you know what form he's in?' Nancy asks. 'You have to get the results from his form teacher.'

'Yes, 11MNT,' I say, joining the back of the queue.

The two girls have seen friends further up and they go to join them with a parting 'I hope Alfie's results are okay.'

'Thank you,' I say, as if they're my own. 'Good luck with yours.'

I pick up the envelope with Alfie's results and go outside again, into the sunshine and the groups of young people, hugging each other excitedly or looking fed up. It takes me back to Beth's GCSE-results day. She'd gone with Chloe to pick them up and I'd gone to the supermarket to buy her flowers and a bottle of champagne, anticipating they'd be worth celebrating, and knowing that even if they weren't, she'd worked hard and if the exam board hadn't recognized this then I would.

I was in the car park about to drive home when Beth called, and to begin with, when I answered, she hadn't said anything. Then I'd heard a stifled sob and gone straight into reassurance mode. It doesn't matter. Whatever your results, I know how hard you've worked. In a few months' time no one will be worried about how you did anyway.

Eventually she'd stopped my torrent of platitudes. 'No, Mum,' she'd said, still tearful. 'I'm not crying cos I messed up. I'm crying cos I did really well. I can't quite believe it.'

She'd reeled off her grades, and even though I knew she was bright and had worked hard, I was blown away by just how well she'd done. I was so proud of her.

But today is Alfie's day. I'm to open his envelope and then call him on his mobile. He'll be waiting at their apartment on Lake Como. I hope there won't be any tears.

I open the envelope, scan the list of exams taken and the corresponding marks, and relax as my eyes go down the list. They're good results. A mix of grades but he's passed English and got nines for maths and art.

Brilliant. I'm so relieved and pleased for him I can't help grinning every time he says, 'Seriously, I thought I'd really messed that one up,' to each and every result I read to him.

'Well done, Alfie. You're a star.' I notice Nancy and Sasha in my peripheral vision as I speak to him.

Nancy puts her thumb up and down and raises her eyebrows, questioning.

I put my thumb up. 'He did really well,' I say.

'Who are you talking to?' asks Alfie.

'A couple of your friends,' I tell him. 'Nancy and Sasha.'

'Can I speak to them?'

'He wants to talk to you.' I motion them closer and hand Nancy my phone.

'Hey, Alf. How did you do?'

I listen as they exchange congratulations and Nancy reels off her own impressive results. I try not to be distracted by thoughts of Beth, of the possibilities her results had opened up for her, paths she might have gone down but never would.

This is their moment, these young people's, and it's hard, surrounded by their smiling faces, not to feel happy for them.

'And is everything okay with your parents?' I hear Nancy asking Alfie but not his reply.

'Oh, well, I guess that's something,' she says, in response to whatever his reply was. 'Anyway, I'd better give the phone back to your aunt. See you when you're home.'

A short silence while she listens and then, 'Ha-ha! *Arrivederci!*

'Thanks,' she says, handing my phone back, and then handing me her phone. 'Could you take a picture of us?'

She slings her arm round Sasha's shoulders and they hold up the pieces of paper with their results, incline their heads towards each other and smile, big smiles bursting with so much possibility that I find it impossible not to smile too.

The Following Weekend

'How are you doing?'

'I'm okay,' I say, finding the pace we're running at easy, just fast enough to feel I'm pushing myself but not so hard that I can't speak. I've finally committed to joining Emma, occasionally, on a Park Run.

Running is no longer something I do to punish myself. I've begun to enjoy it. It helps clear my head and I'm getting fitter too. The last couple of times I've come with her we ran three kilometres. This time she'd suggested we do five.

'Do you want to speed up for the final push?' Emma asks, as we pass a marker point that tells us there's only another half-kilometre to the end.

'Okay.' I nod and Emma sprints, fast, so fast that I struggle to keep up with her.

I'm out of breath, red in the face, sweating when I bend down to recover at the finish and hear someone say my name. 'Cate?'

I stand up, wipe my brow and look at the tall, tanned, bearded young man standing beside me, perspiring gently, as if he too has just finished the run but for him it had been a walk in the park.

'Evan?' I know it's him but was thrown by the beard and his height. He's several inches taller than when I last saw him.

'I thought it was you,' he says, breaking into a smile now

and stepping forward to hug me, as if there's never been any bad feeling between us.

'I'm really sweaty,' I say.

'Everyone is,' he replies, as Emma eyes him curiously.

'This is Evan. He's a friend of my daughter.' I'm surprised it didn't feel odd to introduce him in that way.

'Hey.' Emma nods.

'Hi.'

'You've grown so much.' I couldn't help the maternal remark but Evan doesn't seem to mind.

'Mum said it must have been the sunshine while I was away!'

As if he's a plant. 'I've never done this before,' I tell him. 'Are you a regular?'

'Dad's one of the organizers so he forces me out of bed when I'm around.'

'And when did you get back?'

'A couple of weeks ago,' he says tentatively, aware perhaps that we're moving towards uncomfortable territory.

'I'll get going now, Cate,' Emma says, putting her hand on my arm. 'I'll see you on Monday.'

'Okay.' We'd planned to go our separate ways once the run was finished.

'Nice to meet you,' she says to Evan, then jogs in the direction of the car park.

'Dad's going to be a while, finishing up here,' Evan says. 'I was going to get something to eat at the café. Do you want something?'

'Okay.' I begin to feel slightly awkward as we walk towards the café next to the children's playground but Evan appears relaxed, at ease with me despite everything.

'I don't think I've been to this café since Beth was a toddler,' I say.

'It's changed hands a few times since then.' Evan holds the door open.

'Thank you.'

Inside, where once the interior was very basic in a way I can't quite remember, it's now all brightly painted walls and wooden tables with primary-coloured chairs. A little too familyish for comfort.

'What do you want to drink?' Evan asks.

'I'll get them.'

'No, really. Let me buy you a drink, Cate,' he insists and I scan the blackboard beside the turquoise wood-panelled counter.

'I think I'll have a ginger beer.'

'Anything to eat?'

'No, thank you.'

I find a free table amid the clusters of toddlers with dads doing their Saturday stint at the park. There's a large tin of crayons in the centre of the table and I can see some children using them to colour in paper placemats with pictures of unicorns.

'This is all much more child-friendly than it used to be,' I say, when Evan joins me with the drinks.

'I guess.' He looks around, as if he hasn't noticed until I mentioned it.

'So, did you have a good time travelling?' I ask.

'Mostly, yes. There were times when it was a bit hairy but it was a great experience.'

I try not to stare too hard at him, as he tells me his passport and all his money were stolen in Bali. He's changed during his time away and it isn't just his physical appearance: he seems to be much more than he used to be – a bigger person somehow.

'I guess those are the things that make it more memorable.' I raise my voice to be heard above the toddler at the adjoining table who has started to rap, 'I want white bread. I want white bread.'

'Listen, Evan, I'm sorry about the things I said.'

'It's over. Finished. Forgotten.'

'But seriously . . .'

'Seriously, Cate,' he says, and the way he says it seems newly mature, as if he's talking to me as a friend now, rather than the mother of his former girlfriend. 'It really is in the past.'

I incline my head to one side slightly.

'I mean our Facebook exchange and the girl in the picture too,' he added hurriedly. 'It's not that I've forgotten Beth.'

'It's okay, Evan. I know that.'

A lump is forming in my throat and it isn't because the mention of Beth has made me emotional: I feel a sudden surge of warmth towards this thoughtful young man.

'I know it's been difficult for you too,' I say. 'It's hard to lose someone you were close to at the age you did. But it's great to know that you've had a good year and to see you looking so well.'

'Thank you,' he says, looking directly at me for the first time. I can see the emotion behind the confident exterior.

'Evan!' A tall, fit-looking middle-aged man in running shorts is approaching our table.

'Hey, Dad! This is Cate, Beth's mum.'

I'd met Evan's mother a few times but never his dad

255

and I register a momentary look of uncertainty as he realizes exactly who I am. But it only lasts a split second.

'Bill.' He puts out his hand. 'It's lovely to meet you at last. We loved Beth. She was an amazing girl.'

'It's kind of you to say,' I murmur. 'She had some amazing friends too.'

'Evan?' He raises his eyebrows. 'I guess he's not so bad. And he was lucky to have had Beth in his life.'

Evan looks down, a little awkward now.

'I'm afraid we need to get off, young man.' Bill seems deliberately to lighten the atmosphere. 'I've got to pick your sister up from the hairdresser.'

'Sure.' Evan stands up. 'It was really good to see you, Cate,' he says.

'It was good to see you too,' I say and I mean it, even though I feel a pang of loneliness as I watch his dad put an arm around his shoulders as they walk out of the café together.

Life, Going On

Alfie had missed out on the general results celebration but had asked if he could stay one evening, when they were all back from their holiday, so he could go out and belatedly celebrate with a few of his friends.

'Of course. Where are you going?'

'Probably just to the park or something.'

There weren't many places people their age could go. They were too young for pubs or clubs and either met in parks or at other people's houses, which, unlike Alfie's, were easy for people to get to and from.

'How many people are you meeting up with?' I'd asked him.

'Probably about eight.'

'Do you want to ask them round here?'

'Are you sure you don't mind?'

'No. I'll go out for the evening.'

The gesture was apparently 'totally awesome', and 'insane' when I left a few bottles of Prosecco in the fridge and enough bread and cheese to soak it up with whatever else they drank.

Alfie had turned up earlier in the afternoon and helped me put together and distribute a few missing-cat flyers. Tiger had been gone almost two weeks now and I was giving up hope, but Alfie was immediately proactive.

'We can do it before you go out.' He'd lifted pictures

I hadn't even known existed from Beth's Instagram account, and helped me push the flyers through the letterboxes of the neighbours and those in the adjoining street.

'Now they've got your number to call, if we're too noisy this evening,' he'd joked, as we walked home, adding, 'Don't worry, there's only six people coming. We won't go totally mad!'

I hadn't had a plan of where I might go when I offered to be out for the evening but, by coincidence, Mum came up with one. It's their wedding anniversary. She and Dad are going to an exhibition and wondered if I'd like to meet them for an early supper before they get the train back to Portsmouth. It's a convenient plan.

Mum and Dad are already at the restaurant, sitting next to each other at a table for four, tucked away in the corner beside the exit to the kitchen, clearly not good-looking enough to be placed in the window. They're hunched over the same menu and don't see me until I reach the table.

'Oh, it's Caty,' Mum says, as if surprised to see me. 'You got here promptly. Joe said he might be a bit late.'

'I didn't know he was coming. On his own?'

'Apparently Sophie's on a late shift.' Mum looks at Dad, as if expecting him to confirm this, and he nods.

'Happy wedding anniversary.' I'd stopped at the florist on my way, picked up a small bouquet of carnations, roses and baby's breath arranged in a glass jam-jar, and put it on the table.

'Oh, aren't they beautiful? Thank you, love.' Mum beams with delight. 'Are they from your garden?'

'No. The florist on South Street.'

'Well, they're still lovely.' Mum smiles again. 'Now, what would you like to drink?'

By the time Joe arrives, we've ordered a bottle of red and are halfway through it, staving off hunger with a selection of *antipasti* while Dad tells me that there had been a parrot in the quiet carriage. 'And it kept talking! I mean, why would you sit in the quiet carriage with a noisy parrot?'

'Mum, Dad, sorry I'm late,' Joe says, tanned from his holiday but somehow tense. 'Hi, Caty.'

'We've not ordered yet,' Mum says, a reminder to Joe that we've been waiting for him, denying ourselves in the meantime.

I kick Joe under the table and nod towards the flowers.

'Oh, sorry. Happy anniversary,' Joe says, as if he'd forgotten this is why we're assembled.

'Why don't you have the beef?' Dad is saying to Mum. 'Help you get your strength back up.'

'Have you been unwell?' I ask.

'No. No,' Mum retaliates. 'Of course not.'

Of course not. Mum is never unwell, not that she'll admit to anyway. I can't remember her ever being ill in bed when we were growing up. I don't even remember her sitting down, and even in old age her health is resolutely robust.

'It's been a long day,' Dad says. 'There were only two carriages on the train here so we had to stand and it's exhausting looking at pictures.'

I nod, watching the way he touches Mum briefly on the wrist as she examines the menu. Concerned and kindly, aware of each other in a way I don't remember them being when we were children. I remember tension, bickering, and the anticipation of Dad's home leave tinged with dread too. We'd all be glad to see him but he'd disturb the equilibrium. In retirement and old age it appears to be fully restored. They've found a different way of being together.

'I think I will have the steak. What about you, Cate?'

'I'd like the risotto.'

We order our mains and Mum carries on chatting, as if it's required of her.

'We bumped into Tessa and Frank Staples on the way here. Do you remember them? You were at nursery school with their daughter Clare.'

I do remember Clare. I remember she threw a cricket ball at me the summer before I started school. It hit the side of my face and my first week at infants was spent being asked what was wrong with my face. I'd developed a lump the size of that ball. I put my hand to my cheek, without realizing, to check for any residual trace of it.

'They send their love,' Mum continues. 'I told her you'd been having a tough time.'

Dad puts his hand on hers with a gentle shushing, which creates an awkward silence, into which Joe clears his throat.

'I've been trying to find the right moment to tell you this,' he says, picking up his side plate, turning it over, examining the writing on the bottom, as if he's here on business, thinking about bidding to supply the crockery, getting an idea of what they already use first. 'But there never seems to be one.'

'Tell us what, Joe?' Mum asks.

'Sophie has a new job,' Joe says, putting the plate down

but still looking at it, as if the plain white surface is covered with the most mesmerizing pattern.

'Well, that's good,' Mum says. 'Is it a promotion?'

'Not exactly.' Joe looks up and at her. 'It's in Lincoln.'

I look at her too, register that she's taken aback, that Dad has reached out and touched her hand and that she's already regaining her composure, trying to react in the right way.

'Well, that's good for Sophie,' she says. 'She'll be near her mum. But does that mean . . .' She pauses, sips her wine.

'When does she start?' Dad asks.

'October,' Joe says. 'She's a month left to work her notice here, then a bit of time to get settled in up there before she starts the new job.'

'So, will you all be going?' Mum asks wistfully.

'I'm not sure,' Joe says, picking up the plate again, spinning it round in his hands. 'We could go with her. I mean, I'd have to come down here and travel a bit for work still but I could base myself there. It's possible. But, well, to tell you the truth, we've been finding things a bit difficult lately. It might help if we have a bit of a break from each other.'

'So you're separating?' Mum's voice rises a pitch or two.

'Well, Sophie will be up there during the week and I'll be here with Alfie. He doesn't want to move, especially not now he's got a place at college.' He looks at me and smiles as if this was all my doing.

'And Sophie will come down at weekends, when she's not working.'

'I see,' Mum says, and adds, with effort, 'I'm sure it'll work out all right in the end.' But she does not seem convinced and she barely says a word for the rest of the meal.

Instead it falls to Dad to carry on the conversation. He asks Joe how business is and how Ned's getting on at university.

'He's loving it there. I'm not sure he's doing any work but he seems to be enjoying himself.'

'Well, that's good,' Dad says, with an air of resignation.

'I saw some photos of him on Facebook,' I say. 'Dressed as a chicken on some charity run.' I realize it actually cheers me to think of Ned happy at university, getting on with his life, living as kids his age should be.

'It was in aid of dementia or something,' Joe says.

'Excellent,' Dad remarks. 'I expect we'll have that soon.'

It's a joke and we laugh, but there's fear beneath, of old age and what it will bring. It's not right that Mum and Dad are still fretting about their children when they're at the age where the roles should be reversed. We should be worrying about them.

Joe and I walk with them to the station where he has left his car.

'Shall we have a drink somewhere?' he asks, when we've seen them off. 'Unless you want to get back and check on the party? Thanks for that BTW.'

'It's a gathering! But I don't think it's a good idea to interrupt it just yet.'

We go to the nearest pub. I have another glass of wine and Joe orders a coffee.

'So,' I say, when we sit down, 'is this a sort of trial separation?'

'It seems to be.' Joe stares blankly into his coffee. 'It's about Sophie's mum and her wanting to be nearer but by default, yes, we're not going to be living together and I've no idea if absence will do the proverbial or if it's the start of us going our separate ways.'

'Maybe a bit of space will help.' I wish there was something more I could do or say to help.

A Pleasant Interlude

'It's definitely a date,' Emma says, looking over my shoulder at the email I'm reading.

It's from the author of the instant gardening book. He has two tickets for a rare-plant fair near Winchester and wonders if I might like to come with him.

'I think it's more of a thank-you,' I say.

'"Thank you" is saying thank you, maybe buying you a bottle of wine or sending you a card – "Thanks for all your work on the book." That's "thank you". This is him asking you on a date.'

'I'm not sure.' It seems odd and out of the blue. We met up a few times, over the course of the year, as the book was coming to fruition. 'There've never been any signs that he was at all interested,' I tell Emma.

'That's because it was a professional relationship and he kept it professional,' she asserts. 'And now the book is out, he's going to take a chance!'

'What if I work with him on another book?'

'So you admit it *is* a date?' Emma smiles triumphantly.

'No, I'm just saying . . .' But I have to admit to feeling ridiculously flattered and tempted by the offer.

'So will you go?' Emma asks, going back to her desk.

I tell her I'm thinking about it.

*

A week later Mark Catton, horticulturalist and author of *The Instant Garden* meets me at Winchester railway station.

The rare-plant fair is at Gilbert White's house and gardens, about half an hour's drive. I've been in Winchester to meet Mark once before, when the proofs of his book were ready and we'd been to a café in town to go over them.

This meeting is different. I feel nervous, awkward and a little fraudulent, too, because I'm not really ready to date anyone, not even sure if I want to.

It was Emma who persuaded me – at least, that's what I keep telling myself but, if I'm honest, it was the unfamiliar feeling of excited anticipation that convinced me to go ahead. Every time I thought about it, no matter how abstract, I started smiling, looking forward to it in a way I'd not looked forward to anything much for ages.

'You look nice,' Mark says, when I meet him waiting just on the other side of the ticket barrier.

'Thank you.' He'd never commented on my appearance before, never noticed it, as far as I'd been concerned, but clearly I was wrong.

I look at him now, in dark blue chinos and pale khaki shirt leading me towards his car. I notice the gold strands of his hair that I'd previously thought mousy, as he turns to look behind him before pulling out of the parking space, and I register the slight indent on his ring finger when he changes gear, where I presume he once wore a wedding ring.

And I warm to him – even more than I did while he chatted easily during the car journey – when we arrive at the fair and he suggests wandering around at our own pace and meeting up later for lunch.

It works, as a plan. I'm happy browsing stalls selling grasses and perennials and have been looking at one selling damson trees when someone touches my elbow. 'We should have a walk through the orchard here after lunch. It's really lovely.'

'That sounds great.'

He drifts off, finding me later looking at alpine plants this time. 'Are you getting hungry yet?'

I am and we go to the café in the old stable block and find a quiet table in a shaded corner where I sit while Mark goes to get lunch.

'Thank you for all of this,' I say, when he comes back, carrying two plates laden with a variety of salads.

'It's only salad.'

'I meant the fair, and bringing me here. I've never been before.'

'I know,' he answers. 'I mentioned it when we were working on the book and you said you hadn't.'

'Did I?' I have no recollection.

'You did.' He smiles. 'And you said you were interested in rare plants too.'

'Were you taking notes?' I laugh.

'I kept a few.' He grins. 'Did you see anything that might fit into your garden today?'

'I've not really been doing much gardening recently.' It seems like an opportunity to let him know a little more about my home life.

'No?'

'No.' I hesitate. It's always difficult for people to hear. 'My daughter died. Just over a year ago. It's been a really difficult time and I haven't been up to much.'

'I'm really sorry,' he says. 'I had no idea. I can't even begin to imagine. God, I feel guilty now that you had to put up with me and my silly book.'

'It's not a silly book!'

'But it's not important. I'm just trying to remember all the annoying emails I sent you over the last few months, worrying about chapter headings, and all the time, I had no idea you had much bigger things to deal with.'

'To be honest, it helped me, being back at work. It gave me something else to think about.'

'Do you have other children?' he asks.

I shake my head. 'You?'

'Two girls,' he said, 'fifteen and thirteen, but I don't get to see them very often any more. Their mother's French and she moved back when we separated.'

'That must be hard.'

'It is,' he replies, and I'm grateful to him for not saying anything trite about how it's nothing compared to what I must be going through.

'I really miss them,' he adds. 'But they came over for a couple of weeks this summer and we had a good time, the three of us.'

I ask him a bit about their mother, his ex-wife, how they met and why they split up a couple of years ago.

'And what about your daughter's father?' he asks.

I tell him we'd separated years previously.

'What did he do?'

There's something about Mark Catton, something that makes me open up to him. I find myself telling him about Patrick, how he's often away and somehow we let things slip. 'When he told me he wanted to separate, I was knocked for six. But I always thought we'd end up getting back together again.'

'And you still miss him.' Mark is looking at me with an expression that I can only describe as frank.

'Yes, I do. It probably sounds strange but I actually find myself missing him more since Beth died than I did before.'

'That doesn't sound strange at all,' he says kindly. 'It sounds perfectly reasonable.'

'But he's with someone else now,' I say abruptly, wanting to move on, as I've taught myself to do whenever my thoughts turn to things that make me sad but I can't do anything about.

'But you're not ready to be,' Mark says, not as a question but as a simple statement. 'Not yet, not after what happened.'

He reaches his hand across the table a little. I take it and feel comforted by its warmth.

'I'm sorry,' I say. 'But no. I don't think I am. Not yet.'

'So how was it?' Emma asks excitedly, when I'm back in the office, the following Monday.

'It was lovely,' I say truthfully. 'He's a really nice man.'

'Will you be seeing him again?'

'Perhaps, but just as friends.'

'Why? He obviously likes you and you like him.'

'It's too complicated –'

'Oh, no! Is he married or with someone?'

'No, nothing like that,' I say.

'Then what?'

Emma is young. She doesn't have children. Could she

even begin to understand how losing one damages your capacity for love?

'I can't really explain,' I say, and she shrugs and leaves the subject alone.

Uncertainty

When Rachel calls a few days later I'm at work, searching the internet for information on what to do with cremation ashes and coming up with some fairly outlandish suggestions: blasting them into space, turning them into jewellery, even a story about someone who mixed his spouse's ashes with tattoo ink and emblazoned her name across his chest. None of these are right but I'm determined to come up with some ideas to talk through with Patrick.

There's been the odd text from him since we brought Beth's ashes home and walked by the river but I haven't seen him. I want to and don't want to.

My phone is in my bag when I hear it ringing and I root around, wondering if perhaps someone has found Tiger. When I retrieve it, I see the outline of a face for which I don't have a photograph – and the name, RACHEL.

I stare at it. Why is Rachel calling me? Rachel doesn't call me.

'Rachel?' I ask, as if it might be someone else.

I don't have to go. I might not. I could just not show. I have these conversations with myself in the days before we meet. Rachel wants to talk. Easier face to face. There's an exhibition she wants to see at the local museum, by a photographer she was at college with. I've seen the posters around town. 'Tide and Times', it's called. The posters have an image of a vast sandy beach, not unlike ours, with a curious line of white shells running from the shoreline up into the dunes. I noticed the poster and wondered who had made the line of shells.

I suggest a café in the street adjoining the gallery. It's rarely busy and it has a small garden.

'Perfect,' she says. 'I'll see you there, unless I hear from you.'

I could cancel. I'm tempted, but I don't.

Rachel is already there when I arrive, resting back against the ubiquitous coffee-sack cushions that line the bench running along the wall. There's a large painting of a woman weeping fish on the wall above her. The café doubles as a gallery. They all double as something in this bit of town: yoga studios, or microbreweries, or hairdressers.

Rachel looks minute and monotone beneath the vibrant reds and yellows of the weeping-fish woman. She's wearing a cream shirt and black trousers. Her blonde bob has grown out. It's not really a bob any more. She's staring ahead, lost in thought.

'Cate.' She waves as I approach, as if it was me who hasn't seen her.

'Hi.' I sit opposite.

She doesn't get up to greet me and I don't bend awkwardly to kiss her.

'I ordered a latte at the counter,' she says, calling the waiter over.

I pick up the menu. I feel uncomfortable. I smile. 'English breakfast tea, please. And a cinnamon bun.' He has green eyes. He reminds me of Patrick. Does Rachel see it?

He takes the menus, so smiley.

'How is Patrick?'

'He's away,' Rachel replies. 'But, if I'm honest, he's not good in a way I can't even begin to understand. He doesn't really talk to me. He keeps so busy with work but I don't think he talks to anyone. Does he talk to you?'

'When I see him,' I say, a little hesitantly.

The smiley waiter comes back with our drinks and my bun which he puts on the table between us. Rachel breaks off a tiny piece, a morsel, and puts it into her mouth. I don't say anything and leave the plate where it is.

'I've got an exhibition coming up,' she says, swallowing. There is a pause before she adds, 'In Seattle.'

'That's great.' I don't anticipate where this is leading.

'It's for six months at a prestigious gallery.'

'Congratulations.'

'And I'm planning to go out and base myself there while it's on.' She looks at me. 'Perhaps for longer.'

'And you want Patrick to go with you?'

'It could be a fresh start, for both of us,' she says.

'No.' I hadn't meant to say this out loud.

'I know it will be difficult, Cate. I'm not making him join me. It's a choice. I thought it might help, being somewhere else, being somewhere different. I thought it might help him . . .'

'What?' The edge in my voice could slice the cinnamon bun in half.

'Put some of this behind him,' Rachel says.

'Put it behind him?' I practically shout. I know other people are looking but I don't care. 'Beth's death isn't something either of us can just walk away from, Rachel.

Do you think he wants to forget his own daughter ever existed?'

'No, of course not. I didn't mean that at all. I just thought it might help to move away. Just all the pain and sorrow, all the anguish surrounding her.'

'The hardest thing is actively remembering her. You've no idea. After a while, people stop talking. They don't want to talk about her. Everyone wants you to move on. You start to forget some of the details. All the memories you have, they start to slip away. He needs to remember her, Rachel. We both do.'

I'm practically weeping fish myself now. I take a deep breath. I'm livid.

'I'm sorry.' Rachel clutches the edge of the table as she speaks. Her cheeks are flushed, her voice is agitated. 'I didn't mean to upset you. And I know that this is something that will always be there, of course, for both of you. But at the same time Patrick needs to start living again.' She toys with the bun on its plate. 'And I do too. I'm going to take the job but I don't know what Patrick will do.'

'He hasn't made up his mind?'

'No. He said he needed time to think about it.' Rachel turns her face towards the wall so that her profile matches that of the weeping-fish woman and I can see she is holding back tears. Normal ones.

'He's been in Kenya.' She exhales as she speaks. 'He's back in England now but he hasn't come home. He said he needed time alone.'

'Right.'

'He said he's staying with friends but I'm not sure who or where. I thought you might know.'

'No. I've no idea.' I start to worry.

'I thought he might be staying with Joe or . . .'

'Me?'

She nods.

'No. He's not with me.'

'I'm sorry. This was probably a bad idea. I just thought you should know what's going on.'

I'm afraid that if I speak I'll be unable to keep the bitterness out of my voice. How dare she? How dare she even think about taking Patrick away? She has no right. And yet she has every right.

'I love him too, you know,' Rachel says, and it sits there uneasily between us, this articulation of the fact.

Rachel picks up a green silk scarf from the bench beside her and winds it around her neck, destroying the monochrome effect as she takes her purse from her bag. 'I'll get the bill. It's on me.'

'Listen, Rachel . . .' I begin, but I have no idea what to say.

'It's okay,' she says. 'You don't have to say anything.'

Then she bends down towards the floor and picks up a large carrier bag. 'I almost forgot,' she says, putting it on the table and pushing it towards me.

'What is it?' I feel suspicious.

'It's something Beth was making for you,' Rachel tells me. 'She hadn't quite finished. It needed a few more . . . Well, you'll see if you open it. I wanted to give it to you myself.' She nods towards the bag, which is sealed at the top with a narrow strip of Sellotape.

I peel it off slowly, then open the bag and take out the contents.

It's a miniature house, made entirely from wine corks.

'It's a bird feeder,' Rachel explains unnecessarily. 'We saw some on a stall in the Columbia Road flower market. It must have been a couple of years ago. Beth said she wanted to make one for you. We started saving corks but there never seemed to be quite enough. So many wine bottles have screw tops, these days.'

I recognize the nervousness of Rachel's chatter. 'It's lovely,' I say, stopping her, feeling the sponginess of the cork in my hands. The lightness of this physical object. 'And it looks finished. It's beautiful.'

Rachel looks at the table, oddly embarrassed as I have never seen before, stripped of her innate poise.

I raise my eyebrows quizzically.

'I finished it for her,' she says. 'It was just the roof really. I thought you'd like to have it, and Beth had been so excited about making it for you.'

'Thank you.' I feel a surge of warmth for Rachel. I don't know what else to say. Life is so complicated.

Someone Else's Decision

I can't get to sleep after my meeting with Rachel. I lie awake, in the early hours, telling myself that it won't make any difference if Patrick is living on the other side of the Atlantic. Asking how often I would have seen him anyway. And yet I know that it would make all the difference. That it would mean the end for us, that what very little of us remains would cease to be.

I get up just before two a.m., go to the kitchen and make myself a cup of chamomile tea, which I carry into the sitting room. I take a couple of photograph albums down from the shelves above the television, early ones, stuffed with snapshots from before Beth was born, when Patrick and I first got together. Patrick on a ridge above the clouds in Nepal, focusing his camera across the valley towards Mount Everest in the distance, unaware that I was capturing his outline from behind. Patrick outside our tent in the Serengeti, where he'd been to document the zebra migration and taken me with him. It was where I got pregnant with Beth. Patrick on the harbour front in Portsmouth, as we walked from the station to my parents' house, a nervous look on his face as he smiles at me. It was the first time I had taken him to meet them.

Eventually I go back to bed and drift into sleep, just as the house-martins nesting under the eaves are waking and chattering and the grey dawn is filtering through the curtains.

I'm woken, only a few hours later, by the sound of a chainsaw, forcing me up and to the window. Men with hard hats are halfway up the elm tree on the pavement outside Joyce's house, lopping off branches, too keenly and too early. It's not yet eight o'clock. Isn't there something in the byelaws that prohibits excessive noise before eight on a Saturday?

I go downstairs, make coffee and bring it to the living-room window. They've taken some of the branches back as far as the trunk. A ruthless pruning, there'll be no foliage left by the time they've finished. My view, when I draw the bedroom curtains, will be altered, too early, way ahead of autumn when the change would have been slow and kaleidoscopic.

It was one of the things I'd liked about this house, when we saw it: the tree, and that we could see it from our bed, watch buds beginning to appear and the leaves unfolding as we nursed morning coffee. Watch the tree sparrows, flying back and forth with material for their nest, as Beth nestled between us at weekends. Had their nests been lined with her hair? Even the outline of bare branches in the winter gave foreground interest to the sky.

I shower and dress for a day with nothing planned beyond a trip to the corner shop. The bread in the bread bin is mouldy beyond the point that even I will eat it. I put on a jacket, grab my keys and purse and head for the Friendly Stores, shocked as I step outside to see how much more of the tree has gone while I was showering and dressing. It's practically all trunk now.

One of the men holds up his hand, signalling to me to wait as another branch comes crashing down onto the pavement.

'You're cutting far too much off. It'll take years to grow back.'

'It's coming down. It's diseased.'

'The whole thing?'

'Yup. Gotta go before it spreads.'

'Oh.'

It saddens me so much I think I might start to cry. So I move on quickly, reaching the shop just as the fresh bread is being loaded onto the shelves. So many varieties: wholewheat, seeded, rye, sourdough, gluten-free, honey and sunflower seed. And in a tiny corner shop. It's the same with standard milk: it's hard to find it among the almond, soya and other dairy-free varieties.

'People take care of their health.' Ajit grinned as if this was a source of personal pride, when I asked him once why there was not more normal milk. Have they nothing better to worry about? I thought.

I take a sunflower-seed loaf and start to walk out of the shop, forgetting to pay.

'Miss! Miss!' Ajit calls after me.

Another shopkeeper might have been less understanding.

He smiles, wrapping the bread in paper, all part of the new 'artisan' feel. 'Anything else?' he asks, and I look around.

I should buy something to make up for the shoplifting. I spot a pile of *National Geographic*s on the floor beside the newspapers, which have not yet been put onto the shelves. I take one and a bar of chocolate. 'I'll have these too, please.'

I carry them home but am interrupted on my journey by Joyce. 'Caitlin,' she calls from her doorstep, as if she'd been watching the tree-felling through her living-room window and needs to talk to me about it. 'Caitlin.' She beckons me over.

'I can't believe they're taking the tree down.' I'm gutted.

'I know.' Joyce nods sympathetically. 'It's terrible. Terribly sad. Could you come in for a second? It's just . . .' She hesitates. 'Well, there's something . . . It's best if you come in.'

'Okay.' I wonder what's going on. Has her son been granted probation? Is he going to be released? Does he want to see her? Or not?

'Sorry, it's a bit of mess,' she says, leading me through her tidy hallway, orderly but for a couple of pairs of trainers scattered along the side of the striped stair-runner, which extends to the doorway.

Incongruous trainers. Size tens. Teenage.

'Oh, yes,' Joyce says, as if she knows exactly what I'm thinking. 'It all happened a little faster than I expected. I've got a boy from Syria, Samir.'

'Oh, gosh.' I feel a little excitement for her. And responsibility. 'From Syria? How old is he?'

'Seventeen. He's out in the garden.' She appears to be heading that way. 'He seems very pleasant, despite all he's been through. He's been helping me in the garden. Apparently his father owned a garden centre.'

'In Syria?'

'Yes. It's not what you imagine when you think of the

country, is it? Not with everything going on there. But apparently it thrived for a while.' She pauses, her hand on the back door, which leads out of the kitchen into her garden, and lowers her voice. 'Until his father was killed.' She turns to me now. 'He likes being outside. But he's still very sensitive, after everything he's seen back home.'

I wonder what Joyce means by this.

She opens the door and I follow her out. The first thing I see, in the middle of her lawn, is a dead blackbird, its wing splayed across the grass, blood beginning to congeal like red berries against the dark of its feathers.

I swallow and look away, to the edge of the garden where a boy who must be Samir is sitting on the bench, barefoot. I notice this because it's cold and I think he must be. I'm thinking about this and the dead bird. Does it bring back bad memories for this boy, who must have seen a lot of death? My thoughts divert my attention so that I don't notice that he's cradling something on his lap.

'It was a bit of a shock for Samir,' Joyce is saying. 'Poor bird. But I think it might be your cat?'

And then I realize that that is what Samir is holding. It's a cat. It's Beth's cat. It's Tiger. The tears are already forming.

Samir looks at me with soulful, wide, questioning eyes. I nod and he stands and gently passes Tiger to me.

I can't even begin to speak. Tiger struggles slightly as I take him from Samir but I hold him tightly, relieved to feel the warmth of his body and the dampness of his fur.

'I think he was hungry,' Samir says, nodding towards the dead bird.

I feel a new skinniness to Tiger, a weight loss caused by neglect. I've neglected him. The cat Beth loved and I should have looked after. 'Thank you,' I say to no one in particular, to Samir, to Joyce, to the powers that be for letting me find him, giving me another chance.

'Oh, poor Tiger,' I say, stroking his head. 'Have you been fending for yourself all this time?'

'Why don't you bring him in and let's see if we can find him something else to eat?' Joyce suggests, half nodding towards the bird.

'Yes.' I follow her back into the kitchen, aware that Samir is a few steps behind me. Only when he has closed the door behind me do I dare relinquish my tight hold on Tiger. I expect him to wriggle and spring away as I sit down but he remains on my knee, allowing me to stroke him while Joyce roots around in her cupboard, producing a tin of sardines.

Only when she has emptied the contents onto a plate and placed it on the floor does he wriggle away.

'He must have been hungry,' I say apologetically, to Samir, taking him in properly now. He is tall and rather beautiful, wearing a T-shirt that says 'CHALK' and black jeans. I notice a deep white scar, which runs lengthways along the side of his tanned foot. It could be anything. But he is a war child and I feel responsible for the latest carnage he has been forced to witness.

Samir puts out a hand, takes mine, holds it a little longer than anyone British would, and says, 'I am happy you have found your cat.'

There's something about the kindness of the gesture and the words, a generosity in them.

'I hadn't been looking after him,' I confess, and he squeezes my hand reassuringly.

Tiger is wolfing down the sardines as if he hadn't eaten for days. I'm so happy to see him but I can't quite get the image of the blackbird out of my mind. Experiencing death up close has made me less able to tolerate it, in any form.

'It's such a waste,' I say.

'I'll bury it in a bit,' Joyce says, as if she knows exactly what I'm thinking. She's busying herself with the kettle now, making tea, and shortly places a cup, which says Chester Colliery Brass Band on it, in front of me.

'Thank you.'

'It's fine,' she says. 'The important thing is you've got your cat back, dear.'

I don't know if it's the term of affection, or her solicitousness with the tea or the way Samir is looking at me anxiously, with those big sympathetic eyes, but mine are welling again. I'm not sad. I'm overjoyed at having found Tiger. Despite the dead elm tree being removed outside, despite all the awful things that go on in the world, despite how hard life can be sometimes, it is still punctuated by moments of joy.

Tiger has finished the sardines now and is purring as he rubs himself against my legs. It is bliss.

'Do you like roses?' Samir asks, in good but broken English, peering at me anxiously still across the table.

'Of course.' I sniff. 'Everyone likes roses.'

'Then we bury the bird and we plant a rose nearby,' he says solemnly. 'As a sign of new life.'

'What a beautiful thought,' I say, somehow cowed by the simplicity of it.

A little later, Joyce leaves him in the kitchen and walks with me to the front door. 'Samir told me that after the bombings in Syria, people used to come to their garden centre to buy roses,' she said. 'They used to plant them where the bombs had fallen, as a symbol of defiance and hope.'

'Really?' I find myself in awe of such optimism, that people would still take the trouble to grow things while war raged around them, that they would choose the places scarred by bombs to plant new life.

The Father of my Child

When I get home, I lay out my earlier purchases on the kitchen table: the seeded loaf, the bar of chocolate and the magazine.

I make myself more tea and sit down to begin scanning *National Geographic*, as if it will be enough to broaden my horizons, to open up my world, which has shrunk so far in the past year.

The magazine contains articles about disappearing coral reefs in the Philippines, honey hunters in Nepal, plants used in medicine and, three-quarters of the way in, I find Patrick's familiar head and shoulders, unchanged in the thumbnail image that accompanies his photographs.

'Elephantine Emotion' reads the headline in large bold print and a smaller strapline: 'Elephants, like us, are empathetic beings. They help each other in distress, grieve for their dead, and experience many of the same emotions as we do.'

I scan the copy. Elephants are under threat, the population declining to such an extent that some scientists already consider them 'ecologically extinct'. There are facts and figures to back this up: incidents of elephants being shot and maimed for ivory. But there is another threat: drought affects the wildlife population as much as it does our own. Patrick details the threats to elephants matter-of-factly. But then the tone of the piece changes. 'And the horror of all of this is compounded by the fact that we know elephants to be emotive and empathetic beings,' Patrick writes, and I can hear him saying this, imagine him just back from a trip, recounting a little of what he has seen, trying to convey some of what he felt.

Elephants, just like us, feel emotional pain and distress. They too grieve for their fellow creatures. They also suffer sorrow and loneliness in the aftermath of the terrible things done to their friends and relatives.

We will never know exactly what goes on inside the mind of an elephant, just as we will never know what goes on inside the mind of another person.

My eyes are drawn to a pull quote, an extract from the article, printed alongside the main body in a bigger, bolder font. There is an image of a mother elephant, standing over the body of a baby, pushing against it with her foot.

This mother stayed with her baby, trying to lift the body and move it for several hours as she tried to come to terms with what had happened. For me, it was impossible not to think that what I was witnessing was grief. The mother's bereavement transmitted itself so strongly.

There's another picture: a group of elephants standing around the baby's body. They look like a regular group of mourners, paying respects, their expressions sombre and sad.

In another, the mother appears to be crying: tears are streaming down her face, from both eyes.

The image is heartbreaking, the sense of loss evident.

My eyes move between the images and the words. I can see the distress and heartbreak on the faces of the elephants Patrick has captured with his camera and I think I can hear his own in the accompanying words.

I read it again. I look at the images again. I reach out and run my fingers along the image of a male elephant standing beside his dead calf and I try to read the expression on his face, just as I try to read the spaces between the words that Patrick has written.

I want to talk to him. I desperately want to talk to him. The idea of five senses dates back to classical times.

You'd have thought by now that we'd have added a few more, more than the ubiquitous 'sixth sense'. Why not a sense of the way we perceive time or register a presence without it being tangible, or the way we know something that has not happened yet is about to?

It was either that, or coincidence, that made me take my phone out of my bag before it had even begun to ring.

It was a private number.

'Am I speaking to Caitlin Challoner?' the caller asked.

He sounded young, with a slight accent. Irish? Only a few words to go on so far.

'Yes. It's Caitlin.'

'I'm calling from Scarborough Hospital,' he says. 'On behalf of Patrick Challoner.'

'Patrick? Is he with you? Who is this?'

'I'm calling from the hospital in Scarborough,' he repeats. 'Patrick was admitted this afternoon, suffering from severe hypothermia.' He pronounces it as if it's two words, with the emphasis on the first. Definitely Irish, I think.

'In Scarborough?'

People never ask the right questions or say the appropriate things in these circumstances. That the hospital Patrick is in is in Scarborough is not the salient fact.

'Yes,' he says. 'Are you nearby?'

'No. I'm on the south coast.' Possibly as far away as I could be. 'But I can come up if he wants me to.'

'If you can,' he says. 'We'll be keeping him in overnight.'

'And does Rachel know?' I ask.

'You are the only person he's asked me to call,' he replies. I reach for a notepad and a pen and write down some of the details the Irishman is giving me over the phone.

A list of words that don't make sense to me but all beg the same question.

'Is he going to be okay?'

'He'll be fine. He's going to be fine.'

I find myself momentarily reassured but how can I be? Not after Beth. I look at the scrap of paper where I have written 'heart and chest unit'. Why is he there? How can he be fine if he's there? 'He can't be fine,' I say.

'He's okay,' the Irishman says. 'He's been treated and we expect him to make a full recovery. Really there's no need to worry. It's probably best if you talk to him yourself, if you can get here. He's been asking for you.'

'Yes,' I say, and despite the circumstances I feel something akin to relief. Because he asked for me. But it's mingled with fear, for Patrick, and a slow, simmering anger. I try to remain polite and calm on the phone as I promise that I'll drop everything and travel to Scarborough, but I'm furious when the call is ended. How could Patrick have done this to me? How could he force me to make another journey to another hospital to hear another set of doctors and nurses tell me that someone I love has been brought in after being pulled from the sea.

How can it come to me, with such clarity, how deeply I love and need Patrick? If anything were to happen to him, I don't think I could go on.

It's a journey of nearly five hours to Scarborough by train, during which I go over the details of what I was told on the phone. None of it makes sense: Patrick being in Scarborough in the first place. Patrick being plucked out of the sea by a lifeboat and brought to hospital suffering from extreme hypothermia. Patrick being given a cardiopulmonary bypass. I wrote it all down on autopilot.

I take the piece of paper out of my pocket now, look at the words and allow them to start to sink in.

'It's a way of warming up the body,' the Irishman had explained. 'Doctors remove blood from the body and heat it before putting it back.' Patrick had responded well to the treatment, he'd told me.

I'd phoned Rachel, as soon as the call from the hospital had ended, and went straight to her voicemail, to a message saying she was out of the country 'and several hours behind' but would respond as soon as she could.

I hung up the first time, thought briefly what I would say before calling the number again and leaving a brief message: Patrick was in hospital in Scarborough. He'd been swimming and he was okay. The hospital said there was nothing to worry about but he'd been treated for hypothermia. I was on my way. She should call me when she got the message.

*

So I'm heading to the hospital. It's all so similar yet not the same at all. Awful. Better. I don't know. I can't believe this is happening. Not again.

The walls of the ward are painted in a green several shades lighter than scrubs. It feels medical but I'm sure it's supposed to be soothing or healing. Patrick is propped up in a bed at the end of a bay, looking better than I'd expected. I was dreading a mass of wires and a deathly pallor again, but there are neither of these things and, with his eyes closed, he looks almost peaceful.

I'm relieved but furious still.

He opens his eyes when he senses my approach, smiles and shifts a little. 'You came.'

'Of course I came.' I stand beside his bed and he stretches his arm towards me. Unfurls his hand. I take it, swallowing my emotion and my anger.

'Patrick.' I want to ask him what happened but the question feels too intrusive.

'I wasn't trying to kill myself,' he says, squeezing my hand.

'I didn't think . . .' I stop because I had thought it. On the train, on the way up. What was he doing swimming so far out to sea that he couldn't get back? So that he was so cold by the time the lifeboat picked him up that he needed a cardiopulmonary bypass? I was furious with him but it's gone now that I'm here. Well, not gone, but subsided.

'What were you doing?' I let go of his hand, pulling a chair closer to the bed.

'Give me your hand back.' He holds his out again, as I sit. 'I need some warmth.'

He takes my hand and I'm reminded of something my mother had said to me when I was a child and had asked her why grown-ups got married.

'So that there is someone to hold your hand as you go through life,' she had replied immediately, as if this was something she had thought about and her answer was definitive.

I'd thought about it, after Patrick left, when I started to envy my friends with partners, the presence of a significant other in times of difficulty. And of joy.

'Tell me.' I feel Patrick's palm warming in mine.

'I thought maybe if I came home,' he jerks his head towards the window, as if the rooftops outside constituted home, 'that things would feel different.'

Patrick grew up in Scarborough but he rarely refers to it as home. He's always been so transient, too nomadic even to think of the house he used to share with his wife and daughter as home.

I wait for more.

'I'd booked into a B-and-B for a couple of days. I meant just to walk on the beach, but when I was there, I wanted to get away, to get out into the water, to look back at the land. It was a kind of compulsion.' He held my hand tighter, as if squeezing it would force understanding. 'And I'm sorry. I didn't think. Of what might happen. Or the parallels. I just wanted to get away. I didn't want to be rooted on land, and when I was out, it was cold. It was freezing after a while, but it didn't seem to matter. It just felt like a reminder of how much you can endure, of how much a person can go through and still somehow keep on.'

'Yes,' I say, as if I understand, and I half do, although I couldn't articulate what I understand.

'I've been telling myself,' Patrick continues, 'I keep telling myself, that I just need to keep going and I'll reach a point where it'll be easier to keep going. But every time I think I've reached it, it moves further into the distance. Am I making any sense?'

'Yes.' It's what I've been doing.

'I'm tired.' He closes his eyes. 'I'm so tired of keeping on going and never getting there.'

'I know what you mean. I'm tired too but we have to carry on.'

'It's not easy. I know it can't be easy for you either. I do know that. But sometimes, during the past year, I've envied you.'

'Envied me? For what?'

'For your ability to turn to others.' He looks directly at me now, fixing me with the green of his eyes. 'It seems so simple for other people to turn to those around them but I've never been able to do it.'

And this is the moment when it starts: when we begin to communicate properly, openly, when we stop hiding feelings from each other because we're afraid of what the other will think.

'Oh, Patrick,' I say, knowing how true this is, wishing he'd admitted it years ago.

'I've been so lonely, Cate. I've felt so alone.'

'What about Rachel?'

'No.' He shakes his head. 'It's too much. It's all been

291

too much. Too much for her even to begin to comprehend.' He closes his eyes and we sit in silence again for a while. I'm tired too, from the journey and the day. I lean back in my chair. I close my eyes for a while and stay silent.

'When the hospital called,' I say eventually, 'they asked for Caitlin Challoner. Why did they think that was my name?'

'They asked if there was anyone they could call, a partner or a child. Rachel's in the States,' Patrick says. 'I told them you were the mother of my child.'

PART FIVE
Two years on

Things get broken. Sometimes they get repaired
and in most cases you realize that no matter what is
damaged, life rearranges itself to compensate for
your loss, sometimes wonderfully.

— Hanya Yanagihara, *A Little Life*

Time. Slowly Healing

I can look at the photos hanging on the walls of the staircase now without that awful knife-twisting feeling. I can smile at the memories, which are still there, without them hurting quite so much: newborn Beth, first-birthday Beth, geese-feeding Beth, all the way up the stairs to eighteen-year-old Beth, studying.

People don't cease to exist when they die, only when you stop remembering them, and Beth is remembered, very much, even though her presence is fading and many of the physical reminders of her are dwindling too.

Beth's bedroom is now Alfie's. Her desk is still there but her books and files have been replaced with tubes of paint and pots of brushes. Her spotted pyjama bottoms no longer hang on the back of the door. Alfie's grey check ones are abandoned on the floor. His electric razor now sits on top of the chest of drawers, where Beth used to leave her hairbrush.

Everything, until the night Sophie and Joe came round together, saying they had something to ask me, had pointed towards a separation: Sophie's new job in Lincoln starting just as Alfie began his A levels at the local sixth-form college; Sophie being up in Lincoln while Joe remained with Alfie; Alfie still spending the odd night at my house and Joe, dropping by more often than he used to, wanting to chat, clearly not happy.

The evening they arrived together, they'd brought wine even though Sophie wasn't drinking. 'I'm driving and I've got an early shift,' she'd said, looking at Joe as he told me the previous few months had made them both realize they wanted to be together but that the logistics were now more difficult.

'I don't need to be here to manage the business,' Joe said. 'I'd have to come down but I can do most of what I need to do wherever I'm living, but we don't want to uproot Alfie, not now that he's started his A levels.'

The unspoken question hung in the air. And, without pausing to think, I'd said, 'Why doesn't he stay with me during the week? He can walk to college from here and go home at the weekends if you're coming down.'

Joe had looked at Sophie, and she'd given an almost imperceptible nod.

'We'll probably come down most weekends and he's old enough to stay in the house on his own now anyway, but it would help enormously if he could be here during the week. Are you sure it wouldn't be too much for you?'

'I'd like it.' I'd felt more sure of that than I had of anything. 'But what about Alfie?'

'We'll have to ask him, of course, but I think he'd like that,' Sophie had answered, and I'd watched Joe take her hand and squeeze it – Sophie and Joe again.

Alfie had apparently jumped at the suggestion and I'd called Patrick to tell him.

'I'm going to have to sort Beth's room properly.' All her clothes were still in the cupboard or folded in drawers, all her books in the bookcase, her work files and notebooks in her desk. And her ashes, her tangible remains, still there on the shelf above it.

I'd wondered whether Alfie was disturbed by them being there on the nights he slept over but he'd said nothing and, for the time being, that was where I'd felt they belonged. So I'd said nothing either and left them there.

'I'll come down, if you like,' Patrick had replied. 'I can help you with her room.'

I'd made a start without him. I'd taken things out of drawers and cupboards, stacked notebooks and papers on her desk, piled clothes in mounds on her bed, brought empty boxes home from work, thinking that the obvious thing to do with her possessions was to store them elsewhere, in the attic, in storage, perhaps, or maybe Joe and Sophie would exchange house space: I'd have Alfie to stay if they'd keep Beth's clothes in one of their many floor-to-ceiling wardrobes.

But Patrick was a little more selective in his approach. 'GCSE history books?' He queried what went into the boxes destined for the attic. 'She didn't even like history and they're just textbooks.'

'I know, but . . .' I relented.

It was the same with clothes. 'I don't remember her ever wearing this.' Patrick held up a rust-coloured shirt.

'I don't either,' I admitted.

It went into the charity-shop pile.

'Can you take them to a shop in London, though?' I asked Patrick.

It was one thing allowing her things to go, but the thought that I might bump into someone wearing something of Beth's was quite another.

'Yes.' He didn't need to ask why.

'Oh, I remember buying her this in Iceland.' He held up her Icelandic sweater. 'Did she wear it much?'

'All the time. She said it had cost you a fortune.'

'Like everything in Iceland.' He shrugged. 'She wasn't very well prepared for the trip.'

'No,' I assented, half responsible.

She was around twelve at the time, beginning to take an interest in fashion and lose interest in practicality.

'Does it fit you?' Patrick asked.

'Probably, but I don't think I could wear it. Put it in the charity-shop pile.'

'Sure?'

'I think so, but not that.' Next on the pile was a green linen top that Beth had worn almost daily in the summer before she died. I could picture her sitting in the garden in it, her shoulders visible and golden in the sun.

'Here.' Patrick handed it to me and I put it in the zip-up clothes bag, with a few other items I could still clearly see her wearing.

'Her ashes?' Patrick asked, looking at the shelves above her desk.

'I'll put them in my room,' I said. 'Unless?'

'No,' Patrick replied.

It still felt too difficult to decide what to do with them.

The drawers of her desk were easier: a dusty jumble of pens, a lot of which Patrick had stolen from around the world, paperclips, phone chargers and iPod leads, Tupperware boxes containing nothing, a few beer mats, their significance lost on me.

In the top drawer were her passport, purse and a few

other things she used daily. 'Everything in there's for keeping,' I said to Patrick, as he opened the drawer.

'Sure.' He took out her passport, opening it, looking at the picture for a while, putting it back, then opening her bus pass to reveal another forgotten Post-it. An enigmatic note Beth had written to herself this time. 'Mum and Dad?' was all it said.

Patrick closed the pass and replaced it.

'What's this?' He took out the leather jewellery box that had once contained earrings.

'It's her hair. I took it from her brush.' My voice cracked. It was suddenly too much.

Patrick looked at it for a few moments, then put it back.

'I think we need a break.' He'd put out his hand. I'd taken it and let him lead me from her room, out into the garden where we had lunch.

This was how it started to happen, slowly, as we dealt with practicalities, side by side and beat by beat. We started to mend ourselves.

'Thanks for coming down,' I'd said to him when he went back to London. 'I couldn't have done it without you.'

He'd held me then for a few moments before kissing the top of my head. 'Come up to London soon.'

And I had, a few weeks later.

We meet at London Zoo. It isn't the first time we've spent the day together in London. Over the past year, since Patrick's short stay in hospital, we've had a series of meetings, embarked on mini-pilgrimages to places we'd been to with Beth.

Rachel had taken the job. She'd gone back to the States

but Patrick had stayed here, not wanting to leave the place where his daughter had grown up, where her memories lingered on.

We've done our separate grieving.

We need to do it together now to start to move on.

Also, I have something to discuss with him when we meet at London Zoo. 'Do you remember how she wanted to walk up the ramp in the penguin pool when we brought her?' Patrick asks, as we sit on the terrace of the zoo's restaurant, despite the cold.

'Did she? Was I there?' I pause, forkful of quiche on its way to my mouth.

'Yes. It was when we still lived here. At least, I think it was.'

'I remember her being scared of the wolves.'

'I don't. Just the penguins. You were holding the hood of her jacket, trying to stop her pulling away.' Patrick bites into his burger. 'I can still see her face when she first spotted them. She couldn't stop smiling or clapping her hands.'

'"One cannot be angry when one looks at a penguin,"' I say.

'What?'

'It's a quote. I think it was Ruskin who said it.'

'Well, she wasn't, was she? She was delighted.'

It's easier to recall when there's someone to do it with. Memories are like jigsaws. Sometimes you need someone to find the missing bits.

'There's something I wanted to ask you,' I begin, looking at Patrick, who has opened his bun and is adding a layer of chips to the burger.

'Yes?' He's absorbed in the task.

'I started this savings account for Beth when she was a baby and now it's matured. There's a few thousand. I've had to fill in a few forms and send copies of Beth's death certificate, but they're transferring the money to me now.'

'Is there something you want to do with it?' Patrick looks up. 'You should use it to do something for yourself. You could visit Laura in Indonesia.'

'No. It's something I want to do for Beth, for myself too, and hopefully others will benefit.'

'Go on.' He picks up another chip, which hovers in mid-air, tempting a seagull from nearby Regent's Canal to swoop and Patrick to swat. 'Bloody birds!'

'Ugh.' I cover my plate.

'What is it you want to do?' Patrick asks, keeping half an eye on the scavenging birds.

'I want to create something. I've been thinking about it for a while.'

New Beginnings

It was much earlier in the year when the idea first struck me. I'd been going to the letterbox but was distracted by a profusion of snowdrops nodding gently from the hollowed-out centre of the dead elm's stump, and the clusters of newly opened primroses around its base: life springing forth from dead wood. Beautiful flowers, unfurling in the weak spring sun. I was moved by the sight in a way I had not been moved by anything for months.

I stopped, looked more closely at the snowdrops' milky heads bowed over the glistening green of their stems. Who had done this? When had it happened? Why had I not noticed before?

'It was Samir's idea,' Joyce told me, when I ran into her later.

'How lovely.' I remembered that Samir's father had run a garden centre back in Hama.

'And Samir is still planting them,' I said, more to myself than to Joyce, marvelling quietly at the resilience of the teenage boy.

'He's been trying to get a weekend job at the nursery but they say they don't need anyone,' Joyce told me. 'He loves gardening. There's not really enough to do in mine to keep him busy.'

It hovered for a moment and then Joyce said it. 'It would be good for Samir if he could help you with yours. I think he'd like that. It might make a difference.' She looked at me expectantly. 'And he seems to like your nephew.'

I'd made a few half-hearted efforts to breathe some life back into my garden but working on it never felt quite right.

I had wanted to punish myself by letting the garden go to seed, by shunning the thing that hitherto had given me hours of pleasure. How could I tend it when I had allowed my daughter to die? How could I allow it to flourish when she had been denied the chance? How could I take pleasure in its growth when Beth's life had been cut so tragically short? I kept asking myself these questions, even as I began to start work on it again.

It was the emphasis on Samir that brought about the shift in my attitude. Joyce wasn't suggesting that Samir help me for my benefit. It was for his. If gardening gave a boy who had lost everything some pleasure, if he could see optimism in the small shoots of spring, then who was I to deny him?

It was a few months after Samir had helped me cut back the tangle of overgrowth and clear the undergrowth, after the daffodils had pushed out into the light and the magnolia buds had begun to reappear, that I opened the letter, which was addressed to the 'parent or guardian of Beth Challoner'.

In the aftermath of everything, I'd forgotten about the savings account, had had no idea that the paltry amount I'd put aside each month was now worth a couple of thousand. But as I held the letter, and watched a blue tit resting on a branch of the magnolia, a plan began to form.

*

'I want to use the money to create a garden in the grounds of the hospital where Beth died,' I tell Patrick, as he bats away another seagull with eyes on his lunch. 'I've done a little research into costs, and Sophie has told me who to speak to at the hospital.'

'By "grounds" do you mean that awful space where everyone went to smoke?' he asks.

'Yes. It was so soulless there,' I say. 'The only place there was to go when you wanted to get outside, out of that awful ward. If we could create a garden there, something in Beth's memory, it would . . .' I can't find the words to articulate my need to do this. 'What do you think?' I finish lamely.

'I think it's a wonderful idea,' he says. He reaches across the table for my hand. 'It's absolutely right.'

We finish eating in silence, but with a new awareness of each other. Patrick has been concentrating on his food but every now and then he looked at me, caught me looking at him.

There's something and I'm not sure what it is, until a young man, who's probably about the same age as Beth would be now, comes and asks if he can take away our plates.

'Leave anything for long and the seagulls swoop,' he adds conversationally, a slight accent. Polish, perhaps.

'I've got something for you,' Patrick says, when he's gone, fumbling in the pocket of his jacket. 'I wasn't sure whether to give it to you today but I brought it anyway.' He removes his hand from his pocket and it contains a small box.

'Open it,' he says, pushing it across the table.

'It's a lovely box.' I delay the moment, feeling the soft-ness of the burgundy leather.

'Open it,' Patrick repeats.

I raise the lid and inside is a ring: it looks like a signet ring but its face is a small oval disc, with a gold surround and a crystal face. Inside, several strands of golden hair are woven together.

I can't speak. It's beautiful.

'It's a Victorian mourning ring,' Patrick says. 'I found it in a jeweller's in Shoreditch and asked if they could remake it. I took some of the hair from the box in Beth's room. I hope you don't mind. I know I should have asked but I wanted to surprise you. You don't mind, do you?'

'No.' I shake my head, tears welling. 'It's beautiful.'

'Try it on.' He takes my hand again. 'I think it goes on your middle finger. If it doesn't fit, I'll get it altered. Here, let me.' He takes the ring and puts it on my finger. It fits perfectly. It is perfect.

'Thank you.' I'm at a loss for any other words.

'It's a mourning ring officially,' Patrick still holds the tip of my middle finger, 'but I wanted it to be something else. Something less mournful.'

I smile. 'Such as?'

'You're better at this than I am,' he says.

'What?'

'Words. Finding the right ones. Expressing things.'

'I don't seem to have any at the moment.'

Patrick takes my hand, holds it properly. 'These last cou-ple of years have been hell,' he says. 'I know they've been hell for you too, but I don't think I could have got through them without knowing you were there, that someone else

305

was going through what I was. And I know that's selfish and it would have been better if you'd been spared, but it helped that you were around because you're her mother and always will be.' He pauses. 'Am I making any sense?'

'Yes.'

'I didn't want to think of this ring as a mourning ring.' He touches it on my finger. 'I wanted it to be something that said, no matter what has happened, we had a child together. That was the most wonderful thing that ever happened to me and it happened with you. I will always love you for that.'

'Patrick,' I say quietly.

'I still can't think about the future clearly,' he says. 'The only thing I know is that I need you to be in it. I'm not asking if you'll think about us being together again. But can we try to find a way forward together? Can we see what happens?'

I nod, because the lump in my throat is too big to allow me to form words. I nod, and I squeeze his hand, and I don't know what emotion I'm feeling. It's not happiness. I don't know if I can ever be really happy again, but it's overwhelming and it's good.

Time Flying

The speed with which the next few months go by surprises me. Perhaps it's having Alfie around: getting up and off to college each day, needing to be fed each evening. And the flow of teenagers that goes with having him in the house, colourful boys and girls studying art and design A levels with him, smiling, laughing, asking if I have any bubble wrap because it's integral to some project or other.

The days begin to pass quickly. I can hardly find spare moments for household chores, like replenishing the food that Alfie gets through at an alarming rate. It's increasingly hard to find a spare day on which to meet up with Patrick. And there don't seem to be enough hours to work on the garden project. But suddenly it's actually happening.

Patrick stops, stands up and clutches his back.

'Are you okay?'

'Yeah, just a twinge.' He grimaces.

'Lightweight.' Alfie grins, continuing to shovel compost into the newly constructed frame he and Patrick have made from bits of reclaimed wood, while Samir and I were at the nursery buying plants. It is now lined with polypropylene, and for the past hour we've all been lugging compost sacks several hundred yards across the hospital grounds from the car park.

'It's okay for you.' Patrick flicks compost off his forearm at Alfie. 'You're young.'

'Oi!' Alfie chucks a small clod back at him.

Samir joins in.

'Boys!' I admonish, smiling.

I'm smiling.

I'm tired from the physical exhaustion, and my back is suffering the odd twinge too, but this is the closest I've felt to content for so long that none of this bothers me.

Alfie glances in my direction, as he slits open a fresh bag of compost and pours it into their newly created flowerbed. Samir brings another over. 'Are we doing this all on our own now?' Alfie asks.

'Just give us a bit of a breather,' Patrick says, and to me, 'It's looking a whole lot better already.' He flaps a hand towards the cluster of flowerpots, which I have filled with dianthus, lavender and lobelia, and a couple of planters containing miniature Japanese maple trees. When Evan came to see me during the university holidays I told him about the garden. 'I'd like to donate something towards it,' he'd said.

'You don't have to.' I worried I'd put him on the spot.

'I'd like to,' he'd told me, adding, 'If she had a grave I'd have been to put flowers on it. But this is better.'

'I'm sorry, Evan.'

'What for?'

'For not really thinking about you. I know it's been hard for you.'

'She was the first girlfriend I really loved,' he'd said unembarrassed. 'She'll always be special. I want to donate something in her memory.'

I look at the Japanese maples now with their fiery spread

of deep pink leaves and say a silent thank-you to him, for those words, as well as the plants.

'"Instant gardening reaps instant rewards,"' I say to Alfie now, and I'm quoting Mark Catton. I met up with him, as friends, a couple of times after our 'date'. I found him good to talk to. He's met someone else now but he still emails, every now and then, and asks me how I'm doing.

The last time, I told him the book we worked on was coming into its own.

It feels like cheating, this purchase of full-grown plants, but they're what's needed. No one who comes out is going to be here long or often enough to observe the slower process of nature at work, the tiny shoots of spring, the unfurling of buds, the slow creep of climbing plants or the thickening foliage of greenery.

The entire project has come about faster than I could possibly have imagined, without any of the envisaged stumbling blocks. It's given me a renewed sense of purpose and some satisfaction, as I survey the results.

It should make a difference, I hope, thinking back to the moment when I'd had the idea for the garden, which had felt like a turning point for me, a small one but significant nevertheless: a tiny shoot of spring, a hint of a new beginning.

'Do you want something to eat before you go?' I ask, when we get back to the house after dropping off Alfie and Samir.

Patrick needs a shower before he gets the train back.

'That would be good, if you've got something. Thank you,' he says, heading upstairs.

My fridge is fuller, these days. I have to keep it stocked with Alfie in the house.

The supermarket deliveryman has noticed the change.

'Got people staying?' he asked, one evening, carrying boxes into the kitchen, where I unloaded the contents on to the table.

I take a packet of mince from the fridge now, switch on the radio and begin preparing meatballs while listening to talk of a new play about Galileo. 'Some scenes work excellently,' a reviewer is saying. 'In particular, the excitement of Galileo's endorsement of the Copernican theory that the earth revolves around the sun, which he demonstrates to a pupil with the aid of a chair, a lamp and an apple.'

I smile to myself as I mix fennel into the mince and form it into balls. It reminds me of Beth's demonstration.

I pause mid-mixing. It reminds me of Beth's demonstration without tearing at my heart.

'Do you want a drink?' I ask Patrick, when he comes down showered, shaved and fresh despite the day's hard work. 'I've got some beer. Or there's wine.'

'Food and drink!' He grins. 'You having Alfie to stay is great. Could I have a beer?'

I take one out of the fridge and hand it to him. 'So,' I say, when we're sitting on the bench just outside the kitchen, 'you've got a few viewings tomorrow?'

'Three or four but the agent said there might be more. I haven't checked today.'

'That's good?'

'Yes. Rachel wants to buy something in the States. The sooner we get it sold . . .'

'And you can stay with Simon when you're in London until you sort something else out?'

'Yes. I've got a few more trips coming up so I won't be there much. He says he'll be glad of the rent and it'll give me time to decide where I want to be.'

'You can always stay here when you need to. I mean, I realize it's not so easy with Alfie here but . . .'

'I know.' He puts out his hand and rests it on my knee, just as the oven-timer calls me back into the kitchen.

We don't talk much over dinner but the silence is companionable rather than strained. When he's finished, Patrick looks at his watch.

'Do you need to get going?'

'Yes, I should.' He stands, takes his plate over to the dishwasher, then comes to where I'm sitting and puts his hands on my shoulders. 'Thank you, Cate.'

I stand up and allow him to take me into his arms. At first he holds me tightly, so tightly I can hardly breathe, but then he loosens his hold and steps back a little so I can look up at him. He appears older now. His hair is almost completely grey but still thick and wavy, and his face is heavily lined but it makes him seem kinder. And his eyes have a sadness they never had before, but he's still Patrick, still beautiful.

He bends down and kisses me.

The Next Frame

A few days later he's back to finish the garden. There's not much left to do. A few brackets to be inserted in the wall, a few planters to hang from them, a couple of window boxes to attach to the sills, amid a steady trickle of patients and their relatives coming out to smoke or simply escape the confines of the hospital ward.

It didn't really matter to me if they noticed the change. It was enough knowing we had effected it, that there was more evidence of life in the area. Not just the plants but also the butterflies that fluttered around the lavender, and the bees that alighted on the abelia. The garden was a gentler echo of what was going on inside the hospital, a microcosm of life and how everyone and everything strives to preserve it.

'Are you going to have some sort of official opening?' Alfie had asked, when we'd planted the final bed.

The hospital manager had asked the same question but we'd decided not to, preferring simply to leave the garden, agreeing first to a few photographs, taken by Ella, the hospital press officer.

We shuffle into photo formation, Patrick, Alfie, Samir and I, standing in front of the newly planted instant trees. Patrick puts an arm around Samir's shoulders, and the other around my waist. I feel the warmth of him across the small of my back as Ella asks us to smile and I tell Alfie not to spoil the picture. 'Don't make your Snapchat face! Just smile normally.'

'Thank you. That's lovely,' Ella says.

She shows me the image. It's not bad. 'Could I have a copy?' I ask. 'I'd like to show my parents and my sister. She's recently moved to Sumatra. I'd like to send her a copy.'

'Of course,' she says. 'And I wondered if we might have a chat sometime. There's something I thought you might be interested in.'

'I've been offered a new job,' I tell Mum over lunch, a few days later. 'It's not full time but they guarantee a certain number of days each year.'

I tell her about the offer from the hospice garden charity, which Ella had told me about. 'I'll be helping to manage teams of volunteers to create gardens at several of the children's hospices in the south-east.'

'It sounds perfect for you,' Mum says. 'Have you accepted?'

'Not yet,' I tell her. 'They gave me a few days to think it over. It wouldn't start for a while. I'd need to work my notice out at the publisher's and they have to get the finance in place. I won't be earning as much, but I don't really need to.'

'So what is there to think about?' Mum asks.

And she's right.

I feel excited about having the chance to create something that might make a little difference to people at extreme times of their lives.

It wasn't unusual for Mum to insist I go to have lunch with them. 'We haven't seen you for ages. When are you coming to see us?' she'd say, even if I'd just driven home from having lunch with them.

But there was something about the way she'd said it this time, a level of insistence beyond the usual, that made me feel slightly uneasy.

I wasn't really listening to the radio in the car on the way over. It was on and people were talking but I hadn't tuned in until the news and a report about the parents of a six-week-old terminally ill baby, whose request to take her out of the country for experimental treatment in America had been turned down by a judge.

I slowed down, deliberately concentrating on the road while also giving the radio my attention. It was a tragic story. The world is too full of them but somehow it goes on.

The newsreader was quoting the judge, who had denied these parents the chance to cling to a few final straws.

'It's impossible,' she had said in her ruling, 'to have a philosophy of life that does not include death.'

I found myself nodding, despite my sympathy for the parents, despite their desperate plight. I was further ahead down this path, beyond the stage where I beat myself up for not having fought harder for Beth, at the point where I now accepted that her death came too early, far too early, but that death is inevitable.

'How was the drive, love?' Mum opens the door before I've even knocked. And, almost immediately she's telling me she'll get the potatoes on now. And Dad, asking if I'd like something to drink, asking Mum if she needed help, taking dishes out of the dresser, telling Mum the potatoes need turning down.

Most people have three significant relationships in their lives. Emily Ewing had told me so in my last session with her, when I'd said I'd started to see Patrick again. 'Often they're all with the same person.' The one Mum appeared to be having with Dad now was sweet. Touching. Hopeful.

'Have some more ham, darling.' She pushed the plate of cold meat across the table towards me. 'I'm afraid I haven't done anything for pudding.'

'I'm okay.' I held up my hand, stopping the plate mid-track. 'That was lovely but I'm full.'

'There's the cake I bought in the village yesterday,' Dad said, getting up, clearing the plates, a new man in his older age. 'Why don't you go into the living room with your mother? I'll bring the coffee through.'

I look to Mum for guidance. This is irregular. My parents take their coffee at the kitchen table after a meal. They always have.

'Thank you, Bill.' Mum gets up slowly, leaving Dad to clear away the remains of lunch and sort coffee and cake.

'You look well, Cate,' she says, adjusting a picture on the wall, which is slightly wonky. 'Is it straight now?' she asks, and I nod.

Satisfied, she settles into the armchair by the window. 'Very well,' she adds.

'I've been outside a lot, what with the hospital garden and everything.'

'I'm looking forward to seeing it,' Mum says. 'It's a lovely thing you've done, and having Alfie as well. I know it means a lot to Joe and it's been a real help to them.'

'Good,' I say, looking out of the window, at the rose bed

315

in the centre of the lawn, where we used to cut our nails as kids because Dad said it made the roses grow better, and am momentarily overcome by the profusion of pale pinks and yellows.

'We've got a bit of news.' Mum's voice crackles in a way I've not heard before, which brings my attention back to her.

'Mum?' I'd been wondering what the reason was for lunch and the coffee in the living room.

'Oh, it's nothing to worry about.' She's detected the note of alarm in my voice. 'Your father and I have just reached the time of life when we needed to start making a few decisions.'

'What sort of decisions?'

'We're not getting any younger and we're not as fit as we were.'

'Are you ill, Mum? Or is it Dad?' I suppose all children with elderly parents are anticipating this moment.

'No, darling. There's nothing wrong. It's just that the house and the garden are getting a bit too much for us, so we've decided we're going to sell and move somewhere more suitable.'

'Oh.' I'm not quite sure what to say. This is not what I had started to worry about but I find myself strangely upset nevertheless.

'I know, love,' Mum says, putting her hand over mine. 'I know this is where you all grew up. This has been our home for nearly fifty years and it's sad to think of leaving but it's better to make the move now, when we're still young enough to adapt to somewhere new and we've still got each other.'

'Oh, Mum.' I sniff and she strokes my hand with her fingers.

'We won't move far,' she says. 'We'll still be close by, just somewhere a bit smaller and more manageable, but I know it'll feel odd, not having the family home any more, for all of us.'

'It will,' I reply and we both gaze for a moment out of the window across the garden, towards the outline of the Downs in the distance.

'There's something I'd like you to do for me,' Mum says.

'Yes?'

'You know the cherry tree you gave us for our fiftieth wedding anniversary?'

'Yes.' I look out of the window again but the spot where I planted it is not visible from here, only from the kitchen window. Mum had asked for it to be planted where she could see it when she was doing the washing-up.

'We don't want to leave it here,' Mum says. 'It's still young enough to move and it's such a lovely tree, so special to us. I was hoping you might transplant it to your garden. Now that you're working on it again, it would be lovely to see it there, and I know you'll look after it. Do you think you could find the space for it?'

'I've got another idea,' I say, as it occurs to me, wondering if the thought running through my head is something I should discuss with Patrick first.

'Yes?' Mum looks at me.

'I'm not sure about my garden because I suppose I might consider moving myself one day, but if we could find somewhere else to plant it, somewhere we could always visit, maybe I could bury Beth's ashes with it. What do you think?'

'I think that's a lovely idea, Caty,' Mum says, taking out her handkerchief and dabbing the corners of her eyes, 'That would make me very happy.'

'Oh, Mum.' I laugh.

She laughs too, and I feel something like calm in the strangeness of the moment.

'There's something else,' I say. It's like being at confession, not that I've been since I was thirteen.

'I hope it's good news,' Mum says, smiling, twinkling a little.

'Yes. I hope it's good. I think it's good. It's early days yet but . . .' I feel anxious now, halfway through my sentence.

'Go on, love.'

'It's Patrick. We're going to give it another go. We're not quite sure how, or what form it will take, but we need each other.'

'Yes.' She nods.

'You knew?'

'No. But I hoped that in time you'd realize you needed each other.'

'I'm scared, Mum.'

'I know, love. After all you've been through. You're scared of getting hurt again.'

'It feels like a huge gamble.'

'Putting your coat on in the morning is a gamble,' Mum says. 'But it's life, Cate. You have to accept that everything you love you might lose. You never know what's going to happen but you can't allow yourself to stop living.' She looks out of the window at the garden again. 'Do you remember when you fell into the rose bed when you were learning to ride your bike?'

'No.'

'Joe was trying to teach you, holding the back of the bike, but he wasn't really strong enough. It would have been easier if your father had been around.'

'It must have been difficult for you, Mum, with Dad away so much.'

'Not really. It meant I didn't have to worry about your father too. There was time for that later, when you were all a bit older.'

'Time for what?' Dad asks, coming in from the kitchen, carrying a tray.

'Nothing that concerns you,' Mum says, with a smile.

And then, looking out of the window again: 'Oh! See that? Two for joy!'

I don't need to look to know she's spotted two magpies.

'Now, Cate,' Mum says, as Dad sits down with us. 'Tell us how Alfie's getting on at college. He's invited us to see his end-of-year exhibition.'

'Oh, that's nice. He's been very secretive about what he's doing for it.'

A Week Later

'You look smart!' Samir arrives wearing a white shirt, black trousers and black jacket. He looks a little like a waiter, or as if he's dressed for a funeral, but I don't say this. He has clearly made an effort, too much, perhaps, for the viewing of an end-of-year art project but it's nice that he's come, nice that Alfie wanted him to come.

The two of them have changed the dynamic of the street by being out in it, often: kicking a football, like a couple of eight-year-olds, or sitting on garden walls, talking like much older men. An unusual friendship, which has blossomed and grown over the past eighteen months.

'These clothes belong to Joyce's son.' Samir sounds slightly apologetic, as he shifts on the doorstep and I wonder how it must have felt for Joyce to see the boy who had arrived with nothing going out in her son's things.

'Alfie's gone for scruffy,' I say. 'Come in. We're in the kitchen. Sophie and Joe have just arrived.'

Joe gets up when Samir comes in. 'We should probably get going now. We don't want to be late for the art event of the year.'

'Dad,' Alfie mutters, but he's pleased by the hype, I can tell.

'Patrick's going to meet us there,' I tell Samir. 'We'll go in Joe's car and Pat can bring us back after.'

'Mum and Dad are going to meet us there too,' Joe says. 'And we'll take pictures for Ned and Laura and Dan.'

So much interest in Alfie's final-year art project, perhaps because he's been so secretive about it. 'You'll have to wait and see,' he repeats, each time I ask him what the latest package of art supplies contains, and 'I want it to be a surprise,' when I ask him how it's going.

Samir, I suspect, has been in on it. Is this the reason for his semi-suited appearance, I wonder, as he tries to coil his long legs into the space behind where Sophie sits in the passenger seat?

The art room is busy with parents and students, the walls covered with paintings: nudes, lots of them, still lives and interior landscapes – vast oil canvases of suburban living rooms – eighteen-year-old art students' take on life. In the centre, a huge wire sculpture and another made from Coke cans. To one side, a shopping trolley covered with images of young children. I don't know what it signifies. There is no time to stop and look.

Alfie leads us to a small separate room, just off the main one, the art cupboard, I suppose, but it's bare, except for a table in the middle.

On the table is Alfie's installation: a beautiful representation of a magnolia tree, its distinctive pink and white petals laid out in concentric circles, interspersed with green leaves. All of this is made from grains of coloured sand, painstaking pushed into place over the past few months by my nephew. It's beautiful and fragile.

'Alfie, it's incredible,' I whisper. 'It's amazing. It must have taken you ages.'

He points to the pictures on the surrounding walls, photographs documenting this piece of art's construction. 'It's based on the sand mandalas made by Tibetan Buddhist monks,' he says, becoming older and more knowledgeable as he speaks. 'Historically, they made them with tiny granules of crushed coloured stone.'

'It's so delicate.' I stand back, afraid to go too near in case I disturb it.

'That's why it's in this room. So it didn't get knocked about too much. Try not to sneeze!'

'Can't you fix it with something to keep it in place?' Joe asks.

'That's not the point,' Alfie says. 'It's supposed to symbolize the transitory nature of life. Dismantling it afterwards is part of it.'

'So you're going to destroy it?' I ask. It seems such a shame. So much work has gone into it. People should see it.

'I'm going to break it up, just as soon as everyone is here. It's the final part of the project. Samir's going to film it and I was hoping you might draw the first line in the sand.'

'I don't know if I could bear to. All that work.'

That's when I notice the small handwritten piece of card pinned to the side of the table: 'In memory of my cousin, Beth'.

Alfie watches me reading it. 'Do you mind?' he asks.

'No,' I say, looking from my nephew's anxious, expectant face back to the table, with its carefully crafted coloured sands. 'I think it's wonderful, Alfie. Really incredible.' My voice trembles slightly as I speak.

'Really?' He's still concerned. 'I worried it might upset you.'

'I'm touched, Alfie. I'm really touched that Beth was your inspiration. You're an amazing boy.'

I go to him and hug him, blinking back the tears as I hold him and he allows himself to be embraced, briefly.

There's an audible hush in the room now, where we have been joined by the head of art and a few of Alfie's fellow students and their parents. His teacher says a few words, and then Alfie explains, more fluent in front of a crowd than any of us ever imagined he would be, that he's now going to break up the image he has created in the sand.

'I'm not destroying it. It's a reconfiguration. The sand will still exist but not in this form.'

I notice, out of the corner of my eye, Joe reaching out and taking Sophie's hand, and I sense someone else coming into the room but I don't turn, not until after Alfie has handed me a ruler.

'Cate?' he says tentatively. 'Do you want to push it through the centre, to divide it in half initially?'

Despite Alfie's words about reconfiguration, it still feels like an act of vandalism to be breaking up something so beautiful.

Others look at me.

'I can't.'

'Oh, okay. Sorry.' Alfie seems crushed, his moment destroyed by my refusal. He's unsure now. He's a child.

'I'm sorry, Alfie.' I have to do it, for him. 'I just need a moment.'

I look at the mandala again and at the card. I'm touched

beyond words that Alfie has done this, and privileged that he has asked me to make the first line in the sand. And then I see, out of the corner of my eye, who has just joined us in the room.

It's Chloe. She meets my eye and smiles and nods towards the mandala, as if to say, 'Go on.'

I push the ruler into the coloured granules, destroying the shape of the magnolia. Alfie makes the second line and continues, pushing the sand apart into separate piles, as Samir films, dividing the image diagonally so that the sand no longer resembles a flower but a fractured Union flag.

He takes a paintbrush and sweeps the remaining piles of sand into a small dustpan, then empties them into a large jar, as the crowd begins slowly to disperse.

'Well done, Alfie,' Joe says.

He speaks quietly but I can hear the pride in his words.

'Yes, well done, Alf,' Sophie echoes, putting an arm around Joe's waist. 'You've amazed us all.'

The latter sounds heartfelt.

'Cate?' Chloe is standing beside me now and I cannot believe just how pleased I am that she's here.

'Chloe.' I blink back the tears and hug her. 'I didn't know you two had kept in touch.' I step back and take her in. She looks well.

'Facebook.' She smiles.

I'd never imagined. They'd met on numerous occasions, of course, Beth's best friend and her cousin who lived nearby, but Chloe's older. I thought they'd gone their separate ways.

'It's so good to see you,' I say. Too often we think of

people living on through their descendants, but that's not the only way. They live on, too, through their friends, through everyone who knew them, whom they touched while they were still alive.

'It's good to see you too, Cate,' says Chloe, and she dabs at the corner of her eye with her sleeve as she speaks.

'It's not quite finished.' Alfie interrupts our tearful reunion. 'The final part of the installation is to tip the sand into the sea. It's what the Tibetan monks do and I want to do that too, at some point, return the sand to the sea.'

'Why not do it now?' I say impulsively.

'Really?' Alfie asks, unsure. 'I don't want – I mean I don't want for you to have to go to the beach.'

'I'd like to,' I say, determined. 'Why don't we go now?' I look around at everyone.

'Yes,' Patrick agrees. 'Let's go now.'

The beach is nearly empty, and cool after a hot day. We walk together, a small group of family and friends, towards the sea, and stand on the shore in the dusk.

'We need to be further out.' Alfie glances around. 'Where the sea is deeper.'

There's a small fishing pier, further along the beach. Alfie inclines his head towards it, questioning.

I nod. 'I'll come with you.'

'Are you sure?'

'Yes.'

It's only sand but it feels strangely liberating pouring it away, watching the coloured grains being mixed with the moon's reflection in the water. From the corner of my eye I can see my mother crossing herself.

Samir films from the shore, a respectful distance away.

We stand for a while, watching the water dancing round the wooden struts of the pier.

'Shall we go back and join the others?' Alfie asks, after a while.

'You go. I need a moment.'

I stand on the edge of the pier. I want to prolong the moment of appreciating the beach for what it is, for what it used to be, a place of beauty, not for what it became, the scene of a tragedy I hadn't been able to revisit.

Watching the sea, being lulled by the waves, trying to spot the tiny flecks of coloured sand being churned absorbs me and I feel a sense of calm, which is an absence of pain.

'You okay?' Patrick is walking down the pier, concerned.

'Yes.'

He puts his arm around me and we stand for a moment, looking at the water, before rejoining the rest of the family.

A Step Back in Time

'These?' Patrick beckons me over to the kitchen table where he is arranging a portfolio of photographs. He points to one of a spoonbill perched on a branch, another of a heron standing on the bank alongside a wooden fishing boat, pulled half out of the water.

'Yes,' I say.

'And this one?' He shows an image of cormorants and pelicans flying together over the surface of a lake. He has applied for a job with a local wildlife conservation charity. It's freelance but a guaranteed number of days per year. They need someone to document the work they do, someone with experience of wildlife photography. Patrick is more than qualified. He would earn less than he does now but we don't need much money. It will still involve travel but mostly in the UK.

'I might still do one or two overseas trips as well, if I get it. If anything interesting comes up.'

'Of course.'

I don't want to stop him doing what he loves. But he's said himself he's tired of all the travel. He wants to stop, to have more time, to spend more of it at home, which is here now.

Alfie's doing an art foundation course in Lincoln and hoping to go to art school next year.

I rest my hands on Patrick's shoulders, as he carries on

sifting through prints, bend down and put my cheek next to his, absorbing its warmth. He reaches up and briefly touches mine as the letterbox clanks to the tune of the postman shoving something through.

I leave Patrick and go into the hallway, pick up a couple of envelopes, junk mail, I think, and a slightly battered one with an American stamp and a faded postmark. It's written in a hand I don't recognize.

'Anything interesting?' He looks up as I go back into the kitchen.

'I'm not sure.' I put the junk straight into the recycling and open the handwritten one, removing two sheets of thick manila laid paper, covered with the same neat script as the envelope. There's an address, scrawled in the corner, a street name and house number. It does not resonate. 'Dear Mr and Mrs Challoner,' it begins.

'This is to both of us,' I say.

'Who from?' Patrick asks.

I go to the bottom of the second sheet. 'Someone called Tom Shapiro?' I look to Pat for elucidation. 'Is he something to do with you?'

Patrick shakes his head. 'Read it,' he urges.

'Out loud?'

'Well, I'm curious now.'

'"Dear Mr and Mrs Challoner,"' I read. '"Forgive the time it has taken me to write this letter."'

I look at the date of the letter, expecting it to have been written a few weeks beforehand.

'What's up?' Patrick asks.

'It's dated October the year before last.'

'That can't be right.'

I look again. 'It is.' I peer at the worn envelope, its post-mark too faded to make out the date. 'I guess it must have got stuck in the post.'

'I suppose so,' Patrick agrees. 'But for such a long time? It's weird.'

I start reading the letter aloud again: '"I am the professor in charge of the Nuffield placement scheme at Stamford University and I was very much looking forward to welcoming Beth to the university and to the physics department."'

Patrick stops what he's doing now, stands up and comes over to where I am, leaning against the work surface.

I hold the letter between us, like a shared hymnbook or song sheet. We read in silence together.

When we interviewed her by Skype we were impressed by her academic ability but also by her articulacy and personal charm. Beth was enquiring and engaging, a gentle humor shone through and we were unanimous in our decision to offer her the place here.

I was greatly saddened by the news of her untimely death and I cannot begin to imagine what you must be going through.

'He sent it a few weeks after she died,' I say to Patrick. 'But it's only just arrived. How extraordinary.'

Patrick picks up the envelope and examines the creases and slight rips along the edges. He screws up his eyes, better to read the faded postmark. 'It's taken over two years to get here.'

We continue reading.

I realize that there are no words, especially now, that will offer you comfort at this terrible time, but these words, often cited among the physics community, may in time, I hope, offer some solace.

I pause, waiting to see if Patrick has finished reading before placing the second sheet of paper on top of the first.

$E = mc^2$. It's the world's most famous equation, Einstein's big idea that energy is constant – it's always conserved or converted into mass. I hope that by talking about the conservation of energy you will understand that Beth's energy is still there in the universe; every vibration, every bit of heat, every wave of every particle that was her remains in this world, all the light that shone from her eyes, all the heat she gave off, all the warmth that flowed between you in life is still here.

According to the law of the conservation of energy, not a bit of Beth is gone.

'Life everlasting, amen,' I murmur.
'What?' Patrick asks.
'It's just beautifully put, isn't it?'
'Yes.' Patrick puts his arm around my shoulders and we read on.

This is an extract of a famous speech but there's something else, a concept that helped me following the death of my father a few years ago. It has more to do with time than energy.

I remember thinking about it, when my brother and I were going through family photos, leafing through moments in time that

*stretched back many years, wishing we could have some of the days
with Dad back again. I remember saying to my brother that if
Einstein was right and if the past, present and future really do all
exist simultaneously, then all of those moments captured in the
photographs are still out there, all those precious memories of
people and places are still out there, somewhere in space-time.*

*I'm rambling now but I hope this letter reaches you and I hope
that, in time, some of this will be of some comfort.*

I am so sorry for your loss.

Yours

Tom Shapiro

'He sent it so long ago,' Patrick says, looking at the date
again.

'And yet it's probably arrived at just the right time.'

A New Beginning

Patrick's new job began at just the right time too: after I'd worked out my notice but before I took up my new position with the hospice garden charity. It meant I could go with him to Scotland, to the Galloway Forest, for a few days in the early autumn.

'I think I might take a shower,' I say, although I'm almost too tired to get up, comfortable on the sofa, watching Patrick light the wood-burning stove. But I know when he's finished he will ask me if I want a drink, pour me a glass of wine or perhaps a shot of whisky, and that once the stove begins to heat the cabin and the alcohol my blood, I'll be even less tempted to stir.

It's a beautiful evening, crisp and clear, the sky above the forest streaked with splashes of coral. 'I can't believe how beautiful this part of Scotland is.'

The cabin is built high into the hillside in the Galloway Forest. Sliding glass doors run the entire length of the living room, offering views over the canopy of trees. A goshawk is hovering, its wings spread wide as it looks for prey. The red squirrels are under threat from these birds and their grey relations, who are more efficient feeders.

Patrick is here not to photograph them, although inevitably he has, but black grouse, the game birds that feature on Scotland's famous whisky, which Patrick is pouring now.

'Do you remember when Beth drank your whisky thinking it was apple juice?' I ask Patrick, suddenly remembering her face, screwed up with the unexpected assault on her senses.

'Yes.' He smiles, recollecting.

And I smile at the two of us recalling our daughter with pleasure, not pain.

'How many fingers?' he asks, sloshing it into one of the crystal glasses that come with the cabin.

'Do you always stay in places like this?' I asked, when we first opened the door and I took in the deep Harris Tweed-covered sofas set around a low oak coffee-table, the sheepskin rugs that covered the wooden floor, the television, stereo, drinks cabinet, and the framed wildlife prints that hung on the walls: red deer, otters, nightjars and the famous black grouse, which Patrick has been capturing with his camera. He's documenting the work that the RSPB is doing here to ensure their numbers, which are dwindling, do not fall further.

'No. I usually stay in a bothy or a tent.' Patrick threw down the bag that contained his clothes, while carefully placing his camera equipment on top of the drinks cabinet. 'I asked for somewhere nicer because you were coming with me.'

'This is lovely,' I said looking around.

I'm still thinking that after three days, during which Patrick has been staked out on the moors. While he's been working, I have been reading and walking. I even hired a bicycle from the forest centre and rode around Loch Bradan, pausing to eat a packed lunch of smoked-salmon sandwiches and toffee, suitably Scottish picnic fare, on a bed of purple heather.

Beth would have liked it here, I think and sometimes say to Patrick, spurring him to take my hand. But she probably wouldn't have wanted to come with us. I conjure up an idea of her as a little older, more independent, a young woman who has spent a year in America and is now away at university. This young woman wouldn't want to be away with her parents. Would she?

Earlier Patrick had told me that the baby cocks had already left the nest and soon the hens would go out into the world too. The mother would start again, mating, egg laying, sitting and raising her young for another year but she'd never see those chicks again.

He's shown me a photograph of her, standing amid the heather, two younger hens not far away but not close either. And I've shown him a few shots of the loch, which I had taken on my phone. It's on the table now and I shove it slightly with my socked foot as I put up my feet and sip the whisky. It rings as I nudge it, vibrating loudly against the table so that I jump.

Laura's face appears.

Patrick goes out onto the terrace while I talk to her, allowing me privacy although I don't mind if he listens. He's happy to watch the sunset, whisky in hand, and I go out to join him when I've finished the call.

'How is she?' he asks, half turning but his attention is still focused on the forest.

'She's good.' I try to keep my voice steady.

'Yes?' Patrick senses something. He turns to me.

'Yes.' I take a deep breath. My heart is racing. 'They're coming back.'

'For a visit?'

'No.' I begin to gabble. 'For good. I don't think it's really worked out the way they hoped. She felt they were running away and not really ready to start a new life somewhere else. They miss their friends and family.'

'That's understandable.' Patrick is searching my face, as if he knows there's something else. 'But it's good, right? That they're coming home? You'll be glad to have her in the country again.'

'Yes, of course. Of course. I've really missed her.'

'But?' Concern in Patrick's eyes. Damn him.

I look away, catching sight of a red kite, which hovers in a pool of light above the forest. I managed to keep it together when I spoke to Laura on the phone, to keep my voice even, to say all the right things and keep my own emotions in check when Laura asked if I was okay.

'Caty?' He moves closer.

'She's pregnant.' I burst into tears. I can't tell him any more, none of the details that Laura has told me, for the huge body-racking sobs that overwhelm me.

Patrick takes me in his arms, holds me tighter, strokes my hair, tells me to 'Sssh', tells me 'It's okay', pulls a tissue from his pocket, which I take, moving away from him a little and blowing my nose. 'I'm sorry,' I say to him now.

'There's no need,' he says. 'It's great for Laura but it's understandable that you're upset.'

'No.' I wipe my nose. 'No. You don't understand. I'm not upset.'

'No?' Patrick looks confused. 'Then tell me.'

'Can we go in?' I'm shivering slightly in the cold air.

Patrick follows me inside, closing the windows onto the balcony and sitting beside me on the sofa.

I try to compose myself. 'She's three months pregnant. It's a miracle, isn't it? All those years of trying and the attempts at IVF and the unexplained infertility, and they give up hope and go away and then she gets pregnant. It's amazing.'

'Yes.' Patrick puts his hand on my knee. 'I've heard other stories like that. People who couldn't conceive and then, as soon as they'd stopped trying, it happened.'

'She's not young either.' I sip the waiting whisky, savouring its smoky warmth. 'But she had a scan and they say everything's fine. She wants to have the baby here and Dan has to give notice but they plan to come back in three months.'

Patrick takes my hand. 'It's okay. I know you're pleased for her and I know you said you're not upset but it's okay if you are. You can be both.'

'It's not that.'

'Then what?'

'It's just that . . .' I'm afraid I won't make sense as I try to explain, '. . . it's just being here, being with you, knowing I've got the new job to go back to and that Laura will be coming home and that she's pregnant. When she told me, I felt . . . I felt . . .'

'What?'

'It doesn't feel right to say.'

'Just say it, Cate. Whatever it is it's not going to make any difference to me.'

'I felt almost happy,' I say, and I'm crying again, as Patrick draws me to him so that my teary face feels the warmth of his cheek and his chest.

'Oh, Caty,' he kisses me, 'you're allowed to feel happy.'

'It's just . . .' I begin, but he silences me, putting his fingers to my lips.

'I know,' he says. 'I know.'

After we've eaten, Patrick suggests a walk.

I'm exhausted but also charged with emotional energy. 'Okay. That's a nice idea.'

I go to our bedroom, pull on a sweater, my fleece jacket and warmer socks. When I emerge Patrick's already in his coat and boots, waiting by the door, a miner's lamp strapped to his forehead.

'Not too far,' I say to him.

'Down the trail to the clearing where we saw the deer the other day?' he suggests, as we walk down the wooden steps.

It's not far by day but it feels further in the dark, with the forest floor invisible beneath us. The night is clear, bathed in the soft shine of stars, and after a while our eyes adjust to the dark and I'm beginning to feel I could walk further when we reach the clearing.

There's a bench for walkers. We sit. Patrick puts his arm around me. 'Maybe the deer will come back,' he says.

'Have you got your camera?'

'No.' He looks up at the star-filled night sky. I rest my head on his shoulder and close my eyes, suddenly so tired I think if we stay here much longer I might fall asleep.

I stir when Patrick shifts. 'Look!'

I open my eyes, peering into the clearing and beyond into the trees, for deer, I think, but it's something else entirely.

Patrick points to the sky and I look up to see a slow

surge of yellow light pulsating slowly across the sky, followed by flames of green. 'The Northern Lights,' Patrick whispers, as they strobe in gaseous formation high above us, morphing from inky swirls to rivers of light and great shafts of colour.

I can't speak but only marvel as we watch their perpetual motion and the amazing spectacle caused by particles in the earth's upper atmosphere, driven by the energy of the sun. I think of Beth and the letter from the Stamford physics professor, Tom Shapiro: the letter I've read so many times that I know the lines off by heart.

'All your energy,' I recite inwardly, as if in silent prayer, 'every vibration, every bit of heat, every wave of every particle that was your child remains in this world.'

After several minutes the lights gradually die down, like the dying embers of a fire, fading until once more the sky is lit only by stars.

'It feels like a sign,' I say, as we walk back to the cabin.

'Of what?' Patrick asks.

'Hope,' I say, feeling the word expand and take shape as I repeat it.

A short word with the ability to encapsulate so much more than those four letters, to sum up whatever makes you want to keep going, keep moving inexorably through life, no matter how much pain it throws at you, keep travelling forwards in time.

Those memories that are out there in Einstein's universe, where time is not linear, they allow us to travel back, but it's hope that lets us move forward.

'Hope,' I repeat.

Epilogue: Four Years After

Bessie is cradling a spider in her hands, cupping and recupping them so it cannot escape, but carefully, protective of it. 'Can I bring it home and have it as a pet?' she asks.

'I don't think so, love. Spiders aren't really meant to be pets.'

'Why?' she asks.

'Well, they're not really house animals.'

'Why?'

I'd forgotten how much three-year-olds like to ask why.

'Because they need to be outside. They need space to spin webs.'

'But they can spin them inside too. Our house is full of spiders' webs.'

'Well, yes, some spiders like making them in houses. And maybe one of those could be a pet. But I think that one's an outdoor spider.'

'Why?'

'Why what?'

'Why is it an outdoor spider? Why are some spiders outdoor spiders and some indoor spiders?'

'I don't really know.' I admit defeat. 'You'll have to ask Uncle Patrick later. He knows more about spiders than I do.'

'Will he be home later?' she asks, not looking up, still cupping the spider and allowing it to crawl around her palms, not scared of spiders the way Beth used to be. She used to scream the house down if there was one in the bathroom, refuse to go to sleep if she spotted one in her bedroom. In summer I was forever collecting house spiders and depositing them outside but 'Baby Bessie', as Patrick and I still refer to my niece, even though she's now three, is curious and unafraid of the natural world.

'Uncle Patrick will be back by supper time,' I tell her. 'And you're staying for supper tonight.'

It's one of my days for having her, while Laura teaches at the primary school we all went to in the village where we grew up.

It's funny the way things turn out: Joe and Sophie moved back, together, permanently, after Sophie's mother died, and Laura and Dan moved to the village when they came back from Indonesia. They live a mile away from Dad and Mum. It makes Mum so happy and proud. 'Joseph, Caitlin and Laura all live nearby,' I've heard her telling friends, as if this is her greatest achievement.

And it is: that we're all still close, that we've been able to help each other through the worst of times. That we're still there for each other now.

Dan is working at a vets' practice in the city. He will pick Bessie up on his way home this evening.

'Do you want to help me put these in?' I ask her.

We're at the woodland burial site where Beth's ashes lie at the foot of Mum and Dad's cherry tree. I'm planting snowdrops around the base. Bessie toddles over still cradling the spider.

'Why don't you put the spider in there?' I suggest,

gesturing at the box that contains my gardening gear. 'It can crawl around for a bit while we plant these bulbs.'

'In here?' she asks, kneeling beside it and opening her hands, allowing it to crawl free and probably away.

I'll deal with that later, the worry about where the spider has gone. Maybe she'll forget, in the meantime.

'Here, take the bulbs out of the bag.' I hand her the mesh bag containing handfuls of snowdrop bulbs. 'Do you want to put them in the ground, with the pointy bit facing up?'

She squats beside the hole I have just finished digging, her face serious, intent on the task. She places the bulbs carefully, one by one in a circle in the ground.

'Do you want to push some of the earth back over?'

'Okay.'

She scrapes the disturbed soil over the bulbs with the trowel.

'Now can you fetch the watering can and give them some water?'

She wanders the few feet to the can, which we filled earlier at the tap on the edge of the site, and starts sloshing it over the ground, satisfied when all the water has gone. 'There.'

'That's great. Thank you, sweetheart.'

She smiles, happy to be appreciated, then looks up at the bursts of pink blossom springing forth on Beth's tree. 'That tree's pretty,' she says.

I look up at it and can feel my eyes beginning to smart. 'It is, isn't it?' I blink back the tears.

There's something particular about cherry blossom, a spark of something we don't have a word for, some essence of life and the universe unleashed as the buds unfurl and burst into blossom, something about the way it seems to symbolize Schrödinger's paradox: that every individual must die and yet life itself endures.

'I love that tree,' Bessie says, with feeling, clapping her hands.

She's too young for me to explain about Beth, my daughter, her namesake, too small to take in the significance of the tree we planted in the spot where her ashes are buried, too full of childish wonder to understand that we will all die, and yet we remain in the memories of those we leave behind, in the things we have done, in the people we have touched, in the lives we have lived, however long or short. Our lives continue to echo through space-time, to reverberate around the universe.

'I love it too.'

I scoop her into my arms and hold her up so she can see the blossom better and I can feel the warmth of her small compact body and luxuriate in everything that is contained in this particular moment.

Do not stand at my grave and weep
I am not there. I do not sleep.
I am a thousand winds that blow.
I am the diamond glints on snow.
I am the sunlight on ripened grain.
I am the gentle autumn rain.
When you awaken in the morning's hush
I am the swift uplifting rush
Of quiet birds in circled flight.
I am the soft stars that shine at night.
Do not stand at my grave and cry;
I am not there. I did not die.

Mary Elizabeth Frye

Acknowledgements

Thank you to my editor Jillian Taylor for bringing this book to life, to my agent Sheila Crowley for her belief in it, and to Araminta Hall and Mick Finlay for their early readings and enthusiasm. Also, to Kitty Perrin for her later reading and support. As always I am endlessly grateful for the many conversations with friends that have given me food for thought and generally sustained me during the writing of this novel.